The Good Thief

The Good Thief

JAMES BUCHANAN

mlrpress

Copyright 2008 by James Buchanan

Published by:
MLR Press, LLC
3052 Gaines Waterport Rd.
Albion, NY 14411

Visit ManLoveRomance Press, LLC on the Internet:
www.mlrpress.com

Cover Art by Deana C. Jamroz
Editing by Maura Anderson
Printed in the United States of America.

ISBN# 978-1-934531-44-0

First Edition
2008

Reviews for The Good Thief

"The Good Thief is a superb mixture of hilarious dialog, an outstanding plot, and passionate love scenes. James Buchanan illustrates real life circumstances with realistic characters that draw you into the action. Caesar is savvy with a good heart, and Nate is honorable and determined to do the right thing. Even Caesar's dog Ponchito is loveable. Together they make fascinating characters in this electrifying story. I enjoyed The Good Thief immensely."

Chocolate Minx, Literary Nymphs Reviewer

"The Good Thief is an incredible story that left me in awe. The dynamics of the relationship between Caesar and Nate, the cultural flavor that peppered the story and the suspense of seeing if justice will prevail while all sides seemed to be converging to rip Nate and Caesar apart truly kept the story alive and vibrant for me....The Good Thief had me on a roller coaster of emotion all the way through and like any good ride, the ending left me breathless and happy."

Xeranth, reviewer at WhippedCream2.blogspot.com

CHAPTER 1

"I think you're just what we need for this project."

Caesar looked over the lip of his beer can to stare at one of those Hollywood-earnest faces. Two of them in fact. The woman speaking to him was all expensive dental work smiles, collagen lips, breast implants and a body sculpted by equal parts starvation, plastic surgery and some guy named Lars down at the gym.

Caesar expected the aging man at her side to flip him a peace sign and pass over a joint. Just as earnest, her partner jumped in, "Housebreaker is going to be the next big thing in reality TV." Head shaved to hide the fact that he was balding; earrings and trendy clothes couldn't hide the fact that he was in his early forties. It wasn't the years but the mileage that gave that one away.

A hot night in the Hollywood hills blanketed them. From Caesar's vantage on a porch slung off the side of the cliff, it was hard to tell whether the sky was overcast or merely smoggy. The only stars visible were the twinkling lights on the freeways of the Los Angeles basin. Well, there were a few minor celebrities roaming about the house. Mostly of the one-shot and has-been variety that tended to gravitate to studio wrap parties. For the most part it was a gathering of regular studio people: working actors, grips, light techs, and camera guys. His brother, Angel, always managed to con him into tagging along to these things. And he was so pissed that Angel had tricked him this time; promising a party, but setting him up for a casting session instead.

"Don't they already have a show like that on daytime?"

The woman sipped her chardonnay as her cohort leaned into Caesar's personal space. "Not like this one, baby."

Unlike the pair he was talking with, Caesar had dressed in a low-key, not-meant-to-be-noticed fashion. Well, noticed, but not the *Studio* type of noticed. New, but somewhat faded, and loose jeans contrasted with the tight white T-shirt. A thick, black belt pulled the pants in at the waist enough to illustrate that he had one. His boots were of the steel-toed construction variety.

Caesar attempted to set his can on the rail he was leaning against. Misjudging the distance, his beer went spiraling down into the canyon behind them. Damn, that meant fighting the crowd inside for another drink. Trying to remember how many beers that made for the night, Caesar pushed his thick, black hair behind his ear. It was one of the few vanity points he allowed himself, letting it grow down to his shoulders. "Maybe." He stalled. "It might work."

"Oh no man, you're perfect." Cigarette stains flashed when he smiled, and Caesar wondered why his partner hadn't introduced him to her dentist. "Trust me, you are one-hundred-and-fifty percent of what we need. You're good looking." His slow once-over clued Caesar into the fact it wasn't a merely professional appraisal. "Hispanic—ethnicity is so big right now. And," he drew out the word like a sales pitch, "your brother Angel says you used to be really good," the guy's voice dropped to a near whisper as he finished the thought, "at, you know, breaking into peoples' homes."

Angel was so dead when they got back to his place. "Yeah, I used to be."

"Well, as long as it's in the past. The bonding company for Housebreaker," bald man cooed, "requires that you don't have any convictions for that kind of thing in the past five years."

Behind the bald man, framed between the sliding door and his shorn head, an argument caught Caesar's attention. The female half of it he couldn't give a damn about. Now the guy... whole 'nother story there. Too bad he was with a girl. The one good thing about these studio parties Angel tended to drag him to was the chance to meet a guy or two. And that one was so worth meeting. Not much taller than Caesar, but with nice, broad shoulders and an ass that made his mouth water. Either light brown or blond hair—dim light made it hard to pin down—was cut military fashion. It set off his square-jawed profile just perfect. Maybe a stunt man—he had that kind of look about him: —rough and tumble and used to playing hard.

Absently, Caesar toyed with the fringe of his not-quite-goatee and mumbled his answer. "Nope. No arrests, no convictions." He'd been pulled in for questioning a few times in the past five years but no arrests.

The argument was quiet, but hot, if the guy's grim face gave any indication. They split in a huff, the girl heading towards the rail where Caesar stood being hounded, the guy heading back into the house. Shit!

"Well, good then. See, it's just perfect." It was the woman's turn to over-stress her vowels. "You have my card, call me. We'll bring you in for a screen test."

"You simply must do it." Bald man's hand hammered his shoulder like they were old friends. "We had our doubts when Angel mentioned you. But just meeting you, it feels like it was meant to be."

That brought him back from the rapidly-disappearing eye-candy. "I'll think about it. Really, I will."

"Do that." Twin, not quite skin contact, kisses to each cheek from the plastic surgery queen, and the pair was off. Caesar slumped, relieved, against the rail. He couldn't believe there were people who sought out those kinds of conversations. Any more of that and he would have jumped into the canyon to escape.

Caesar turned to his left when a warm laugh sounded. The female half of the argument studied him, her wine glass held loosely over the edge. "Making your big break, huh?" Emerald eyes appraised him with critical curiosity. Eyes that clear a green were rare. This was Hollywood central casting, they could be contacts, but somehow this woman didn't seem the type. Hell, she didn't even dye her hair. And while she was partied up, with tight jeans and one of those gauzy shirts that were all the rage, it didn't scream *notice me*. The fake girls all screamed that.

"Them?" He shook his head. "They're pimping for some kind of reality show. My little brother works camera on one of their shows. He's just trying to get me," Caesar racked his brain for a moment coming up with an innocuous enough dodge, "steady work."

"Really," she said, tucking her longish, natural blond hair behind one ear. "Sick of waiting tables?"

"Actually, I don't act." He always felt a little embarrassed saying that. Everyone in Los Angeles wanted to act. It was almost a city ordinance. "I'm in construction."

"Oh. Thank God." Swigging the wine, she let out an exaggerated groan. "I'm so sick of talking with actors and wannabe actors. I manage talent, mostly voice-over talent right now, but the agency is starting to groom me to go up the ladder."

"That's good." What people do for a living and why it sucks. Caesar chuckled. In Southern California, that type of conversation was often odd, but much more human, than just industry talk. "Nice to move up."

"So much better then baby-wrangling, where I started." She mimicked his laugh and took another large gulp of her Zinfandel. "Our agency has a good relationship with Jeff and Millie. They produce a bunch of those daytime TV how-to shows. They treat their people well—all of them, not just the talent." She took another swig. "If they're offering you a job, you should jump. I guess you're talking about one of their home improvement gigs?"

"Something like that." He really didn't want to get involved, but this woman was hitting it pretty hard. Getting too drunk at these types of parties could be hazardous to your career. Say the wrong thing to the wrong person, and you'd end up on a studio blacklist. "You okay? Looked like you and your boyfriend had a kinda nasty fight."

The woman offered a long-suffering sigh as she waved toward the sliding glass door. "Oh, the goon?" Then she laughed and wobbled slightly. Not overly steady either, Caesar stepped in to catch her arm before she could topple off her heels. "He's not my boyfriend. He's my brother."

Not her boyfriend. His non-committal, "Oh," must have packed too much interest because her green eyes sparked.

Inebriated, but seductive, a soft turn at the corner of her mouth sent warning bells ringing for Caesar. "Really." Her hand ran across his where he still held her arm. "I'm single."

Trying for casual, but coming off as strained, Caesar choked out, "I'm gay."

She blinked. Her shoulders slumped. "Well, hell, this *is* Los Angeles. All I ever meet are gay men... or really ugly ones." Then he got a broad, friendly smile. "So you were watching us fight? That means you were checking out one of the two of us, hmm?" Caesar failed miserably at trying not to be embarrassed. Again, the seductive look came out. "My brother's single, too." Her eyes got even brighter. "And we have the exact same taste. We're twins, you know."

Uhng, he had such a thing for blonds. Especially ones with tight asses and green eyes. The mental image sent his hormones into overdrive. "Really?" His gaze slid toward the door where that sexy, tight ass had disappeared.

"Yep, exactly the same taste in *men*." Looking at her empty glass, she sighed. "Come on." An arm threaded through his. "I need another drink, and then I can introduce you." She smiled. "By the way, I'm Carol."

He returned the smile. "Caesar." They stepped back into the house and the crush of people. First he snagged another beer for himself and more wine for Carol. Then they were on the hunt for a blond man with a tight, fine ass. "Are you sure this is okay?"

"Oh, hell, yes." She smirked, squeezing his bicep. "Trust me, Nate will just adore you. And he's got to be just frustrated as all hell by now. I bring him to these gigs, he wanders around drooling over everybody, goes home alone and then tells me about what he should have said over the next week. He just needs to get laid. Oh!" With a jerk on his arm Carol stopped dead. "I didn't mean it like that. It sounded like I'm pimping him out or something."

Caesar almost contradicted her, then thought better of it. No sense humoring a drunk too much. "You make him sound pretty desperate."

"Not desperate." Blushing hard, she lifted her glass to cover her mouth. After gulping down more wine, she continued. "The one place we're not the same," her free hand fluttered up and down her torso, "besides the obvious, is I'm the party girl. Outgoing. Gregarious. Nate's more the quiet, shy type. He's no bumbling virgin, had a few longish relationships." Blond hair whipped loose as Carol shook her head and led him down a narrow set of stairs. If he remembered correctly there was a game room on the bottom floor. Caesar was very good at memorizing the floor plans of houses he visited, even when he didn't mean to. "But his current job makes it real hard for him to meet people. They change up his shift a lot."

Caesar missed a step and had to grab the rail to keep from toppling onto Carol. "What does he do?"

Since she was in front of him, Caesar couldn't get a read on her face, but he thought she hesitated before responding. "Security." A shorter pause. "I'll let him tell you about it. Nate hates it when I ramble about his life to other people." At the bottom of the stairs she looked back at him and smiled. "I see the wallflower now."

Caesar did, too; a well-built guy holding up a piece of wall and cradling a beer. The guy absently watched the pool game in progress, in which two chorus-line starlets were skunking a pair of guys. Big meaty guys, in crummy clothes: Caesar pegged them as either grips or set construction.

Carol danced around the pool cues and headed for her brother. "Nate," she burbled, "you've been hiding from me. I want you to meet someone."

Nate's whole body slid into a long-suffering slump. Then he rolled his eyes. "You're drunk."

"Yep." She slid under his arm. "And you're gay." Bumping his hip she added, "Gay Nathan Reilly meet hot, gay guy Caesar whose last name I don't know."

Nate's green eyes went wide as he glared at his sister. A comic, wide-eyed stare met his, with the addition of a tongue half stuck out of her mouth. If Caesar had any doubts on their twin status, that little exchange of sibling love put them to rest.

"But," Carol drew out the word, "who was checking out your butt earlier on the patio."

This was the most unusual, and funny, introduction Caesar'd ever had. "Hi." He took a swallow of his beer and hooked his thumb in his jeans' pocket. "You have quite a sister."

"You don't know the half of it." Nate growled.

Now Carol wiggled out from under her sibling's embrace. "My work here is done. You're talking to someone. Ciao, boys." A finger dance of a wave dismissed them. "Use condoms."

Nate chewed on his cheek. Shame, tempered by obvious interest, tightened his square jaw. It gave his ears just the slightest pink tinge. Caesar took the opportunity to really look the man over. Everything was tight, not just his ass. And Nate was packed, solid... not gym rat going-for-competition solid, but with a working man's broad shoulders and biceps. It was the kind of body that said "I work out because I might actually need to bust someone's head in." Where the V of Nate's collar exposed his chest, a slight tufting of blond hair curled over the fabric. Fuck! Blond, green-eyed, muscled and with chest-hair... Caesar was going to blow in his jeans.

Finally, Nate growled again. "I'm going to kill her." That growl was damn sexy.

"Really?" Caesar gave his best come-on smile. "I was thinking of sending her a box of chocolates and some roses." More pink crawled up from Nate's collar. It was just edible.

Actually, he was almost as desperate as Carol made Nate sound. Given what Caesar did for a living, long-term relationships were out of the question. Finding someone who would buy the lifestyle of a housebreaker... well Caesar'd never even gotten close to having that discussion. Anything past three dates constituted long term for him. The moment a guy started in with "what do you really do?" it was over. However, a couple dates with Nate might be a doable plan.

"My sister messes in my life too much." Nate shifted. If Caesar had to guess, Nate was checking him out.

"So, is that a bad thing tonight?" Caesar knew what he had; not as buff as Nate, but tight. And even with loose jeans, there was something there to see; especially with the direction his thoughts had been going. Caesar figured he was a little vain, but enough guys had confirmed it for him. Landing a date hadn't ever been much of a problem. He'd just have to draw Nate out a bit to hit paydirt "Maybe we should go find somewhere quiet to talk." He stepped in close, almost, but not quite, touching.

"Talk?" Nate shifted so that their hips bumped.

"Or make out, I'm good with either." He was a little drunk himself to let that slip out. Caution—the trademark of a professional burglar. Maybe tonight he could let it down a little. Or maybe he should stop drinking, ask for a phone number and put it off until he was a bit more sober.

"There's a…" Nate's tongue stroked the edge of his teeth. Then he swallowed. "There's a kinda private patio outside the guest room down here. We could talk there."

The hell with later, now was good. "Lead the way."

CHAPTER 2

They didn't talk, not a bit. Nate slid through the door, Caesar slid his hand across Nate's ass, and Nate's hesitation vanished. He grabbed Caesar and pulled him into a hard, heady kiss. Maybe, Caesar mused, Nate just wasn't into public scenes. Whatever, because the way Nate's tongue moved in Caesar's mouth drove him nuts. Completely wrapped up in tongues, lips and inappropriate public touching, Caesar lost himself in the moment. At least until someone walked out for a smoke and yelled, "Jesus, get a room!"

A few sputterings followed before Nate suggested moving to his place. Caesar texted his brother that he'd see Angel in the morning while writhing in the passenger seat of Nate's old Taurus. How the man could feel him up and still manage to drive was unfathomable in Caesar's current condition.

Then he shoved his cell onto the clip, leaned over and unzipped Nate's jeans. Two could play that game. Nate hissed, "Holy shit!"

For a moment Caesar could only stare. Nate's cock throbbed hard under his shorts. There was already a little wet spot staining the gray cotton, dark from the desire leaking out the tip. It had been way too long since Caesar had seen anything so delectable. He licked his lips.

Hooking his fingers in the band of Nate's shorts, Caesar pulled them down enough to draw out Nate's cock. God damn, Nate had a good looking prick. It wasn't terribly long, but nice and wide, something that would fill you up good. That prick looked stiff enough to burst. Thick veins stood out in hard relief under light brown skin. Nate's dick was about a shade darker than the rest of his body. It contrasted so nicely with the blond curls spilling out of his jeans. Caesar's mouth watered and his prick throbbed like mad with just the thought of tasting Nate.

Finally, desire got Caesar moving and he ran his tongue over the silky skin. Caesar wrapped one hand around the base of Nate's prick and slid the other into his own pants.

"Fuck! In the car?" Nate moaned and the Taurus revved. It must have been awhile for the blond hunk as well.

Caesar mumbled, "Mmmhmm," wrapping his lips around Nate's purple head. His tongue toyed with the slit. It tasted so good, salty and slightly sweet. Caesar sucked down until he buried his nose in the blond curls crawling up towards Nate's navel. His own prick hot in his hand, Caesar savored the taste. Nate's cock burned his tongue. He loved the way the flare of Nate's head caught his lips as he pulled back. It was like velvet moving in his mouth.

A horn blared and Caesar felt the Taurus swerve. He started, pulling back, but then Nate's hand was cupping the back of his skull and pushing him back down. When Nate's fingers slid through his hair, Caesar arched into the touch. God, he loved when guys played with his hair. It was the main reason he'd never cut it. And Nate knew what he was doing, tugging every so often, letting Caesar know just how he enjoyed being sucked. Shivers ran down Caesar's spine, landing in his hips and his cock.

From above him, Nate's voice drifted down. "Yeah, like that, just like that." Caesar had to smile. He'd landed himself a talker. Talkers turned him on. There was nothing better than hearing a guy beg for what he wanted. He definitely intended to have Nate begging by the end of the night.

Still, it was hard to get the right motion going, wedged between Nate and the steering wheel. Didn't matter much, this would just be the appetizer to the main course. If neither of them got off before they reached Nate's place, they'd be that much more excited. Of course, by the way Nate bucked into his mouth, Nate wasn't going to last much longer.

Caesar slowed it down, pulling off and just licking from base to tip. "Jesus, don't tease me!" Nate's moan rewarded him.

"Tell me what you want. Let me hear you say it." Caesar punctuated his demand with a nip just below the head of Nate's cock. He cupped his own balls, sliding his wrist against his prick. It was difficult keeping the pleasure going without speeding it up. He'd save getting off until later.

"Suck me." Nate panted. "Please God, suck me."

Licking back down along the warm vein, Caesar whispered, "After that?"

"I want..." Nate's fingers tightened in his hair. "I want you to..." The pull against his scalp added such delicious pressure to the fire burning in Caesar's hips. "Shit, I want you fuck me. Pound me hard." Oh good, that was out of the way. Caesar could swing either way, but it was easier not to have to *negotiate* about who topped or bottomed.

Instead of sucking, he licked and teased, tracing patterns on Nate's prick with his tongue. Nate shifted in his seat trying to get his cock into Caesar's mouth. The car jerked as Nate overcorrected and Caesar grabbed Nate's thigh to keep from sliding off his own seat. Each time Nate moved, Caesar moved as well, keeping the contact as tenuous as possible. It was terrible, but fun, keeping Nate on edge like that... hell, keeping them both on edge.

When Nate was all but shaking, Caesar figured it was time to stop kidding around. Sliding his lips over the head of Nate's cock, he sucked down hard. And he kept sucking, keeping the pressure on. Nate babbled nonsense then he tensed. "Oh shit!" was the only warning Caesar got before his mouth filled with cum. Nate tasted just as good as promised: salty, slightly sweet and thick on his tongue.

Caesar pulled back, dragging his hand from his jeans, laughed and licked his lips. A wide, green-eyed, sideways stare caught him as Caesar adjusted his seat belt. "What?"

"Fuck, just fuck." Nate breathed.

Caesar ran his knuckles over Nate's thigh and got a shiver in response. "How much longer?"

"Until what?"

"Until we get to your place?" Caesar slammed his hand against the dash as the brake lights of car in front of them flashed. Instead of slowing, Nate risked a quick glance over his right shoulder and then cut across two lanes of traffic.

Caesar realized they were pulling off the freeway. "I guess that answers my question." A few minutes later they pulled into the outdoor lot of a large apartment complex. Whether or not Nate was open about his lifestyle to his neighbors hadn't been broached, so Caesar decided to play it safe, following Nate with his hands safely in his own pockets. For once he didn't memorize his surroundings. Instead, Caesar focused on memorizing how Nate's butt moved in his jeans.

Finally, they were there, past the small patio and through a door set off-center in a wall full of windows. Nate's place was a typical one-space-for-everything apartment. Spartan described it well: one chair, one small couch and a cheap coffee table to the right. Just beyond that two barstools snuggled under the breakfast-bar separating the living area from the tiny kitchen. You could look through the paltry excuse for an eating area and catch a glimpse of a pool through the sliding glass doors. That's as much of a look as Caesar got before Nate's mouth was on his. They stumbled around the TV and through a door in the left hand wall. Shirts and shoes lay strewn through the apartment in their wake. Nate pulled him into a bedroom barely big enough for the queen-sized bed on a Hollywood frame. They bumped into the dresser, knocking pictures to the floor.

Nate fumbled with the buttons on Caesar's jeans, his mouth drawing up a bruise on Caesar's neck. "You're fucking horny, aren't you?" Caesar teased. Then he glanced up and caught sight of the art above Nate's bed. A framed poster, drawn comic book style—the scruffy, trench-coated detective's hands were held prayer-like before his face. Washed out nightmare assortments of skulls backed him. Pentagrams and other evil symbols were overlaid across his form. That was just plain weird. Well, sharing a guy's taste in art was not a prerequisite to screwing him.

"Suck me off in the car on the way over and you call me horny?" Nate growled again. "Get out of those fucking jeans."

That brought Caesar's attention back to the here and now. Caesar laughed and hooked his fingers into the band of his pants. As he slid them off his hips, he teased. "Want me to throw you on the bed, spread those legs wide and make you take it all?"

"Oh, fuck yeah!" Nate shimmied out of the last of his own clothes before falling back onto the bed. Damn, that *hombre* was *tío bueno*. Nate's thick cock was back up and ready, straining out of the mass of blond curls between his spread legs. Half-lidded green eyes and the tongue running across his bright white teeth screamed "come and get it." That and the way Nate ran his hands across his own belly and thighs. Tight abs, defined chest and arms and suddenly Caesar felt a little self-conscious about his own body. Nate obviously hit the gym pretty often. Caesar lifted a little at home, but mostly just worked.

Too late for second thoughts, Caesar swallowed. "Where you keep shit?"

"Next to the bed. In the top drawer."

"Keeping it real handy, huh?" After digging a box of condoms and some gel out of the nightstand, Caesar crawled up onto the bed. Tongue working along Nate's chest, he fumbled the cap off the lube. Nate's skin tasted of salt and lust. It was one sexy combination.

Nate moaned as Caesar slid two slick fingers around his hole. "Not like it gets used much."

"That makes two of us, then." Caesar snorted, teeth running along Nate's jaw. "So are you a chocolate and flowers kinda guy, or are you ready now?"

"I'm so fucking ready." Nate lifted his hips into the touch. "You don't know how ready."

Caesar pushed one finger against Nate's hole. After a moment's resistance, Nate's body almost seemed to suck him in. Hot, tight and eager, Caesar loved that combination. He felt Nate twist against him. His other hand wandered through the light fur on Nate's chest.

Low and deep, Nate moaned. "Kiss me!" Nate pulled Caesar up to his mouth, driving them together, hard. "Damn, you still have the taste." That made Caesar smile into the kiss. He could feel Nate's hands on him, and his body reacted with a shudder. So hot, the man was rolling the condom over Caesar's raging hard-on. As he pulled out his finger, he couldn't help pushing into the touch. Then Nate wrapped his legs around Caesar and Caesar slid in between Nate's thighs.

He had no idea who made the first move, but fire lit him up as his cock was swallowed by Nate's body. Nate's channel was so tight. Nate's groan of, "Oh, yeah, fuck me good," lit Caesar's nerves like a roman candle. Then Nate wrapped his ankles behind Caesar's ass, letting him go deep and hard. Caesar could feel the other man's hand between them, jerking himself off as he got pounded. Nate obviously knew what he wanted and went for it. And he kept up the stream of "Fuck mes" and "So goods" that sent Caesar to heaven.

Caesar buried his face against Nate's chest, nuzzling against the fine hair and drinking in his scent. There was no way he could keep it going. It had been too long. Two more deep thrusts and he was shaking as he came. His mind dissolved into the ecstasy screaming through his frame. When his senses restarted, he kept moving. There was a little bit left in him. He tried to angle his prick just so and was rewarded with an, "Oh God!" Hitting that spot again and again, he felt Nate's body tightened around him. Then there was warm cream spilling between them.

When both their tremors subsided, Caesar pulled out and rolled over. He was still panting. The room spun slightly and Caesar wasn't certain if it was the booze or the sex which caused the sensation. Too long and too good, a dangerous combination. "Good?"

Nate's head lolled over. "Very." His eyes were sleepy and satisfied. After a moment he licked his lips. "Ah, this is going to sound silly," Nate ran his hand over Caesar's belly, causing afterglow burns. "Do you, ah, spoon?"

He did. Especially with a guy like Nate, Caesar'd wrap him up all night. "You bet."

CHAPTER 3

Caesar woke to a world that was just a little too bright on the other side of his eyelids. And his head hurt. And his tongue felt like it was coated in fur. An electronic bell screamed against the inside of his skull. It took a moment to realize it wasn't inside but outside. The phone was ringing. Caesar rolled left, arm out and searching, and ran into a warm, muscled back.

He jerked upright, eyes wide open, covers falling across his bare legs. The other man slammed himself against the wall behind the bed. Apparently embarrassed, the blond grabbed a pillow, pulling it over his lap. The man's clear green eyes said he was as startled as Caesar to find himself in this situation.

Nate. The guy's name was Nate something-or-other. There was nothing to be ashamed of between those legs, if Caesar remembered correctly. Oh fuck, he'd gotten way too drunk last night. It had been years since he'd been shit-faced enough to just pick someone up at a party.

The phone rang again. Swallowing, but not taking his eyes off Caesar, Nate fumbled it off the nightstand. "Yo, Reilly here." His glare said if Caesar so much as breathed hard, Nate'd knock his teeth out. "Yeah, okay, I can make it in half an hour, forty-five minutes at the most. Just got to shower and pop some aspirin." He punched disconnect and dropped the phone into the tangle of sheets. "Holy shit!" The words came out as a strangled whisper.

"Ah..." Maybe Caesar'd been drunker than he remembered. "Isn't your name Nate?"

"Yeah, Nathan Reilly." Nate palmed his jaw. "You're..." Eyes skittered back and forth as he searched his brain. "Caesar?"

Caesar tried to laugh. It didn't work well. "Well at least neither of us was so drunk we didn't get names."

"Small consolation there." Offering up a tense smile, Nate slid off the bed. "Look, ah, that was my work." Nate tossed the pillow back onto the mattress. The initial shock seemed to have worn off. When he bared himself, Caesar's cock perked back up. There really was *nothing* for Nate to be embarrassed about with that body. Backing towards the bathroom, Nate said, "I've got to hit the shower and go in."

"I need a ride."

One hand on the vanity cabinet, the other on the closet door, Nate stopped. "What?"

"My truck." Caesar slid to the edge of the bed and swung his legs off the side. Running one hand through his wild hair, he let the other dangle between his knees. "It's at my brother's. I need a ride."

Nate grabbed his temples, fingers meeting over the top of his buzz-cut head. Caesar didn't know if he was trying to think, fighting off a hangover, or both. "Shit, I gotta book. Five guys called in sick today and I've got to cover a shift - on my fucking day off. If it weren't for the overtime..." Looking beset he added, "Why don't you just grab a cab or something?"

That suggestion bordered on ridiculous. Being a slave to someone else's clock was exactly the reason Caesar went into *business* for himself. "I gave my brother all my cash last night for beer."

"Damn," Nate yelled from the bathroom. "Take a twenty out of my wallet. I've got to hit the shower." Then the door slammed.

Caesar sighed. Well, not quite biting your arm off, but, hell, he'd had better morning-after receptions. Nate could have offered him some coffee. At least the sex had been incredible. What he could remember of it. He dug his shorts out of the pile of briefs and pants. Picture frames on the floor caught his attention as he hopped into his clothes. Oh yeah, he remembered running into the dresser while trying to get Nate out of his pants. The memory twisted up one corner of his mouth.

He might as well do a guy who could fuck that good a favor or two. He'd clean up a bit and then see if there were makings for coffee in the kitchen. Nate was probably just startled at the rude awakening, not like Caesar wasn't himself. He knelt down and picked the largest frame up off the floor. Then he damn near dropped it. One of those graduation headshots, Nate's hair was buzzed to almost non-existent. The only things holding up his hat were his ears. On the left side of his deep navy uniform shirt was the silver and gold badge of the Los Angeles Police Department.

For a moment Caesar forgot how to breathe. He dove back into the tangle of clothes, yanking Nate's wallet from his discarded jeans. It opened to the standard California drivers' license on one side and an LAPD ID card tucked in the other. Fuck, he'd just had mind-blowing sex with a *pinche* cop! Shaking, he pulled a bill from the back. He so did not want to take the money. Hitchhiking, however, was a worse plan.

Caesar bolted through the door, still shoving his hands through his sleeves. Better to use his cell and call from down the street. Then he stopped and spun. Before it closed behind him, he grabbed the wood and stepped back into the apartment. He had no clue what part of the city he was in. They'd driven a good ways from Hollyweird. Hopefully a twenty would get him back to his truck. Mass-mailed flyers were piled on the coffee table. Snagging one for the address, Caesar fled into the hazy Los Angeles morning.

CHAPTER 4

Caesar's alarm called him from a restless sleep. A sleep filled with dreams of a green-eyed man begging for "more" and "harder." A hot blond lounged on the bed behind his eyes. Uniform shirt hanging open, police cap pulled over his eyes, legs spread, the vision called to Caesar with a tongue licking his lips and hand stroking his cock. It was the same dream he'd had the night before. The night before that it'd been reality. All of it, except for the uniform.

With a groan, he rolled over. Christ, he'd fucked a cop…one really hot cop, but a cop nonetheless. Caesar still couldn't believe it.

He kicked the covers off. A low growl came from within the folds of the blanket. Ponchito's black muzzle nosed out of the covers. Dark, doggy eyes accused him of all sorts of cruelties…all stemming from being woken too early. The little terrier mixed with God-knew-what would sleep until noon if Caesar let him. "Go back to sleep then!" Caesar growled back and Ponchito snorted. The Saint Francis medal jingled against his rabies tag as the dog wiggled back into the warmth of the covers and Caesar headed for the shower.

Why hadn't he seen it? Being around cops was hazardous to his health. Because no matter what Caesar told his family, he was still breaking into houses. Why did he have to keep thinking about Nate? He'd done the one night stand thing before and never quite been this thrown. If only he wasn't a fucking cop. Caesar shuddered as the spray needled into his skin.

He knew guys with *that* fetish. His uniform fetish, however, involved staying as far away from them as possible. The kind that meant crossing as quickly, and surreptitiously as possible to the other side of the street whenever he saw the police. No cops as friends, no cops as family, no boys in blue, period. Definitely no crawling into bed and fucking them senseless. It was unhealthy, just plain trouble.

He cut off the water, grabbed a towel and stepped onto the mat. His sister, Caesar mused as he toweled off, she always dated guys who were just trouble. Caesar never understood it. Broken hearts and blackened eyes couldn't seem to get her off the kick. When he'd asked her why, Maria-Elisa told him that good boys weren't *exciting*. There was something to a bad boy that just started her heart thumping, got her all worked up before they'd even said anything.

Terrycloth wrapped around his waist, hands clutching the vanity, Caesar stared into the mirror. Maybe that was it: forbidden fruit, dancing with danger and not consciously realizing it. He, like most kids from the barrio, had an innate sense of who the *policia* were. How they walked and talked... just standing behind a random guy at a burger stand and Caesar could tell he was *one of them*. Nate hadn't set those warning bells ringing.

Or he had, and Caesar had been just drunk enough to ignore them. Maybe he'd wanted to ignore them.

Berating himself, he yanked a pair of painter's pants over his hips. Fuck! How could he have been that stupid? He grabbed the T-shirt from the other night off the floor.

As he lifted the shirt to chuck it into the hamper, Nate's cologne rose from the cloth and overwhelmed him again. Memories of those lust-filled green eyes staring up at him crowded in with the scent. He could almost feel Nate's fingers gripping his arms as he moved beneath Caesar. One part of his body had really fond memories of that blond, muscled man. It reminded him, hot and hard, just how good that night had been. "*Chingame!*" Caesar yelled, tossing the shirt into the back of his closet.

Today was planned out ages ago...in a loose, half-assed way. He was going to hit the improvement stores in the Hollywood area. That could lead to jobs in the Hollywood, Los Feliz or Silverlake areas. It had been awhile since he'd worked any of those neighborhoods. If he caught a one-day gig he'd put the cash in his pocket and call it fate. What he was looking for was something that would last closer to a week. That would give him time to scope things out, get a feel for the area and find a mark.

To get there, Caesar had to catch the 5 a.m. bus to the Metro and switch trains once. After a good walk, and over an hour's trip, he was exchanging handshakes and jokes with a dozen other guys looking for work. They were the early crowd. There would be more before eight waiting for whatever jobs came from the contractor's supply. It paid to get there early.

Morning traffic whizzed by on Santa Monica Boulevard. Every make of car in every conceivable condition passed by in the space of twenty minutes. Caesar stood with about twenty-odd men dressed in the uniform of the casual laborer: T-shirts covered by grungy flannel, jeans and cheap steel-toed boots. Whenever a car slowed, they surged into the street and swarmed the windows looking for the signal of how many men were needed.

Caesar could do just about anything. Painting, plastering, bricklaying…all of it learned during brutal Texas summers working beside his dad. Until the day his dad stepped through a tarp-covered hole in a roof while carrying two buckets of tar. It netted him burns over ninety-five percent of his body and a work-comp claim that stretched over five years. By the time it was settled, his family had lost everything. His parents' marriage was wrecked and Caesar was living in Los Angeles with a distant relative.

That's when he started stealing shit.

White, battered and full of five-gallon buckets, tarps and ladders, a full-sized truck slid to the curb. This was what Caesar had been looking for all morning. He lunged through the crowd, yanked the passenger door open and slid onto the bench, beating out a dozen other men. "*Pintura? Un casa?*"

"Yep," the thin man in a baseball cap nodded. "*Dos mas.*"

Caesar leaned out of the window and called to two other men he knew marginally well, Ramon and Miguel. Really good house painters, both of them, they'd worked together a couple of times over the years. One guy had six kids, the other five. They needed the work as bad as any. Plus they covered for him on occasion. They knew that Caesar would work twice as hard when needed and that, like today, he'd pick them out if there was a chance.

The three crowded into the cab. Caesar tried not to push against the driver as he swung out of the parking lot and headed over to Vermont and then East into the Los Feliz neighborhood. Caesar liked that just fine. The area was filled with condos, high-end apartments and expensive homes. Majestic, lacy pines lined Los Feliz Boulevard proper, although palms were prevalent on the more residential avenues. Narrow, winding streets pushed back into the hills above Griffith Park. It was the kind of place where pickings should be good.

Part of Los Angeles proper, it was one of the last places that still held the Hollywood-era glamour. Artists, movie producers and music moguls lived across from doctors, lawyers and other traditional professionals. Young moms jogged the hills, their kids strapped into expensive L.L. Bean strollers. Older couples tended flower gardens overflowing with bougainvillea. You were apt to find modern houses slung off the hills and braced with stilts sitting side-by-side with twenties-era adobes and slapped-together boxes from just after the war. Many were in the process of the gut and rebuild phenomenon typical of Southern California.

As they drove, Caesar negotiated for the group. Although he spoke English just fine, it was better to pretend he didn't. Broken English and the contractor's half-assed Spanish worked well enough. Eighty bucks a day each, four days worth of work scraping siding, prepping surfaces and painting the house. The pay was utter crap—barely half of his month's rent. Caesar was glad the only mouth to feed besides his own was Ponchito's. How guys like Miguel and Ramon raised their kids on these kinds of wages was beyond him. And not his problem.

They bailed out of the truck at the work site. One of the older homes on the wrong side of Los Feliz Boulevard was due for a paint job. Not that it was a bad neighborhood, but the homes on the south side ran close to half a million while to the north, the same type property would top a million easy. And damn, it was one of the cedar-shingled jobbies. Those were hell with all the scraping and prepping they took. It might be longer than a four day gig.

That first day, all Caesar did was keep his eyes and ears open as he worked. He needed to take in the pulse of the neighborhood. Every place in the city had its own feel. Like the ebb and flow of the tide, after a day or so, he could start to see the patterns. Three houses held promise. The first was an antiquated craftsman whose upstairs windows were always left open. While it would be a bit of a trick, Caesar could manage getting to the second floor. Another had boxes from new electronics piled by the garage—a good sign of stuff worth taking inside. The last was a two story English Tudor. What made it so attractive was how invisible it was from the street. Only one window had a street view. All three homes were vacant most of the day.

His preference was always an unoccupied house with easy access, lots of cover, and a couple of escape possibilities. An open window would make him damn near hard. Even without that, Caesar knew to watch the kids and maids. They often clued him in to the allegedly hidden keys in planters, under doormats, and above the ledge. The longer he could watch, the more comfortable he felt. The best was to blend into a neighborhood. Caesar always got uncomfortable under too much scrutiny. Once in a great while, a target of opportunity was too good to pass up, but those also carried the most risk of getting caught in the act. The last thing Caesar wanted was to get caught in the act. That carried the potential for things to go really bad.

The third day he hit pay dirt. While he was painting trim under the eaves, he had a decent view of both the Tudor and Craftsman. That morning a man had left the Tudor with a large dog in tow. Although he could charm most any pooch, Caesar often avoided homes with dogs because they were apt to start barking. Attention was not good. Shortly afterward Mom and two kids, a junior-high level boy and a high-school aged girl left for the day. Except for the dog, it was the usual pattern for the house. He filed the information in the back of his brain.

An hour later the man came back, climbing out of the SUV without the dog. His wife nearly ran him over as she pulled into the drive. Usually both were gone all day. It was mid-week and both adults were home. Throughout the day, Mom came and went on errands. They were generally short and quick. The only time she left for any length of time was to get the son from soccer camp. Something was definitely up at that house.

That afternoon, Caesar sat at the bus stop waiting for the local bus that would take him to the Metro Red Line. Each day he varied which stop he chose. Four were within a reasonable walking distance, and with what he'd seen earlier he picked the one caddy-corner from the Tudor. It gave him time to study the target with more detail. The house was brick and siding with ivy growing up the sides. A circular drive wound by the front door although on the left side it jogged back to a garage. Overgrown shrubs blocked most of the windows, other than the formal living room that Caesar could look into as he passed. A large privacy fence enclosed the entire back of the property. Trees and such blocked the view from the few other houses with second floors.

As he watched, a white Honda Del Sol pulled up to the curb. Three girls were piled into the coupe. All three were California-high-school-girl pretty. One of them shimmied out of the passenger side. Blond hair was pulled back into a ponytail and frayed shorts rode up her ass. The driver propped herself up to look out the open sunroof as her passenger trotted to the back of the car and popped the trunk. That girl had short-cut brown hair, the other passenger Caesar couldn't see. "Come on Shay," the driver whined, "you have to come this weekend." All three wore beach clothes. Their white T-shirts were as skimpy as they could possibly get away with.

Caesar's mind flashed to an image of Nate wearing a pair of cutoff jeans. Oh hell, Nate'd look so good in them. That tight, toned ass just peeking from under an edge of raveled denim. A white T-shirt pulled across his chest so tight. Uhng, especially one of those tank tops, a little bit of fur would peek out the top and his biceps would just catch the sun to perfection. Then, he'd bend over that white, little Honda and show his ass off.

What the hell was he doing? Caesar pulled himself from his daydreams and pretended to read the timetable posted under the bus sign. He also watched the girls out of the corner of his eye. With teenaged girls, not watching or watching too much garnered the same level of suspicion. What he wanted was to pass the *some jerk looking* radar so it would be unremarkable. It was a delicate balance…sort of like scoping out other gay guys at Mexican weddings. Do it wrong and someone was liable to bust your head in.

Shay's body went into a long-suffering slump as she pulled a bag from the trunk. "I can't."

Now the other girl piped up. "Why?"

"My dad's got this stupid conference to go to…he's taking us to Disney World." Caesar almost choked at that. People should think about who was around before they said things like that. Of course, he was aiming to blend into the background. Apparently he'd succeeded. "God, it's like he thinks I'm thirteen or something. A week in freaking Florida with my parents and my little brother. They're going to drive me nuts."

"Oh, that is so lame."

"I know." Shay slammed the trunk down hard. "Can you imagine?" She bounced around to the front of the car. "Kisses! We're leaving tonight." She leaned over the seat and Caesar got a shot right down her unsupported cleavage. "Think good thoughts for me while I'm in hell." Then, she skipped up the drive.

Caesar would definitely think good thoughts of her.

CHAPTER 5

The 415E call that broke across the radio landed on Nate's plate to fix. *Highland Park and loud party, who'd a' thunk it.* He swung the Black & White around in the Super-A parking lot and headed down York Boulevard toward Figueroa. From there it was off into the tangle of streets between the Arroyo and Mount Washington.

It was a slow enough evening anyway, which was strange for a Friday. Usually his beat was jumping by four. Shit, in one month they dealt with nearly two hundred violent calls, ranging from a report of shots fired to full out street brawls. Highland Park and the surrounding areas was one of the older barrios. The *Avenidas* gang, allegedly named because the streets in their territory were mostly numbered avenues, held sway on his beat. They were one of LAPD's nightmare gangs: violent, intertwined with the Mexican Mafia, into drugs and extortion and murder for fun. The *Avenidas* had been around forever and were actually made up of a collection of smaller cliques working together. Hell, with Mexican gangs, anything that hadn't been around since before World War II was considered a fad.

That meant that everywhere he went, even if it was just grabbing a soda at a fast-food joint, he had to be on his toes. LAPD was stretched so thin around here that officers didn't even have partners to watch their backs. Any call had the potential to go sour. There was nothing proactive about his job in this neighborhood…Nate was more like a firefighter, rushing from crisis to crisis trying to throw water on the situation before it got out of control.

It was time to go douse a flame. Hopefully, it would turn out to be no more than a quick in and out. He pulled up to an overbuilt stucco house crammed onto its small lot. Traditional Mexican music, with its mixture of brass and strings, was so loud it vibrated the windows on his patrol car. Lemon-yellow icicle lights still up from Christmas and there was no way the structure was code. Mismatched windows were dark. A driveway headed towards a rear garage and a yard paved with concrete. All the lights were back there. Nate checked in with dispatch before getting out of the car.

Somewhere under the throb of the music was the whine of an air compressor. The corner of a Bouncy House stuck out into the drive. Good, a nice, but loud, family party. Those were usually pretty tame, at least before midnight. After that...get enough booze in anybody and things could go bad. One of the worst calls he'd ever been on was when a career officer's wife had told the guy, during their son's bar-mitzvah, that she wanted a divorce. They'd hauled half the adults out of the party under some kind of charges.

The first person he came across was a middle-aged woman in tight, glitter jeans and a tank-top. She dumped a bag in the garbage, her gaze crawling suspiciously across him. Her hair was permed and streaked unflatteringly. She also could have stood a stint at a diet farm before trying to squeeze into those clothes. Bad taste and Los Angeles, the two were meant for each other. Beyond her, knots of people lounged on fold-out chairs and discarded couches.

The scent of *carne asada* grilling made Nate's stomach growl. Damn, it smelled good. He'd head for dinner after this call. There were a couple of decent, late night Mexican joints nearby. Nate's thumb was hooked into his Sam-Brown belt, up near his gun. It was casual. Still, if he needed his weapon, it was right there. Nate would treat this call with caution until he knew otherwise

"*Hola, Señora.*" He greeted the woman, giving her a warm, I'm-not-here-for-trouble smile. Nate's Spanish was serviceable in most situations, although his accent sucked. "*Como esta usted? Es su casa?*" He jerked other thumb toward the house to make his point. She glared at him then shook her head no. "*Donde es el Señor de la casa?*"

Children had gathered by the wall of the Bouncy House and were staring at him. Nate waved and then put his arms casually at his side. He tried to keep his body language open and helpful. Still, he was wary. On this beat he was always wary. The woman shrugged, "Hold on, I'll find him." Her English was better than his Spanish. All the kids laughed. Just to show he had a sense of humor, Nate did an exaggerated roll of the eyes and thumped his temple with his palm. That earned him more giggles. She walked away screaming, "Juan!" at the top of her lungs.

He stayed slightly in shadow at the edge of the party, although he moved to where the building next door was at his back and he could see most of the guests. Prudent, he wanted to have a clear view of them, while keeping to the shadows himself. Somewhere around the back of the house, Nate could hear a conversation. Spanish mixed with English and border slang made it hard for him to know exactly what was said.

A minute or so later a heavy-set man in slacks and a bowling shirt trundled around the corner. His mustache bristled as he considered Nate. "What?"

"Nothing much." Nate flashed the same smile he'd given to the woman earlier. "We just had a complaint about the music. Look, it's almost nine-thirty. Why don't you turn it down a few decibels?"

"Why?"

How come the guy was going to be a dick about things? If he turned it down, then Nate could bail for dinner and they could go back to their party. "Look, just turn it down."

"Big shot cop," the man growled. "Don't like the music?" It sounded like booze, not brains, talking.

Nate chewed on his lip. "Right now I'm asking you, nicely, to turn it down." His smile went tight, not friendly. "In another minute, I'll be writing you a citation for noise. Which would you rather have? It's all up to you."

For a moment they were locked in a stare-down. Finally the guy shrugged and moved off towards the stereo. "Thank you." He shot at the guy's back. Nate would lay odds that they'd be back out to this party in another hour or two. Hopefully, by that time, he'd be off-shift and at the twenty-four hour gym, winding down. Oh well, the fire was contained for the time being.

As he walked back toward his car, Nate again took note of his surroundings. Just because things seemed to have gone well, didn't mean they actually had. Some guy was leaning against the chain link, a beer dangling from his hand over the fence. A small, black dog scurried about the yard, attacking, then retreating from a worn stuffed animal. White T-shirt, jeans, and longish hair, Nate couldn't make out much else as his eyes were still adjusting from the light at the back. He squinted a little to sharpen the outline.

"It's a birthday party, they're not causing problems." Lifting his head, the man glared out from under heavy bangs. "Why don't you go bust somebody else's chops?"

"Why don't you mind your own…." Then Nate realized he knew that voice. That sensual purr had throbbed at the back of his brain for days. "Oh fuck!" He breathed. Caesar.

Last Sunday, Nate had come out of the shower intending to apologize. Gruff on a good day, that morning's hangover hadn't improved his personality. And, well, he'd been a bit blindsided waking up in bed with a hot guy. Usually he was a lot more cautious than that. He was a cop, a gay cop, he had to be cautious. When he realized Caesar had bolted, without even scribbling his phone number, Nate knew he'd fucked up a good chance. Nate kicked himself that entire day, and the next and the next. Just when he'd managed to chalk it up to experience, who did he have to run into? The odds of that, in a city the size of Los Angeles, were staggering.

"Shit!" Caesar must have realized it was him at the same time.

Why did he have to be Officer Reilly right now? He'd give damn near anything to be out of uniform and off duty. He wasn't. "Put the beer away."

Dark eyes glared at him. "Why? I'm in my own yard." Caesar turned and snapped at the dog. "Ponchito, stop yapping." The dog wasn't barking and Nate could tell Caesar was just trying to avoid an awkward moment. The dark-haired man tossed back another swig before turning toward his house.

Nate stood frozen, feet glued to the concrete. He couldn't move. Fuck, he was going to let Caesar just walk away? No way in hell was he just going to let Caesar walk away from him again.

"Wait, hold on a sec." Nate keyed the mike on his shoulder. After clearing the call and giving the code that said he'd be on break for a bit, he jogged around to the front. Caesar glared at him. "Can I talk to you for a minute?" Even that glare was smoking. When Caesar didn't answer, Nate took it for a yes. The terrier mix was all over his ankles as he slid through the gate. "Look, I'm sorry about the other morning. I kinda freaked."

Caesar started walking towards the detached garage. "You think?" His house was small, with beaten dirt for a yard and light-colored paint. Wrought iron bars covered the windows and a dark, metal security door made the place look like a run-down fortress. It was anything but uncommon in this area.

This had to look bad: big, buff cop trailing after some guy like a puppy. Nate hoped this didn't get back to anyone. Keeping his voice low, he explained, "Look, I haven't done anything like that in a while. I didn't handle it well. I'm sorry. Can we re-wind to slightly before that, pretend it didn't happen?"

"No." Caesar disappeared into the garage, slamming the warped, wooden door behind him.

Nate stood adrift in the barren yard. He should just walk away. He'd pissed the guy off and that was that. But there was no way he was going to leave it there. At the very least he was going to apologize properly. He'd rather get a phone number and a date, but he'd live with not leaving things completely fucked up. Hell, if Caesar had treated Nate, the way Nate had treated Caesar, he'd be pretty damn mad, too. Swallowing his pride, he turned the knob and stepped in.

The door opened onto the scent of sawdust and oil. A yellow light hung from the rafters, throwing shadows into the corners. Lathe, table saw, jig, Nate hadn't seen half those tools since high school woodworking class.

Caesar settled onto a stool as he grabbed a piece of sandpaper and a bit of wood. The little dog darted between Nate's legs and crawled onto a pillow under the workbench. It looked like Caesar spent a lot of time in his little shop. Nate shut the door, crossed his arms and leaned against the frame. "Look, I'm sorry."

"For what?" Caesar didn't look at him.

Damn, the man was going to make this hard. "For being an ass. That was shitty, the way I treated you Sunday morning. I'd be pissed, too. I wasn't feeling good and, fuck, I haven't had anyone over in ages. It really freaked me out, but I shouldn't have taken it out on you." Caesar just kept sanding the surface of the wood. *Shit, shit, shit.* "Aren't you going to say anything?"

"Like what?" Caesar slammed the board on the workbench. Turning on Nate, his eyes were dark and narrowed. "Thanks for the lay, get the fuck out of my garage?" They stared at each other for a while. Finally Caesar looked away. He grabbed a peg and some wood glue, twirling the end in the sticky yellow goop before jabbing it into a hole drilled along the edge.

Nate watched as Caesar picked up another narrow piece of wood. "What are you making?"

Without looking up, Caesar answered. "A TV cabinet." He squeezed more glue into the holes in the end of the board.

"You do a lot of those kinds of projects?"

"Some." Caesar sighed. It was one of those, *why haven't you left yet* sighs. "My dad taught me how."

More tense silence stretched between them. Nate broke it. "Okay, look, I was a jerk. I said I'm sorry. But, I had fun, and I want to get to know you better."

Slowly Caesar set the glue back up on his workbench. He put his hands on the surface and pushed back. "You and me, not a good idea, okay?"

"How do you know?"

"You're a fucking cop." It looked like Caesar was thinking hard. Finally, he spat out, "Look around you. This is *Avenidas'* territory. You think that blue uniform and blond hair is going to go over well around here? They'd pop you just because. Nobody bugs me because I stay low. I just try and live my life and stay out of people's way. Being seen with a cop ain't staying low."

"I thought you liked my blond hair?" The moment he said it, Nate regretted the words. Caesar was trying to give him some serious reasons and he was cutting up. "Look, I guess I should have told you what I do, but a lot of gay guys don't like cops. They want to buy the fancy uniforms at the Pleasure Chest and play dress up, but meet some guy who wears the real thing and they're gone."

That earned him another glare. "Gee, I wonder why? Wouldn't have anything to do with the blue gang being notoriously homophobic, would it?"

"Obviously, I'm not." Nate cocked his hip against the workbench and crossed his arms over his chest. "Give it a chance and see how things work out. Maybe after a couple of dates we'll find out we really don't get along, but maybe we will." Tilting his head and smiling with his eyes, he added, "Give me your phone number."

Caesar went back to fiddling with the wood. "Why?"

Up close, Nate realized it was part of a door frame. Caesar would probably fit it with glass when he was done. "So I can have your number, so I can call you?" For some reason he really liked that Caesar worked with his hands. It made him so much more down to earth than the actors and production assistants Carol always introduced him to. The neighborhood, too, it just fit that Caesar wasn't all uppity about working in the industry. He tried to remember exactly what his sis said Caesar did at the studios, but couldn't bring it to mind. Set construction, maybe that was it.

"Why would I want you to do that?" Caesar was stubborn. Nate liked guys who were stubborn. With his tough guy build and blond looks, he didn't have to go after many guys. The working out was more of a defensive strategy. Even if someone in the department figured out he was gay, the fact that Nate was built like a brick wall made them keep their opinions to themselves. The few times he'd hit *the scene* he'd had men drooling all over him. But the kind who came chasing after him, Nate didn't really want.

"Okay, be that way." Nate pulled the pen from his pocket. Leaning over Caesar's shoulder, he scribbled his home phone on the wall. "Now you have mine." Then he tucked the pen back in place.

Caesar reached for a clamp. "My landlady's gonna love you for that." Nate grabbed the end of the board to steady it while Caesar fitted a plastic bar clamp where it would be most effective. "Thanks." Quick squeezes of the trigger tightened it down.

"No problem." Nate's chest was still pressed up against Caesar's back. He could feel the warmth through the heavy cotton of his uniform shirt...at least the portions not swathed in Kevlar. God, the man was sexy, even with wood glue dripping off his fingers. Voice low, seductive, Nate whispered, "You know, I've been thinking about you a lot since Saturday."

"I don't date cops, Nate." Each word was given separate emphasis.

"Why?"

"Cause it's just gonna cause a lot of trouble." Caesar dropped the piece he was working on onto the counter. Then he propped one elbow on the edge and put his forehead against his palm. There was still glue on his fingers. Now it was also in his hair. "It's not you personally. I just don't need that kind of trouble." There was an undercurrent of fear in his voice. Living in Highland Park, Nate didn't doubt Caesar was worried. Still, he knew cops who'd grown up avoiding the *Avenidas*. If you wanted to, you could survive it.

"So I won't come around here in my uniform." With his head dropped forward, thick, black hair fell about Caesar's face. It hid his eyes, but exposed the warm brown skin of Caesar's neck. Nate pressed his lips against that sexy flesh and whispered, "Give me a chance."

Caesar hissed. "It's not a good idea." Then he shook himself out from under Nate's kiss. "Besides, I'm still upset about you."

"Then let me apologize." Nate purred, pressing his lips against Caesar's neck. Caesar tried to pull away, but it was a half-hearted gesture. Desire drifted off his skin. Nate's touch snaked down the soft, thin cotton of Caesar's T-shirt. Pulling the fabric up, he stroked Caesar's belly. The fingers of his other hand worked along the muscles of Caesar's arm. Then he ran his palm over Caesar's crotch. Yeah, Caesar was getting hard.... "Don't you want me to apologize to you?"

Caesar's voice was tight. "What do you think is going to make up for what you are?" It lingered somewhere between *fuck me* and *get the hell out of here*.

Yeah, he'd been a jerk, but that wasn't who he was. If Caesar would give him one chance, Nate would prove it to him.

"I bet I can think of something." He fumbled with the button on Caesar's jeans.

"Shit." Caesar sucked in his breath. He reared back and grabbed Nate's wrist.

"I know you want it." Nate didn't let it stop him. Not that Caesar was making much of an effort. The grip on his arm was loose. "You just don't want to admit you want it." He moved between Caesar and the workbench, pushing the stool back with his knee. Dark maple eyes brooded under heavy brows. Caesar's lips were full and turned down ever so slightly at the corners. The barest feathering of a mustache and goatee contrasted nicely against his cinnamon skin. It was more like he'd forgotten to shave for a week, than he was actually cultivating facial hair. All of it was so sensual.

Nate went down on one knee. Concrete, pressing against the heavy-duty fabric of his uniform pants, was rough on his knee. As he moved, he drew Caesar's zipper down. Both men sucked in their breath to the tune of metal clawing against metal. Slow and easy, Nate spread the denim and freed Caesar's cock. Half-stiff, and still slightly trapped under denim, it begged for Nate's kiss. He used his tongue to drag it the rest of the way out. As he caressed that hot flesh with his tongue, Nate could feel Caesar swell. It was so erotic having a guy come alive under his fevered kisses. He sighed. "Oh fuck, your taste."

His own cock was throbbing under the polyester. Damn, that heavy belt, slung with cuffs and pistol and radio, was in the way. The weight of it pressed against his erection. It was too much trouble to take it off. Too many things were clipped to it and then to him. Nate unzipped his pants and pulled himself free. The cold buckle caught his head and he gasped. One hand pumping his own prick, the other wrapped around the base of Caesar's cock, Nate started to lick. "You taste so good. I've been dreaming about this dick in my mouth." He loved being down on his knees in front of a guy. It was one of those things he really got off on.

Nate looked up at Caesar. The thick prick lay against his cheek as Nate sucked on the side. Deep, musky, God, the man even smelled like sex. Caesar's eyes were fogged with lust. The rest of his expression was unreadable. "Then put it in there and suck." Caesar ordered. Oh yeah, a man who knew what he wanted and asked for it. Nate shuddered and twisted his own prick in his hand.

Nate ran his tongue from base to tip. Then he dipped it in the slit, tasting the salty bead hiding there. "See, I knew you wanted it." His mouth roamed all over Caesar's cock. Nate loved playing with the area just below the head because every time he did, Caesar would tremble.

Caesar's fingers were dancing across the back of his neck sending sparks down his spine. Combined with the heat he was stroking into his own skin, Nate's senses were rolling. And there was something deliciously *dirty* about doing it while he was in uniform. That just threw fuel on the fire.

When Nate's mouth was watering he knew it was time to suck. First, he tickled the tip of Caesar's prick with his tongue. Then he wrapped his lips over the head, sliding down the shaft, long and slow. He used his lips to drag the skin back up over Caesar's head. Each time he did, Caesar would moan. Nate's own hips were bucking into his tight fist.

Caesar's ass was coming off the seat. For the first time, Nate heard him drop into Spanish. "*Chulpalmae.*" Caesar panted... *Suck me.* Hell yes, Nate was going to suck him. Caesar's fingers clawed into Nate's scalp as he drove between Nate's lips. Nate loved the feeling of Caesar's prick filling his mouth. The thought that something could be that hard and that soft, all at the same time was incredible. Nate worked Caesar's balls in his hand. Pulling and sucking that tender flesh, Nate felt the cock in his mouth swell.

Then Caesar was thrusting uncontrollably. His hand yanked Nate hard onto his prick. With a grunt, he filled Nate's mouth with his flavor. As Nate jerked himself hard, he sucked the last of Caesar's spunk down. He twisted his cock once, twice through his own tight fist, then he went over the edge. Grinding his face into Caesar's thigh, he blew all over his uniform.

CHAPTER 6

"I know it's those Goddamn day-laborers out there. Why don't you guys do something about them?" A beleaguered fan buzzed in the background, its flow directed toward the desk. Guy Carson, Head of Loss Prevention, had the honor of at least some relief from the heat. Carson leaned back in his chair and it groaned. His graying, thinning hair was greasy, but at least he didn't try for a comb-over. "They're all thieves and crooks." Hands resting on a belly sculpted by cheeseburgers, his rumpled shirt stained with sweat, he gave Nate a knowing wink. "Every one of them."

Pen out, notepad ready, Nate stood at modified attention in the cramped security office. A fine dust of wood shavings tickled his nose. Shifting his weight from one leg to another, the sweat ran between his shoulder blades and pooled beneath the heavy duty belt. He hated when rent-a-cops tried to do his job for him. Some took their job seriously, knew what to watch for and were pretty bright. Those people were a pleasure to work with. Half the ground work was done by the time the police arrived, and done legally and cleanly. Then there were morons like this guy; all attitude and bluster, they screwed up cases and tried to act like big shots. "Well, Mr. Carson, why don't you tell me what's missing and we'll go from there." Emphasis on the Mr. reminded the guy he was not LEO, just a civilian like everyone else.

Swiveling back and forth in his chair, the security officer considered Nate. "What are you going to do about them?"

With that look, Nate knew he'd been considered and dismissed. Too young, too clean-cut, too buffed-out to have a brain, any of those resulted in the same reaction. Still, he was the one wearing the badge. "Them...nothing right now." Nate tapped the pen against the pad. He hated when people didn't answer his questions. "What I'm going to do *right now*, is get a list of what's missing. Then I'll look at whatever surveillance video you have." Nate had noted a few cameras on his walk from the registers to the back offices. "Then, if I think the situation warrants it, I'll talk to a few people."

That seemed to settle it for the guard and not in a terribly positive way. He glared at Nate and grabbed a set of papers off the desk. "An impact wrench, a small compressor, a couple of nice drill combo kits." Waving the papers dismissively toward Nate, he added, "It's all right here. Probably a good grand worth of stuff." His tone said he didn't think Nate was capable of reading the list.

Nate usually only got this kind of attitude when he gave out tickets. It was best if he just ignored the ass. Slow, easy and outwardly calm, Nate indicated the list with a jerk of his chin. "Can I keep that?" When Carson nodded, Nate took the papers and folded them under his note pad. There'd be time to go over the list in more detail when he filled out his reports. "Now, when we're talking a small compressor, what exactly is small?"

"Oh, 'bout yay big," the man used a set of meaty hands to square off a two-foot box, "maybe a little bigger. Weighs close to a hundred pounds."

"Okay, so not something you just stick under your shirt and walk out with?"

"No." Carson shook his head. "Hell, even the drills were good contractor models. Heavy suckers. My boys would notice someone walking out with one of those."

Nate bit his tongue. Obviously, they hadn't. If they had, he wouldn't be standing in this stuffy little office taking a report and smelling Carson sweat. "Okay, and you became aware of the theft how?"

"Inventory." As he tapped his lower lip with one finger, Carson's eyes followed the path of a fly about the room. "They were missing on inventory."

"When was the last inventory…before that one?" Nate's tone jerked Carson's attention back to him.

"Hmm, 'bout three months ago."

"And how were the items stored?"

"What do you mean stored? They're out on the shelves so people can buy them."

"All of them? You don't keep them in a separate area?"

"Well, yeah, there's a tool area. Someone's supposed to be at that desk most of the time, but sometimes it's not staffed, especially if the rest of the store gets busy."

Nate figured he'd just learned about three ways to rip this place off. And he was a cop, not a crook. There were a few he'd probably missed. "So you're doing regular inventory...?"

"No, they normally only do inventory about once every six months, but the owner wants to start carrying this new line. With our shelf space, they have to dump something that's not selling as well. So they decided to do an inventory of the power tools, see where they were placed and they also looked at sales. That's how we found it."

There were a lot of ways to steal shit out of one of these mega-stores. The easiest was to load up a cart and just leave without paying. Any good thief knew how to defeat a door sensor. Give them a place with controls this sloppy and it was a wonder more stuff wasn't missing.

Nate scanned the list. On top of the power tools were sprinkler parts, pipe fittings and a high end kitchen faucet. "What's your return policy?"

"Return policy?"

Sometimes theft was done by return switch. "Yeah, return policy." Thieves would wander through the store with a bag, grab an item, pull the price tag off and take it up for return. If all they got was store credit, they could then buy stuff and sell it. Even when cashiers asked for an ID, there was no guarantee that it was legit. A lot of times, employees were so busy they didn't bother asking for ID or attempt to verify whether the item was sold previously.

"Thirty days...cash with receipt. Store credit if you don't have a receipt."

Nate jotted his notes. "Okay, and your cameras?" He canted his head in the general direction of the sales floor. "Do you film the checkout as well as other parts of the store?"

"Actually," some of the bluster dropped from Carson's tone. "The cameras have been busted for a year. We keep meaning to fix them, but...." The thought trailed off.

Why that surprised him, Nate wasn't sure. Maybe because, short of security officers on every isle, it was one of the cheaper security fixes. "Do your employees know that?"

"Of course. We've told them so that they know to keep a sharp watch on people."

After that bit of bad news, Carson herded him through the store. It was as badly laid out as the security officer's description had painted it. Too many uncontrolled exits, expensive products within tempting reach…again, Nate wondered why they weren't missing more. When the tour was finished, Nate flipped his pad closed. "Okay, I'm going to make out my report, put the goods in the system. You'll probably hear from someone on Theft Detail soon. But, I'm also going to put in a request to get you some of the loss prevention materials we have that you can give to your employees. I'll bring it out next time I'm nearby. You might want to think about hiring a security consulting company." Nate raised his hands to forestall the protest already forming in Carson's mouth. "They can give you some tips on traffic flow management and product placement from a security perspective…it's always helpful to have another pair of eyes." Smacking the inventory sheet against his arm, Nate thought a moment. "And get the cameras fixed. So unless you have anything else, I'll be headed out."

Carson jammed his hands into his pocket. "Go do something about them."

"Who?" Raising his eyebrows as he messed with his pen, Nate knew who the man meant. He had just hoped the guy had forgotten that subject.

"The day-laborers hanging around out front."

Oh, good, they were back on that. Exasperated, Nate sighed. "Why?"

"Because they're bothering my customers." Carson waved a thick-fingered hand in the general direction of the parking lot. "They're blocking the sidewalks. They're a nuisance."

Nate hated to give this bozo the satisfaction, but if it was true, then it was against the law. At least outside of skid row, where there was an enforcement injunction underway. "Okay." He tucked his pen back in his pocket. "I'll go check it out."

Because it inspired more respect, and had air, Nate drove his unit over to where the laborers were hanging out and pulled up to the curb. The heat hit him hard when he opened the door. Damn, it was hot, somewhere above the hundred degree mark. Broiling didn't half describe it. And it was only marginally better in the shade along the edge of the building. Nate had to feel sorry for these guys. Yeah, there were some hustlers that hid in among them, but for the most part, they were just trying to eat. And on a day like this one, that had to be hell. It was late and hot enough that only a few die-hards were left.

He sauntered around the patrol car letting his body language convey he wasn't there for fun. "*Hola amigos*, we need to talk. *Venga se, un momenta.*" Grumbles in a mixture of Spanish and English floated toward Nate, as the men roused themselves. They drifted over. "That means you too, buddy."

The guy uncrossed his arms and pushed away from the wall. "Sure, Nate, whatever you say."

For the second time this week, he hissed out, "Oh fuck!"

"Really?" Caesar pushed the cap back on his head, giving Nate a clear view of those dark, sexy eyes.

"*Hombres aya!*" With a jerk of his hand, Nate ordered the other men back against the wall. Then he turned on Caesar. "Wait up at the front of the unit." He growled. Nate had no idea what he was thinking, his head was just spinning. What the fuck was Caesar doing here of all places. He watched as the guy settled himself against the front bumper before moving toward the other men. Each one was dealt with, getting ID, running a quick check for warrants writing them up and telling them to move along. Five tickets in all and Nate would bet most would never get paid.

After the last one left he sat for a moment. Drumming his fingers on the steering wheel, he tried to arrange his thoughts. When in doubt, go back to basics. What would you do if you pulled over the chief's wife? Give her a ticket like everyone else. What would you do if it was the mayor? Give him a ticket. What do you do if it's the hot guy... Nate stopped himself there. He got back out of the car. "Okay, Caesar, give me your ID."

As he reached for his back pocket, Caesar asked the question Nate was going to. "What are you doing here?"

"Investigating some thefts inside." He held his hand out expectantly.

Caesar shifted and played with his wallet. "What did they take?"

Nate felt like an idiot standing there with his hand extended. "Why do you care?" He crossed his arms over his chest and spread his feet. It was the classic cop intimidation stance. Given that his biceps were as big as some guy's thighs, Nate pulled off intimidation pretty well.

It didn't seem to faze Caesar much. "Call it professional interest."

"Power tools, air-compressor, that kind of stuff."

Caesar narrowed his eyes and chewed on his bottom lip for a moment. "Inside job, then?"

"Why do you say that?" Nate was definitely curious at the turn of the conversation. Annoyed, but still it scratched at him.

Shrugging, Caesar looked down at his boots. "I don't know, call it a hunch."

"Don't jerk me around, Caesar," Nate barked.

"Thought you liked that?" When Nate glared at him, Caesar turned away. "Not funny?"

Another growl came from Nate, this time not quite as harsh, "Not funny." The situation was awkward for both of them.

"Sorry." Caesar swallowed and fiddled with his wallet.

"Okay, just give me your ID."

"Why?"

Nate sighed. "I'm going to give you a ticket for loitering under 41.18. You're obstructing the sidewalk."

"That's bullshit and you know it."

It was bullshit. Nate knew it was bullshit. "Look, the asshole in that store says you guys are obstructing the sidewalk," Nate gave his next phrase quotes with his fingers, "molesting and annoying passersby." He shook his head. "Look, if it was me, I'd have just told you all to move on, go somewhere else. But he's boiling because someone's ripping off shit out of his store. Sometimes you just gotta do what you gotta do."

"Fine." Caesar handed over a laminated California driver's license. Somehow there was more resignation than Nate was expecting in the word and gesture. He turned it over in his hand as he walked back to the driver's side. Damn, Caesar even photographed well for the DMV. Caesar Serrano was stamped over the seal of the State of California and followed by address and stats. The only one Nate hadn't figured out already was his DOB. That put him at about a year older than Nate himself…and a Scorpio.

Nate slid onto the seat and pulled the computer keyboard toward his knee. The laptop in his patrol car gave him instant access to databases containing information on people, stolen goods, and license plates. It took about thirty seconds to pull a criminal background check on someone. He could confirm a warrant in no time. Clipping Caesar's license next to the screen, Nate began typing.

Nate's patrol car was the typical, not-quite run of the mill Ford full-sized sedan. It wasn't terribly exotic looking under the paint and roof lights. Most people noticed two differences right off, the shotgun and computer bracketed to the dash. What you couldn't see was where the real differences lay. The larger than normal interior light meant he could fill out his paperwork at night. The seats were heavy-duty and backed with steel. A rubber floor mat instead of carpet hid the special circuits and plastic conduit running throughout the vehicle. Hookups for radios, radar, video cameras and computers snuggled behind the instrument panel. Reinforced structure and larger tires bolstered it for the rigors of chases and round the clock usage. The thing barely sat idle except for routine maintenance checks. The officers probably put close to fifty thousand miles per year on the car…hard miles of stop and go traffic, running over curbs and inner-city driving.

This was also one of the ones outfitted with the StarChase global positioning mechanism the department was testing. Trials were due to start in the fall. During a car chase, Nate could fire a small, epoxy-coated GPS device that would activate the moment it struck a fleeing vehicle. Then, instead of endangering everyone else on the road, Nate could sit back and let the satellite track the suspect car.

Nate scanned the history he'd pulled on Caesar. The first thing that hit him was the aka's: *Cesar Jose Serrano, Caesar Jose Payan, Cesar Payan, Jose Cesar Pyan, Jose Cerrano.* He glowered over the hood of his car at *that guy.* And that was just the icing. It spewed screen after screen of arrest, detention, warrant and conviction records.

Nate clambered out of the vehicle and crossed his arms over his chest. He didn't even walk towards Caesar. He might regret doing something if he got close. "Jesus, how many aliases do you have?"

"None." Caesar looked up from studying his shoes and shrugged.

Jerking his thumb towards the computer terminal in the car, Nate stepped around the door. "I got a list that says different...five or six it says. If they ain't aliases, what are they?" Before tossing his ticket book on the hood, he tucked Caesar's license into a random page.

"Probably my name." Caesar snorted. "Wouldn't want to lie to an officer after all. That's a misdemeanor."

Nate sighed. Semantics, they all played it. "Okay, what's your full and complete name on your birth certificate?" Pen poised ready to take down the utter bullshit he glared at Caesar.

"Only because it's you." Caesar blew him a kiss. "Caesario Jose Payan-Serrano. The last two names have one of those hyphen thingies."

Asshole, getting smart with him. "You've done this a lot, haven't you?" If he wasn't on duty he'd reach across the hood and whack that smirk right off Caesar's face.

"No, actually. I tend to try and stay away from the police. Not good for business or my health."

Nate forced himself to be calm. "What the hell are you doing here?"

"I thought it was a donut shop...'nuff cops here for it." Nate tried to accept it as diffusing the situation. It still pissed him off and his attitude must have screamed it. Caesar swallowed and dropped his tone. "Honestly, Nate, I'm looking for work. I'm completely clean on this. Retail ain't my thing."

"Don't play me," Nate tried not to growl again. He didn't make it. "I just had a good look at your rap sheet."

"This wasn't mine."

"Yeah, like I believe that."

"It wasn't me. Shit, look at my sheet." Caesar ticked off the points on his fingers. "No drugs. No violence. No retail. You said they took pipe fittings. That's way too junky for me."

"So."

"I ain't that stupid. I'd never take a place I'd trolled for work…maybe years later or something, but not that quick and not hang around. Neighborhood yeah, down the block or something, but it's stupid cutting it that close."

"Why should I believe scum like you? I could just haul you out back and beat a confession out of you." He glared.

Caesar glared back. "And I could tell everyone at your station that you babble like a girl when you get fucked. What do you think they'd say? If they knew you took it up the ass?"

"I don't hide it." Nate shifted.

A smirk slid across Caesar's mouth. "I bet you don't go waving flags around either."

"Bite me!"

"I did, at least twice." He ran his hands up under his ball cap. Heavy black hair fell about his face. Softer, he added, "What are you so pissed at, Nate? You're pushing way beyond normal cop attitude here."

Nate tried to put it into words as he settled his butt against the side of the patrol car. "I thought you worked for the studios."

"I never said that." Caesar settled his cap back on his head.

No, he hadn't said that. Nate had assumed it. "Then what were you doing at that party? Casing the joint?"

"No! My brother works for the studios."

Jerking his chin back at the computer and the damming list in green LED, "And you do this?" It was more of a statement then a question.

"Yep," Caesar nodded and sighed. "Pretty much."

"Shit." Nate grabbed the citation book and flipped to an unused page. The license slipped out. Plastic clattered against the car's body as it fell.

"So you're going to write me up a ticket?" Caesar grabbed his ID off the ground where it came to rest. "You just dump on me because you're a cop and I'm a crook. It could have been kinda fun if things were different. Trust me, I freaked when I picked up your academy photo. Oh, *chingame*, I thought my heart was going to stop. And then, I think, okay I'm just gone, I'll never see this *ese* again and who shows up at my next door neighbor's house?" For a moment it looked like Caesar might bolt. Half of Nate hoped he did. The other half was glad he didn't. Caesar shoved the card back in his wallet and did a quick scan of their surroundings. "Look I'll give you a lead if you let me off. I don't need a ticket... fines are a bitch and I can't go in and fight it, even though it's a bullshit charge. What do you say?"

Damn, to have a guy like that go from potential love interest to sleazy informant, life sucked sometimes. "Depends on what you tell me."

"Well, call me suspicious…."

"How 'bout experienced instead?" Nate shot back.

"That'll work, too. You know why I asked you what they took? Because the moment your car showed up, one of their sales gals made a real quick trip to the dumpster. It seemed a little strange, 'cause she wasn't dumping any trash. I'd go check the trash if I were you."

"No honor among thieves, huh?"

"How long have you been a cop, Nate?"

That stung. Still it was worth forgoing the paperwork. Nate pushed away from the car. "Get the hell out of here, Caesar." He turned and walked back to the driver's seat. Leaning on the door, he favored Caesar with his don't-fuck-with-me stare. "And don't let me catch you hanging out on my beat again. I know you. I'm watching you…got it?"

Well, he'd planned to bail after he rousted the laborers, but there was no harm in a little more time. Nate did an illegal U-turn in the street, then parked the patrol car in a vacant area near the entrance. He walked back into the store looking for the Head of Loss Prevention and found him by the registers, talking with another heavy-set man, probably of Arabic decent. Must be the business lunches these guys took at the roach coach. As he approached, Nate smiled and nodded. "Okay, I've told them to move along. Passed out some loitering tickets. I've got some ideas on what you can do. Let's do a walk around now. I'm going to point out some things that you need to do that will cut back a little on your shrinkage."

As they walked, Carson introduced him to Ray Jabra, the manager. Ray's attitude said he was more impressed by, and more open to, the things Nate pointed out than the head of security for his store. Some of it was little things, like locking gates. Other items were more problematic, like how to do an outside display without it lending to things walking off. A busted lock on the back loading dock was an open invitation as was the door someone propped open for air in the back and then walked away from. By the time they reached the dumpsters, even Carson's skepticism was waning.

"See now look." Nate thumped on the gate for the dumpster area. "No lock, it should be locked."

"Why?" Jabra asked the question. Eagerly in fact.

Shouldering the gate aside, Nate smiled. "One thing, it prevents illegal dumping. Why should you pay for someone else to get their trash hauled off? The bins should have locks on them, too." One reeked of standard garbage, the other seemed pretty clean. If Nate were a betting man, he'd go for the clean one. He flipped the lid up. Jumbled inside was a collection of sawdust, boards and other building cast offs. He grabbed a longish board and shoved things around inside.

When he heard the hollow plastic thump, Nate grinned. Both he and the manager jumped up to lean into the bin. Brushing aside the shavings and boards, there it was. A nice circular saw hid just where Caesar said he saw the gal checking. Nate pushed back and shook his head knowingly. "Pretty common on inside theft, throw the item in the can, and then go dump it. They probably plan to come around late at night and pick it up. You know, they don't hold up in court, but you might go for a round of lie detectors." Well, his love life sucked, but his informant had paid off. That only left about a thousand marks against Caesar.

"Wow, I would have never thought to look there." The manager grunted as he pulled the case over the lip. With a thump he dropped it on the asphalt. Jabra mussed his salt and pepper hair as he smiled at Nate. "What do you want?"

It took a bit for the question to register. "What do you mean, what do I want?"

"To make this a top priority. I want these people stopped. What do you want to push it up?" Jabra looked at him expectantly. When Nate didn't answer, he prodded more. "Like doing home improvement? Thinking about painting your bedroom? Just talk to me."

Nate counted to ten under his breath. Then he did it again. "I don't want anything, thank you."

"Oh come on, everybody..."

Nate glared. "Not me." The guy started to open his mouth and Nate's hand went up. "Not another word. I'm going now. I'm going to file my report, someone will be following up in the next few weeks."

As he passed the security officer, Nate heard the guy hiss, "Dumb kid." Whatever, if he wanted to think that all cops were crooked, that was his problem.

CHAPTER 7

Trash day; always a good day to hit a house. Caesar rode his old ten-speed slowly down the street. The whir of his chain was the only thing that broke the early morning quiet. He stopped at each blue-lidded trash bin, fishing out cans and bottles. His hair hung in greasy strands down across the shoulders of a grimy plaid work shirt. For two days he hadn't washed his hair. He hated the way it felt, but work was work. Ripped sweats, two sizes too large, covered his shorts. With the June gloom, Caesar was thankful for the bit of extra warmth the disguise afforded him. Beat up sneakers and a pair of cheap sunglasses made him look like any of the hundreds of other trash-pickers wandering through Los Angeles at that moment.

This way Caesar could take his time. Wandering slowly up one side of the street and back down the other, he noted everything about his target. Two days worth of newspapers were soaked through from the sprinklers. There was always a delay when you cancelled delivery, people never realized that. Mail carriers were better, but a slew of flyers hung off the door. The same lights were still on from days ago. A cheap set of Christmas light timers would have solved that. No cars sat in the drive. Again, with parking at a premium in so many places throughout Los Angeles, let your neighbor use your drive for a week. Those little things would have made Caesar just nervous enough to pass the place up.

As it was, the house just reeked of empty.

Satisfied that the family was still gone, he pedaled off. A couple hours later he was back. Nine-thirty a.m., almost the perfect time to hit a house. Still cool enough for a gardener to be working, but not testing the limits of noise-abatement laws. Wage slaves would be off working, playgroups and non-working people's spinning/kick-boxing/yoga type classes tended to start between nine and ten. Maids had already arrived and were busy inside the houses and kids were at day-camp.

Mid-week suburban neighborhoods were as abandoned as a post-apocalyptic movie set. Perfect.

Caesar backed his pickup into the driveway. The empty plastic trash cans rattled in the back. The bike lay on the bed covered by a tarp and saddled with a garage sale lawnmower. Broken blades meant the piece of shit couldn't cut worth a damn. He kept it for the characteristic gas-turbine whirr rumbling from a thousand back yards in the city.

Caesar clambered out of the truck, swiping his arm across his forehead. Damn it was already close to eighty and the bent-billed baseball cap was dripping with sweat. Especially since he'd shoved his hair up underneath. A clean but faded T-shirt clung to his skin. Now he was in working gear, having ditched the over-clothes when he'd retrieved his vehicle. He dropped the gate, pulled the lawnmower out and then donned a pair of work gloves before throwing one can on his back. They'd get tossed somewhere before he got home.

Summer was the most profitable season for his work…right around Christmas and Thanksgiving came a close second. For one thing, people fixed things up in the summer, which meant that people hired day-laborers. It gave Caesar ample, legitimate opportunity to be in and out of dozens of neighborhoods. And then, well, people went on vacation in summer. In the metro hell of Los Angeles, few people knew their neighbors' names, much less their schedules or habits. A yard man's truck in the drive would be noticed by only a few, and most of them wouldn't think it unusual.

A large privacy fence screened the back yard from the street and neighbors. Beautiful really, alternating double slats dripped with Morning Glory ablaze in purple-blue flowers. The side gate was the easiest to access, and any clear view of it was now blocked by his pickup. A quick snip with a small set of bolt cutters and the cheap padlock was toast. Caesar slid the tool back into one utility pocket. Knee-length khaki shorts fit the gardener profile, as did the cheap tan work boots from the mega-chain. Millions like them across the country meant a shoe print would be virtually useless.

As he walked toward the back of the house, pushing the mower ahead of him, he tried every window within reach. All of them had contact switches for an alarm system. It was a pretty cheap model by what Caesar could tell and he'd seen a lot of alarms in his day. It wasn't enough of a problem to scare him off...yet.

Caesar smiled when he reached the back door of the attached garage. The big glass pane would have been easy enough, but even better was the doggy door for a mid-sized pooch. He'd watched the owner take the dog off and come back without it the day before everyone left. Snagging the plastic flap, he thumped on the panel hidden behind it. Either thick plastic or thin particle board. It was enough to keep animals out. Caesar wasn't an animal, although he was sure there were people who thought that about him. He stepped back to the mower, grabbed the pull and on the third try got it going with a roar. Then he clipped the throttle into place with a bit of wire. Back at the door, one swift kick and the access panel shattered. No one would ever hear it over the rumble of the engine.

Rarely did Caesar ever have to use this much force to gain access. Most of the time someone left something unlocked. Writhing and twisting, he managed to get his head and shoulders through. It was not comfortable, but it was doable. With a few grunts and curses he was all the way in. A quick glance told him this entry wasn't alarmed. He unlocked the deadbolt and opened the door. Then he pulled the garbage can into the garage.

The door between the garage and house was the typical hollow-core with an interior lock. Caesar selected a large screwdriver and hammer out of a jumble of tools lying on a bench. A casual appraisal told him none were worth taking for sale. Well, maybe the drill and circular saw, both part of a nice combo kit...the kind that cost close to four-hundred new. They'd fetch ten or twenty for him. After a quick once-over to make sure the tools weren't marked with visible ID, Caesar tossed them into the can.

One quick strike and the lock was punched. The door swung open to the tonal beep of the alarm warning timer. As he suspected, just inside was a keypad. He'd have about five seconds before he'd have to bail. Flipping down the keypad cover he was all set to start punching the standard code. Most people programmed in lines or X's. If it wasn't new, you'd just look for the worn keys and work from there. Caesar didn't have to get that sophisticated. Such an accommodating family, they'd written the code for the maid inside the cover.

As he went through the laundry room toward the kitchen, he pulled open every cabinet. A quick rummage assured him that all the boxes actually held cleaning supplies. Anyone who thought those fake soda cans would fool a thief needed their head examined. If they could think to hide it there, Caesar could find it. Hell, he got those catalogs, too.

Caesar searched the kitchen thoroughly, but quickly. Even though he'd cased the place, the quicker he was in and out the better. Next he hit the dining room. The flatware he ignored…knockoff plate shit anyway. The silver tea service, some nice silver candlesticks and a few heirloom serving pieces got wrapped in a tablecloth and dropped by the laundry room door.

The only room he wasn't going to hit was the living room in front. There was a big bay window open to the street. The rest of the windows were either covered with some window treatment or blocked from view by fences, trees or shrubs. You couldn't ask for better conditions. Well, they could put everything out on the dining room table for him, but why get greedy?

Ducking through the downstairs bath he found himself in a small office. That opened up to a family room. Stereo, DVD, TV, camera equipment and laptop; that was good for the first load. The small stuff went into the trash barrel. A few leaves and such on top was enough camouflage. The TV was slightly more problematic, but an old tarp in the garage solved that. Those went into the truck and the empty can came back to the house. Now it was time to hit the upstairs.

Back through the kitchen, dining room and this time into the entry, Caesar headed up the narrow stairs. The bathroom at the head of the stairs got a thorough search. So did the linen closet. Caesar's searches were neat and orderly. There was no need to rush on this job. On the top shelf, behind an old lamp, Caesar hit pay dirt. One of those military style ammo boxes was shoved in the back. Behind that was a rifle. He popped the top on the box. A small pistol and a few boxes of ammo rested inside. Dropping those at the head of the stairs he hit the left-hand bedroom.

The teenage girl, Shay, owned this space. There'd be some good shit. Caesar figured he'd need something to haul it all. Why bring it, when it was usually already there. Looking around he spotted a gym bag. Caesar dumped the duffle on the floor and kicked the sneakers and sweaty clothes under the dresser. Then he rifled the room, coming up with some hand-held games, a boom-box and a bit of jewelry. Her brother's quarters got the same treatment.

He dumped the bag next to his growing pile. Then he moved to the master bedroom. Again, Caesar needed something to carry it all in. Two nice suitcases came out of the closet. The upstairs TV would merit a pass. He just couldn't carry it down those stairs by himself. Clothes from the dresser packaged the upstairs electronics in the suitcase. The jewelry box on the bureau was empty. Unless they had a safe-deposit box, the contents would be around. The closets were the most likely place. Just for ease, he stuffed the items already collected into the suitcase, even emptying the duffle bag.

That came back with him into the room. The first closet netted him a few pins left on coats, but not anything spectacular. In the other one he hit pay dirt. Behind a rack of men's shoes was an access panel. When he pulled it open, the space held all sorts of fun stuff. Another gun, this one looked to be antique, was in a zippered case. Into the duffle it went. A tackle box was full of jewelry, much nicer stuff than the kid owned. Caesar didn't bother to sort through it, just dumped the box into the bag. The space looked empty after that, but it extended back behind the eves a bit, meriting more than a quick examination.

He stuck his hand into the cubby. The right side didn't go back far before it hit wall. A little shorter space was on the left, and Caesar was about to abandon it when his hand slid down and the bottom wiggled. That was promising. He fiddled a bit and found that if he pushed at the base he could slide his fingers under and push the false wall up. In the recess within a recess his fingers found a metal box. What came out was a small cash box. He almost drooled. What would be so important to put back that far and hide that well?

Disappointment and confusion crawled across his features when he popped the lid. Photos, it was full of photos. What the hell? Sometimes you just found weird ass stuff in people's homes. There was no reason to it. He was about to set it down when a spider crawled over the lid and across his hand. "*Chinga!*" boomed through the room as he fumbled the box and dumped the pictures on the floor. That set his heart pounding.

A total waste of a good hidey hole... well, those were the breaks. He grabbed the photos covering his knees, intending to toss them on the floor. A glossy picture caught the light. Caesar's gut went cold. What he held in his hand was the vilest thing he'd ever seen. Sick, twisted, why would anyone do something like that much less take pictures?

Deep down inside, Caesar knew the answer. Perverts like that liked to keep souvenirs of the hurt they spread around. He gathered up the photos spilled on the floor. Sometimes there was an adult male, no telling if it was the same guy in every one, but always, in every one were kids. Kids doing things that kids shouldn't know how to do. In a few, the children were doing *things* with that guy.

Caesar's stomach churned. What the hell was he going to do with this? He couldn't just leave it. Caesar had no romantic notions about himself...he was a crook. But he was a garden variety crook. This, this was monstrous. It had to stop. Forever.

First thing, no way in hell these people weren't going to know the house had been hit, but he could clean this up. All the photos went back in the box. As he was closing the lid, Caesar reconsidered. No one would believe him. He had to have something to show them, even if he didn't know who the *them* was yet. Nauseated, nervous, Caesar searched through the depraved snapshots until he found two that seemed somehow less awful then the others. They were also near copies of other pictures...maybe they wouldn't be missed. Then he slammed the box of nightmares shut and shoved it back where it came from.

He collected the loot on his way out. Packing his truck, he burned the address into his memory. Not like there was much hope of ever getting that out of his brain anyway. It was ten twenty-five a.m. when he left that hell behind.

CHAPTER 8

"Come on Nate, you need to get out." Carol's voice came from somewhere inside her one bedroom apartment. Nate stood on the balcony overlooking the complex pool. His sister had bugged him into coming for dinner, using all the dirty tricks that only his twin would know. Then she proceeded to quiz him over the intimate details of his hookup with *that guy*. It really wasn't a subject he wanted to talk about. And yet, the one person he could talk about things like that with was Carol.

Poor sis, she'd geared up for one of his moonstruck ramblings. Beer and sushi topped off with a good action flick; their routine since high school for relationship sharing. They'd figured out early on that you couldn't hide things from your twin, even if you weren't identical. Carol had pulled him in with bright-eyed anticipation of juicy details. Instead Nate had hit her with a rant about blown expectations.

That first night had been so good, and he'd figured he'd wrecked it the next morning. Getting called in to take a shift after a night like that just threw him. Caesar had split without so much as a 'thanks for the fuck.' At that point Nate figured it was because of how he'd acted and it ate at him. Then, shit, when he'd hit that call and seen Caesar at the party, oh man…never, ever in his life had he done something like that while on duty. Yeah, he'd also used it as an excuse to give Caesar his number. At that point there'd been a possibility of a future.

Why did it have to get so fucked up? Nate wished he'd never taken that shoplifting call. No, that wasn't true. He needed to know that about Caesar. He needed to understand that it would never be possible to have a relationship with that man. It was just a gut blow. The guy lit up the police system like a Christmas tree. Receiving stolen property, possession of burglary tools, only a couple of old convictions but enough arrests to just make him bad news. As a cop, especially a gay cop, the last thing he needed was to be stuck on a guy who was bad news.

"Call him." Carol's voice at his shoulder startled Nate. He turned to find her smiling knowingly and holding out a beer. "You've got his phone number now…right?"

He reluctantly took the bottle. Not that he didn't want the beer; unfortunately it was attached to a heart-to-heart conversation that he wasn't sure he was ready for. Carol considered herself a full-time sister and part-time shrink to her twin. "No. I don't need to get out." Twisting the top off, he took a swig and tossed the cap into a planter. It took practice to ignore Carol's evil glare. "I'm not calling him."

"Come on, Caesar seemed like such a nice guy." Carol slid into a patio chair and put her feet up on the rail. Ticking Caesar's good points off on her fingers, Carol continued, "So he's a day-laborer right now. He's looking for steady work. His brother's trying to get him on with the studio." She shook her head and sipped her own beer. "It has to be hard though, like you said, he's got a record. That just means he's not an angel…you can't say that you weren't in and out of trouble as a kid."

"Carol, you're my sister, not my matchmaker." One day she'd learn that. "Don't try and sell me on this guy. You just don't understand." *Holy shit did she not understand.* It wasn't as if they were talking about joy riding and a DUI. The guy had a felony conviction for Breaking & Entering. There was juvie shit there that had been sealed, too. "I'm perfectly capable of finding my own dates."

"Not if you only hang out with cops." She snorted. "Not unless you start going to, what is that gay cop organization called?"

"GSPOA. That's not a meat-market, Carol." The buzzer from the security gate interrupted them. Carol fussed with getting plates while Nate shelled out the cash for the food. Then he tossed the latest Pirates flick in the DVD and settled on the floor. His sister folded herself onto the couch, cradling her dinner on her lap. Hopefully a spicy tuna roll and Johnny Depp would get her mind off the Caesar track.

It worked for all of five minutes. Opportunistic as always, Carol waited until he had a mouth full of Unagi. "What's wrong with Caesar then?"

Nate tried not to spit grilled eel across the carpet. "He's a fucking felon!" It came out all mumbled.

"Used to be." She used her chopsticks to rap the top of his head. "How many years ago was that? He did his time. He did probation. That's over, done, past history."

"It doesn't matter. It doesn't change what he is." How could she not understand something so basic? He was the *them* in the *us vs. them* equation of a blue-tinted world.

"That's a nice attitude to have. Once a crook, always a crook. He's trying to go straight and you, of all people won't give him the benefit of the doubt."

"No, he's not trying to go straight…he's happily gay." Nate ignored her stuck out tongue. Chewing on a bit of ginger, he thought about it. "Most guys don't go straight. They don't clean up. They don't fly right. They just get real good at not getting caught."

"Well maybe Caesar is different. Did you ask him?"

"Are you nuts? I'm a fucking cop. You think he's going to answer that?"

"You'll never know until you ask him. Do it like they do in the movies." She pantomimed removing a cap and throwing it across the room. Drawing herself up on the couch, she tried for a stern voice. "'The uniform's off and I'm asking you man-to-man.' I bet if you did that, he'd be honest with you."

He had to pull the bottle away to keep from snorting foam. "You know you're nuts, right?" At least she'd made him laugh. "Carol, if I said that he'd die laughing. And I'd die of embarrassment. John Wayne I ain't."

"You know you're stubborn, right?" Carol shot back. Leaning in over his shoulder, her voice softened. "Nate, ask him. What's the worst that can happen? He could tell you to fuck off and then you'll know. But until you ask him, you'll just stew on it and be unhappy."

"And what if he says yep, I'm still out there doing crap? What do I do then?"

"Then you'll know. You can move on with your life. But, come on, you obviously like the guy. Take a chance. Throw caution to the wind and jump. You so deserve to be happy."

"Know what, Carol? You read too many of those sappy romance novels." Her derisive huff said she thought he needed to read a few of the ones littered through the apartment. "Look, sis, it's not just me. I'm gay and I'm a cop. Most people are cool with it 'cause I pull my weight, I've proved myself and I don't wave it in people's faces. But it's still there—Duncan, Weiner and Smith had their careers trashed because of it. You know what happened the other day? We got a group of rookies and there's about four of us shooting the shit with them. We're razzing them. Giving them hell and trying to scare 'em a little. Then the desk Sergeant asks me to run some papers up for him. I'm like, 'no problem.'"

"And as I'm walking away, I hear one of the rookies say something about it sounds like I'm a stand-up guy and maybe they can work with me sometime. I'm feeling all pumped with that. Then one of the other guys says 'just don't let him get behind you.' The other officers bust up, and the fresh meat doesn't know what's what so another guy says, 'well, for a guy who takes it up the ass, he's a good cop.' The Sarge shut them down right away…but hell, I heard it. Who I fuck should have nothing to do with whether I'm a good cop or not. But in a lot of guys' minds, it does. If I started dating Caesar, even if I could believe he was one-hundred percent reformed, I'd never convince anyone else of that. It would be like I sold my soul to the devil."

"That's not the Nate I know." Carol slid down onto the floor next to him. With a quick punch to his shoulder, "My brother, balls-to-the-wall Reilly. What happened to 'I'll just have to prove that I'm better than they are?'"

Nate shook his head and set the sushi aside. He'd killed his own appetite with his story. "I fought that battle. I'm too old to take on another one."

Pulling back her arm, Carol pretended like she was going to hit him. "Don't make me slap you."

"Assaulting an officer, not good sis." Nate wrapped his arm around her neck then rubbed his knuckles across her skull. She squealed and pushed him away, managing to kick his thigh in the process. What was a twin sister for if you couldn't give her noogies? When he finally had enough breath to speak, Nate added, "It's been hard enough getting where I am. I don't want to lose the ground I've gained."

CHAPTER 9

Thirty minutes past midnight, Nate slid his car into his assigned spot. Once again, the asshole next to him was encroaching on his space. Damn steroid excuse for a pickup truck…no one outside the construction industry needed a vehicle that damn big. He'd complain to the manager again, but it wouldn't do any good. Luckily he had an end spot and a compact car. Still, it irked him.

Plus, he was already irritated. Nate should have known better than to try and talk it out with Miss Happy Endings. His sis could be so dense at times. "Just talk to him." Yeah, right, like that would solve anything. It'd taken him a good forty-five minutes of lat-pulls just to work her voice out of his head.

Heading to his unit, Nate noted that, once again, half the lights were out. What a dump he lived in. His building was one of those square monstrosities so prevalent in Southern California. Flat, oatmeal stucco walls rose from concrete patios, doors opening straight onto other people's lives. He threaded his way past the few planters cradling ficus trees and a random assortment of plants. There was no plan to their arrangement; it was as if whoever brought them in had dropped them when they couldn't carry them any farther. Iron stairs jutted into the maze of courtyards at odd intervals.

Some guy was sitting in the shadows on the bottom stair across the way from his door. Nate did a quick mental rundown: khaki shorts, T-shirt, work boots and stringy hair. He shrugged. Not a threat, just someone waiting. Mentally he filed it for future reference, pulling out his keys and sliding one into the lock. He remained alert and wary. Hearing the guy move, he turned to let whomever it was know he was no one to mess with. When the soft, "Hey, Nate," washed over him, he froze. That voice was familiar. It haunted his dreams lately.

What the fuck was Caesar doing in front of his apartment? Did the asshole have a death wish? "What the hell are you doing here?" Nate growled.

Pushing his hands into his pockets, Caesar moved across the dim court. "I need to talk to you." His voice was low.

"I don't have anything to say to you." Nate crossed his arms over his chest. The move was somewhere between defensive and threatening. "Get the fuck out of here."

"No. I really need to talk to you about something."

"No, you don't."

Caesar stepped in, right up into Nate's personal space. "Look, can we go inside your place and talk? This is really important." There was an edge to Caesar's voice. One of those things that cut right through everything personal and hit Nate square where he lived. He narrowed his eyes. Looking Caesar over carefully, he could see it, smell it—the fear.

"What's going on?" He used it…his *cop* voice.

"Inside, please." Caesar pleaded.

Something was up and he didn't like it. It had all of his nerves jangling. Seconds ticked by. He could smell Caesar's panic. "Okay, you got one minute." Nate removed the key and pushed the door open. Waiting for the other man to pass, Nate flicked on the light before shutting out the night.

Caesar headed for the efficiency kitchen. "Got any beer?"

"This ain't social." He tossed his keys on top of the TV. "What the fuck do you want?"

"I want a drink." Caesar turned and slapped his hands down on the counter. "A really strong drink." The guy looked like shit. Stringy, unwashed hair hung across his face. His eyes jumped about as though afraid of what they might see if they focused on anything too long. Even his hands shook, although Nate could see he was fighting that. Caesar's voice was strained. "Beer will do, but harder would be better."

"Above the sink there's some scotch. Glasses are to the left of the fridge, get two." He snagged a stool with his foot and perched on the edge. "What happened? Did you do something stupid…or more stupid than you've done with the rest of your life? You know, you tell me something I don't like, I'll have to bust your ass."

"Shut up, Nate." He fished the bottle and glasses out of the cabinet. Fumbling, but not dropping them, Caesar managed to right the glasses and pour two belts. He slammed his down and poured another. "I don't know who else I can tell about this."

"What? Two casual fucks makes us good buds? Oh, I don't know how to handle this, I'll go find Nate?"

For a while Caesar just stared at him. "I broke into a house today."

"You're busted." He swirled the gold liquid around in his glass. "You have the right to remain silent…"

"Shut the fuck up, Nate, and listen to me!" Caesar slammed his fist onto the breakfast bar. Nate rocked back on the stool. "I broke into a house today and I was cleaning the place out and I found something." Before Nate could ask, Caesar fished some papers from a utility pocket and then slid them across the counter. Photos. He looked at his unwanted guest and then down at the pictures. They were grainy and out of focus. Caesar's voice caught him as he picked up the first. "I took two of the crappy ones; something I didn't think would be missed. I don't think whoever took them should know I found them. But you can tell what's going on."

Nate could tell what was going on. It turned his stomach. Graphic, homemade kiddy pics…and not those of summer vacation at the beach. One was two kids together, mouths and hands where they shouldn't have been. The other was caught mid-act, the camera held by an adult participant by what parts of his anatomy were visible. "Oh Christ!"

"You have to do something about that." Caesar poured a third belt, having downed the last while Nate was looking at the pictures.

He reached out and caught Caesar's wrist. "Don't hit that so hard."

Putting the glass back down, Caesar stared at his hands. Then he looked back at Nate. "There's worse than those." He swallowed the words.

"Worse?"

This time he picked up the glass and knocked it back. "Yeah." Caesar's eyes said they were a hell of a lot worse. The kind that left scars inside the people who saw them.

"Tell me exactly how you found these." Nate slid into Officer Reilly mode. "Everything. Got it?"

Caesar spilled it. How he'd cased the house and canvassed the neighborhood that day. He described in quick sentences how he'd gone through everything, gone upstairs, found the hidey-hole and then the pictures. As Caesar talked, he drank. Nate let him get it all out once and then took him back through, asking for details, taking notes on the pad he usually kept next to the phone. By the time they were finished it was nearly two and Caesar was visibly fading.

"You're hammered."

"I am not hammered." The words were slightly slurred. After studying his glass for a bit, Caesar nodded. "I shouldn't have drunk so much."

Why had he let Caesar drink? Nate knew the answer, so Caesar could get it out. Well, Nate did it. He had to fix it. "You can't drive like that." Pointing into the tiny living room and his old sofa, he added, "You can crash there and you are so not allowed to hurl all over my couch."

"How 'bout your bed?" Nate upped his opinion of how drunk Caesar was by a few notches.

"Change in plans. Get in the freaking shower. You smell like sweat and booze. I'm getting you Alka-Seltzer Plus and Gatorade. I do not need you seriously hung over tomorrow. I've got to figure out what to do and who to take it to." He stood, pulling Caesar out of the kitchenette and pushing him toward the bedroom. "You're going to show me that house, so I have an address. Then I'm going to figure out a way to put this in an acceptable report. Confidential informant or some other shit."

While the shower droned, Nate made good on his promise. Slipping the tablets and drink onto the vanity, he tried hard not to stare at the shadow framed in the shower doors. It wasn't easy. Damn it, why did that asshole have to be so fine? He struggled out of his jeans, trying to put it all together.

Whatever Caesar was, whatever plane of lowlife he existed on, he'd risked himself. Nate couldn't deny that. The guy had admitted to a felony, a biggie given his record, because this was just wrong. So wrong he was willing to risk jail to put it right. Caesar had to know that he could wind up busted. There might not be a way to avoid that. And yet he'd gone to someone he thought could do something. That someone was Nate. Fuck! Why did he have to turn out to have some Goddamn moral streak buried in that thick head? Why couldn't he just be your garden variety perp?

Lost in his own thoughts, Nate didn't hear the shower cut off. He was pulling his T-shirt over his head when he heard the bathroom door open. Nate could feel Caesar's eyes crawling over his back and ass. He tried to ignore the almost tactile sensation. Heat hit his hips hard. Damn, and here he was standing there in just his shorts, shirt half off and tangled about his arms.

"Got a problem there, Nate?" Caesar purred. Hardly any slur was evident in his words. Good, then maybe he was sobered up enough to throw out. Nate knew better, but he could hope. Being alone, in his small apartment, with the sexiest man he'd met in a long time was bad news. Especially when that guy was a more than a little plowed.

Yanking the shirt the rest of the way off and tossing it into the open closet, Nate turned. Just because you had a hard-on for a hot guy didn't mean you were going to sleep with him. Nate had to remind himself of that, twice. Caesar leaned against the doorjamb, a towel wrapped loosely over his hips. Water beaded on his warm, brown skin. His black hair was slicked back, damp, behind his ears. Taking a swig of lemon-lime flavored sports drink, Caesar licked his lips. Nearly all the willpower Nate possessed went into not following that tongue with his eyes.

Caesar laughed and used the bottle as a pointer, the bulge in his jockey's evidence that Nate's body didn't have any of the moral qualms his brain was fighting with. "I thought you didn't like me. Maybe I was wrong."

He was not going to back down. No way would he let Caesar know he'd gotten to him. "Fuck off." Nate snarled.

"Offering?"

Instead of answering, Nate spat. "Jesus! Put on some clothes, okay?"

"I could say the same to you." Caesar smiled and stepped in. It wasn't like he had far to go in the cramped confines of the bedroom. Two steps and they were pretty much body-to-body.

Nate swallowed. Caesar teased, "Wandering around like that, you'll get a guy all excited."

"You're drunk." The clean scent of soap drifted up from wet skin. Somewhere behind it was the faded ghost of Caesar's cologne.

"What?" Caesar ran the bottle across Nate's stomach. The chilled plastic pulled water across his skin. "I was good enough to do twice before."

Nate had to fight leaning into the touch. "If I were a girl, I'd slap you for that comment."

"If you were a girl," Caesar leaned in, holding his lips inches from Nate's ear, and whispered, "I wouldn't have fucked you the first time."

"You're a felon." With Caesar so near, it was hard to protest.

"And you're a cop. Nothing's changed about that. We just know it now." Again that edge crept into Caesar's voice. A little scared, almost pleading, "I need it, Nate. I want to fuck myself into oblivion tonight, turn off the Goddamn slide show in my head." Caesar shuddered and slipped his free arm around Nate's middle. As he spoke, he kissed his way across Nate's shoulder. "Wrap me up inside you and let me forget about what I saw. This bust is going to make you and screw me. We both know that. Give me a little peace tonight." The last few words were whispered hot against Nate's jaw.

Nate could barely breathe, he hissed, "Don't treat me like some shrink." Damn, if it was anybody else, there was no way he'd be doing this. He took the Gatorade from Caesar and set it on the nightstand without looking. *Don't think too much, just do for once*, he told himself. He slid his hands under the towel and buried his mouth against Caesar's neck.

Terrycloth slipped to the floor, pooling about their feet. "Shit, yeah." Caesar hissed and pushed his hips up against Nate's palm. That wonderful cock throbbed hard against his fingers. Warm velvet slid under Nate's caress. Caesar's tongue traced patterns of heat across his ribs and he hissed. Pushing Nate back toward the bed, Caesar licked everywhere he could reach.

When his knees hit the mattress, Nate fell. Caesar was on him immediately. Wrenching Nate's briefs down and off, Caesar began to lick and suck Nate's sac. He rolled Nate's balls in his mouth. He ran his lips up the shaft, kissing the tip and tonguing the slit. Nate strangled the moan in his chest. Goddamn, why did Caesar have to be so good? Nate grabbed a handful of dark hair and yanked back. "Get the shit outta the table and let's do this."

"Impatient?" Caesar flashed a lopsided grin as he crawled over Nate toward the nightstand.

Nate snapped, "Shut up."

Caesar rocked back on his knees. Liquid chocolate eyes stared down at him. "You don't have to Nate, if you're not into it."

Both of them were hard and throbbing. "I want to." Nate twisted and dug the condom and lube out of the drawer. "It's just late." Why was he making excuses? He was going to hate himself in the morning for giving in. Nate promised himself this would be it. No more Caesar. No more of that warm skin and those dark eyes. He tossed the stuff on the covers near Caesar's knee. Rolling on his back, Nate spread his legs. His hand wandered down, toying with his cock. "Come on, before I change my mind."

"No chocolate and flowers again, huh?" Caesar ran his palm across Nate's own hand.

Caesar knelt between Nate's thighs, pushing back one leg. Then he bent down and flicked his tongue across Nate's balls. As Caesar licked the area just underneath them, Nate shuddered. Desire screamed through his body. He wanted to say "don't," or "stop," something coherent. All he managed was a strangled "Caesar!" moaning and twisting as Caesar's hand spread his cheeks and his tongue found his hole. Nate was in heaven.

Was it so wrong to want Caesar like this? He grabbed behind his own knees, pulling back to give that exploring tongue access. Each time Caesar pushed inside, fire followed. It consumed Nate from the inside out. He pushed back against Caesar's mouth, urging the man deeper with his body.

Caesar's touch was gone and Nate almost panicked. But then he was bending over Nate, cock pressing against where his tongue had been moments before. A light touch, working through the hair on his chest, shredded Nate's nerves. He wanted to pull those full lips down against his, taste himself on Caesar's mouth. Instead, Nate turned his head away and bit his own lip.

Caesar slid home. Nate's back arched as that delicious heat swept through him. Caesar moved to kiss him and he jerked back. He couldn't do that, share that kind of touch. This was just a fuck. If he gave in, if he kissed Caesar, it would be more than that. Then everything would crumble.

It was so hard not to give in. If only there was some way to separate what he was from who he was. Those wonderful, full lips tortured the underside of his jaw drawing fire down his neck in their wake. "Don't be so cold, Nate." Caesar's words had him trembling inside.

Damn, if Caesar only knew how much Nate wanted to tear him apart, drown them both. There was nothing cold about it. He pressed his forehead against Caesar's arm, shutting his eyes tight. "Just shut up and fuck me."

"If that's the way it is..." Caesar growled leaving the thought unfinished. He reared back and slid his arms behind Nate's knees, spreading Nate's legs wide with the weight of his body. Two short strokes seemed to center Caesar. Then he began to pound. Hot, hard, the pace he set was brutal. Nate could barely do more than ride it.

One hand scrabbled back, trying to find purchase on the mattress. Nate grabbed himself with the other and began to jerk. Biting his lip, he forced back the babbling that threatened to overwhelm him. If he let it go, he'd say something he'd regret, something about how lonely, needing, or fallen for Caesar he really was.

No way was he going to let Caesar have that.

His body said too much already. He couldn't help it. Caesar knew where and how to touch him to send him flying. Nate rammed himself back on that solid prick, matching Caesar stroke for stroke. Everything was shaking. He could feel it building in his thighs, spreading out through his frame, overwhelming him. And then he was lost. He was drowning and yelling out Caesar's name like a fool.

CHAPTER 10

"This is so not funny." Caesar sat, fuming, in the passenger seat. He'd borrowed a set of Nate's clothes. Overly cautious, Nate had bagged and tagged everything except Caesar's underwear. There was no telling what trace evidence might be there and might be useful. Caesar, luckily, had a pair of tennis shoes in his truck because even his boots went in a sealed baggy with date, time and Nate's badge number scribbled on the plastic. Two smaller zip-tops held the photos.

Nate had lent Caesar a pair of jeans and a logo T-shirt to wear. L.A.P.D. was emblazoned in bright white letters across the back with a small badge on the left side of the chest. Actually, the navy blue didn't look half bad against Caesar's skin. The shirt was too big on Caesar, but not by much. His jeans fit though. Not sexy tight, but they clung to his frame in that loose, sexy way that Caesar wore his clothes.

"It's very funny." The little tortures, that's what made life special. Nate continued, "And just think I could have made you wear the one Carol got me for my birthday. You saw it, with the handcuffs that said *Cuff Me*." Man, Caesar would have looked too damn good in that shirt. Brown skin set off by red fabric. And that one was too small for Nate's shoulders. It would have been tight in all the right places on Caesar. Oh hell, he needed to stop thinking like that. He would drive himself nuts that way.

For the first time in a long time, Nate had woken wrapped in someone's arms. Being a beat cop meant he was real selective about the guys he dated. Real selective translated into not dating much at all. Bad breakups trashed many a cop's career. One Sergeant, a Medal of Valor winner stationed at headquarters, lost everything when an ex-boyfriend accused him of harassment. The officer was cleared through the Board of Rights, but had to suffer through surveillance, false dereliction of duty charges and unjustified suspensions before he got there. And when all was said and done, they told him his job no longer existed and he had to go back on patrol. That lawsuit was still winding its way through the courts.

Shit, too much thinking and not enough driving. Nate realized he was on the left and needed to be in the far right of the 118 to make the 5. With a quick glance, he cut the Taurus across three lanes of traffic. Punching the gas, he managed to zip in front of a Semi and just make the transition ramp.

Caesar's hand hit the dash. Wide-eyed he yelled, "Jesus-fucking-Christ, Nate!"

"What?" He grinned across the car, one eye on the road the other on his passenger.

It looked like Caesar was shaking. "You drive like a nut job!"

"Oh, come on, it ain't that bad." It really wasn't. Caesar should see how some of the old-timers drove. "I've had more driving courses then a NASCAR driver. I'm in control of the car at all times."

"This piece of shit is not your patrol car." Caesar slid down an inch. His fingers were still locked onto the dash. "I don't think Ford designed it to be driven like this."

They snaked down the Santa Ana. First Burbank crawled by and then Glendale. It wasn't much past ten and the freeway was packed. Thank God there wasn't a Dodgers game on or the 5 would have been a parking lot. Then off onto Los Feliz Boulevard as it cut through the south-eastern tip of Griffith Park. On the right, the miniature diesel train passed them carrying its typical load of families. Nate waved to the kids and Caesar laughed.

"Did you grow up here?" Finally, Caesar let go of the dash. "In Los Angeles, I mean?"

Nate shrugged. "Yeah, I did ... the white slums of Burbank."

"Ride the ponies in the park, then?" Where the train was stationed was a pony ride that had been around since Nate's mom was a kid. When Nate nodded, Caesar smiled with a mouth full of bright white teeth. "I take my nephews and nieces there sometimes, or the zoo."

As they passed the entrance to the park, Nate peered down the street. Not that he could see the L.A. Zoo from here, it was a few miles inside Griffith Park. "Haven't been to the zoo in ages."

"Changed a lot in the last few years. It's too bad the observatory closed." The barest bit of the dome was visible on the hill and then it vanished behind houses.

"They used to take us during school." Nate could remember lying on the floor looking up at all the stars you could never see in the night sky over Los Angeles. "Of course, we always used it as an excuse to beat up on each other when no one was looking. You go when you were a kid?"

That made Caesar laugh again. It was such a warm sound, but with an edge, almost like he was embarrassed at being caught having a good time. "Naw, I was in high school when I moved here."

"Oh." That didn't make much sense. Nate could remember going up through his senior year. Pulling into the center lane, Nate waited for traffic to clear and then turned left into the bottom half of Los Feliz. He started counting streets to the one they were looking for. "Didn't your high school do those kinds of trips?"

Caesar was silent for a bit and the smile faded. "I never enrolled. I had to get a job to help support my cousin's family. I laid asphalt for a few years. Lied and told them I was eighteen and used one of my other cousin's ID and social." Pointing to a street coming up, Caesar pushed his hair out of his eyes with his other hand. "Shit happens like that."

"Oh." Inside Nate cringed. He sounded like a broken record. "You could get your GED." That came off patronizing and he hated it the moment he said it.

"That house." Caesar indicated a sharp roofed house halfway down the block. As they pulled to the opposite curb, Caesar glared. "I did get a GED. I did it while I was in county." It was like he was daring Nate to make fun of him.

There was no reason to make fun of a guy because he'd had a hard life. Nate would never do that. "Good. A lot of inmates don't take that opportunity." However, a hard life didn't excuse the choices Caesar had made...not by a long shot. Plenty of other people with similar backgrounds made the choice not to steal, to live clean. Or they made the decision to stop. Instead, Caesar made the choice to break into houses.

Nate wasn't sure he could ever forgive Caesar for that.

Across from them sat a comfortable middle-class home. The red brick and white siding would fool anyone into thinking it was a decent place. A bright whirly-gig turned rainbows on a small porch. Soaked newspapers were scattered across the lawn. Nate counted three. There were a lot more than three flyers stuck on the doorknob. Whoever owned the place should have asked his neighbors to tidy up a bit. Of course, a guy who took pictures like Caesar found probably wouldn't want other people around when he wasn't there.

A guy like that would have tons of friends in the area. Moms would trust their kids to go over and play with his. All the adults would like him. All the kids would give half-assed warnings to other kids about the weirdo who lived there. And he would be involved in scouts or little league or soccer, something with lots of opportunity. It's how it always was. Nate turned to Caesar. "You're sure it's that house?"

Caesar rolled his eyes. "Yeah, I'm sure."

Nate fished his cell from the cup holder. "Okay, let's see who the perv in residence is." Who was on duty today? Saturday early, which would mean Frank Calvin was on the beat. Cal was a pretty stand up guy. They'd been in some situations together and they'd both been on the softball team last year. Cal had been Captain. Nate flipped open his cell hoping to find Cal's number in memory. It was there. Hitting the dial, now it was just up to whether Cal would pick up. On the third ring a rough voice answered, "Calvin."

"Hey Cal, its Nate Reilly." He smiled and winked at Caesar. "You got a minute?"

Barely audible in the background was the clink and clatter of dishes. "Just having my breakfast." Even though Nate had interrupted his meal, Cal sounded pleased to hear from him.

Cal, if he remembered correctly was a pancake fanatic. It showed in his waistline. "Heart attack special at IHOP?"

"You bet." Vague chewing sounds drifted over the connection. Cal was not terribly good on the manners end of the scale.

"Look, I need a quick favor." Nate leaned forward, looking past Caesar at the house. Bright brass numbers were shaded beside the door. "Can you run an address for me when you're done? I need to know who lives at this house."

"Why, what's up?"

"Not much, you know my sis is in the industry." In Southern California no one had to be told which industry you meant. "She thinks this house might be what the art director was looking for on one of the productions she's working."

"Let me grab something to write on." There were more munches in Nate's ear before Cal came back on, "Okay, give it to me."

Nate read off the numbers on the house. "It's on Turney, Los Angeles, in the Los Feliz area."

A slurp forced Nate to pull away from the phone. He brought it back to his ear just in time to catch the response. "Hell, don't even need to run that one. You're in luck. Belongs to Syd Price. He's a Sergeant, FTO out of the Hollywood Division. Gearing up to run for Sheriff in the next election. I worked with the guy a ways back, he used to do barbeques at his place a lot…invite all the families over. Want me to pass it on?"

Sergeant and a Field Training Officer, holy fuck the guy was a cop. "Naw, not yet," He managed to get it out rather calmly, even with his spine melting through the seat. "They're just scouting right now. If they like it, I'll get back to you."

"No problem, anytime." Muted conversations punctuated with *honey* and *thanks* that weren't meant for Nate. Then Cal's attention was back. "Hey, we'll be starting signups for the fall team. Love to have you back."

Nate swallowed. "Let me think about it." He needed to get off the phone before he said something stupid, gave something away. "Look I got to run now. I'll talk to you sometime next week about the team."

"Sure." The line went dead without a goodbye. Nate tried to remember how to breathe.

"Well?" Caesar's voice startled him and Nate jumped.

He flipped the phone closed as he dumped it back in the cup holder. Leaning in to look at Caesar's eyes, he had to be certain. "Are you sure it was that house?" His hand shot out, pointing at the Tudor.

"Of course I'm sure." Caesar seemed offended that Nate would even ask. "I spent days casing it. It's what I do; remember everything about a house before I break into it. It would really suck to case a place and then break into the joint next door."

Nate chewed on his lip. He drummed on the steering wheel. He fiddled with the air. Then he turned to Caesar again. "That house?"

"Yes, that house!" Caesar was definitely pissed.

"Fuck!" Nate put the Ford in gear, gunned it and pulled out.

Caesar grabbed the support on the door. "What the hell's wrong?"

"That's a cop's house." Trying not to panic, Nate drove. By instinct he found himself back on Los Feliz and headed towards the freeway. Home, he needed to go home and think things over. "Not just any cop, but a pretty high-up cop."

"Oh, shit." Caesar swallowed.

The officer in Nate had to agree with that statement. "Oh, shit is right."

They didn't talk much on the ride back to Chatsworth. Nate made plan after plan on how to handle it. Each one was discarded as unworkable. And it was so hard to think with Caesar sitting in the car next to him.

Nate slid out of his car and started across the lot. After a few steps he realized Caesar wasn't behind him. Turning, he caught sight of the thief heading towards a battered pickup. Crossing his arms across his chest and falling into a wide legged stance, Nate shot out, "Where the hell are you going?"

"Home." Caesar barely turned to deliver his answer.

"Unh-uh. Not right now." As he jogged over, Nate had a good idea as to what might be in the back of that truck. "There's stuff we've got to take care of first."

Backing away toward his truck, Caesar held up his hands, almost physically pushing the problem toward Nate. "No, there's stuff you have to take care of, Officer Reilly. I did my part, I'm done."

No way was he going to let this asshole bail. "Get your ass in my apartment, now!" Nate stepped up into Caesar's personal space. "I am not letting you out of here until we've got a few things straight and you understand some stuff. Plus, I've got a really good idea as to what's in the back of that vehicle. You leave now, I'll call in your plates and have you popped for at least receiving. Then you can figure out how you're going to protect yourself from a seriously pissed off police sergeant while you're stuck in holding. And, when the shit about the photos breaks…you'll be a sitting duck."

Caesar blanched. "Fuck you! That's so unfair."

"Get in the fucking house!" To make certain of compliance, Nate wrapped one hand around the back of Caesar's neck and steered him towards the courtyard.

Caesar swatted his hand away. "Shit, you don't have to push."

Walking helped settle a few things. He'd need Caesar's statement for a warrant. And he should fill out a report now, while everything was fresh in his mind. "Wait a minute," he caught Caesar by the belt loop and earned a glare, "I've got to get something." Quickly, he popped the trunk on the Taurus. His warbag sat in the back of the car. He dug through the spare set of law enforcement necessities: knife, small pry bar, extra flashlight and fully-charged batteries, a first aid kit, disposable gloves, tissues, gun oil, an extra set of handcuffs, disposable cameras. What a load of crap he carried around. At the bottom of the black duffle he found it. A portfolio type folder of the kind high school kids carried. It held a few copies of the forms Nate used on a regular basis.

When he looked up, Nate thought Caesar had run. Then he saw him leaning against the building, taking advantage of the thin shade. It was ungodly hot, but at least it wasn't smoggy yet. Still, the short walk from car to building had sweat running down Nate's back. He tapped Caesar on the hip with the folder as he passed. "Come on, at least I have air."

"Great," Caesar didn't sound enthused as he fell into step. "No good deed goes unpunished." Cool air whooshed out when Nate opened the apartment door and both men sighed with relief. As Nate moved to the kitchen, Caesar collapsed on the couch. "Can I use your phone?" drifted up from somewhere in the cushions.

Nate dropped the forms on the small dinette table. "Why?" Popping the fridge, he grabbed a couple cans of soda before he wandered back to the living room area.

"I need to call my brother." Caesar was face down on the sofa, one hand trailing on the floor. He jumped when Nate set the cold can against his neck. When he turned, Nate held it out. With a rueful smile Caesar took the proffered drink. "Have him run over and check on Ponchito."

That's right, Caesar had a dog. Somehow that made him seem a little more human. "Yeah, sure. I'm going to do some work on this. Give me the phone when you're done." He headed back to the table and his forms. "You can watch TV if you want. Just keep it low."

"Thanks." Caesar popped the can and took a swig. Then he picked up the mobile handset. Nate turned his attention to the notes from last night. First he took what he'd jotted down and wrote it out legibly, making insertions here and there in the narrative so that it flowed in a logical manner. He also kept himself from inserting the "TV cop jargon" that drove people nuts. Standard English, laid out like he was talking to another officer. Nobody exited vehicles. They got out of the car. You didn't proceed. You ran, you walked or you drove down a street. The Adam-12 language just muddled things.

A soft, one-sided conversation in Spanish sounded somewhere behind him. It was soothing in a way. He really shouldn't have been so complacent about Caesar wandering unfettered through his house. But, while he had an unsavory profession, he seemed a decent enough guy. Nate shook his head at the thought. Decent guys didn't steal shit.

Once set, his draft would be transferred onto the actual report form. Then Nate would destroy both the notes and the draft. His first training officer had taught him that. It took a little longer, but in the end his cases held up better than ones based on reports with insertions and scribbled out passages. As long as the report accurately reflected what was in the notes, it was okay to shred them. The practice kept confusion down to a minimum.

He was halfway through the draft when Caesar set the phone in front of him. Nate looked up. "Thanks. Dog taken care of?"

"Yeah. I'm going to get another soda, want one?"

Shaking his head no, Nate hit the numbers on the phone from memory. The line rang several times before a machine picked up and a computerized voice informed him that no one was home. When the beep sounded, Nate called into the receiver. "Dad, it's me, pick up." His parents always screened their calls through the machine. One of these days he was going to force them into the wonder that was caller ID.

A click sounded and a real person came on the line. "Hey, sport."

Caesar raised his eyebrows as he walked back to the living room. Nate ignored the unspoken question. "Hiya, how's mom? You guys all packed?"

"She's fine and we're good to go. It'll be nice to see my brother although I'm not sure I can stand him for two weeks on a cruise ship." They both laughed. "Carol's got the spare key. Maybe you could run up and check on things if she can't?" His dad should know he didn't even have to ask. Still, it was second nature for him to do so. "So what's up?"

David Reilly had retired from the force two years earlier. Nate still couldn't believe it. All his life his dad had been a cop. And, since he joined the force, Nate knew the one cop he could always count on was his dad. "Dad, I've got a situation and I don't know exactly what to do."

There was silence for a moment, and then a reassuring, "Shoot."

Quickly Nate outlined the events, Caesar's involvement and his involvement with Caesar. He did edit out that there'd been three times they were together. His dad didn't need that tidbit. It was enough for him to know that there was a potential conflict there. The rest of it went unvarnished. The photos, the house, and who owned it all spilled out. Finally Nate figured his dad knew everything he did. "So there's the problem."

"Okay," Nate could tell his dad was thinking, "Tell me why it's a problem?"

Nate shifted in his chair. "Well, because this guy is a cop." He wasn't too certain what his dad meant.

"And why does that make a difference on how you handle this?" A smile rose at his dad's voice. David Reilly was using the *don't be a moron* tone he'd always hit Nate and Carol with when the answer was obvious to him.

"It doesn't but," Nate squirmed some more, "he's a high-ranking cop."

Again, his father used that voice, "And why does that make a difference? I know you know the answer."

Nate thought before responding. Dad was right, it didn't make a difference. "I'm just trying to figure out how to handle it."

"I know." His dad sighed. "What about your captain? Do you think he's on the pad? Or do you think he's clean?"

Now they were getting somewhere. "Pretty sure he's clean."

"Well, sport," the tone changed to something more supportive, "you're gonna find out, aren't you?"

It was Nate's turn to sigh. He'd hoped, vainly, that his dad would have a magical cure. "Yeah, I guess I am." He knew better then to expect such things, but he could still hope.

"Good. At least I raised you partway right."

Nate knew what the partway wrong his dad meant was and that hit him hard. It took a bit, but he managed to drive the hurt down. "Hey dad, thanks for listening."

"No problem. Sometimes you just need to talk yourself through the right decision with someone. You already knew what it was 'cause you're a good cop, Nate. No matter what." The end of that sentence was *anyone else thinks about you being a fag.*

He hated that he knew that about his dad. "Look, I got a report to write. Dot all the I's and cross the T's, make it clean, and then I'll give it to him tomorrow."

"In case no one else tells you, Nate, you're doing the right thing."

"Thanks, dad."

"Sure thing. Take care of yourself."

"Will do." Pushing disconnect, Nate stared at the phone in his hands. Why did his dad have to hurt him like that? What was worse, David Reilly didn't even realize he was doing it. As he turned and started to rise, Nate caught Caesar staring at him. The look said *what was that all about?* When Caesar started to open his mouth, Nate stopped him with a glare. "Just watch TV and be quiet." Caesar shrugged in response and went back to staring at the set.

It took a good couple of hours to get everything in logical order. While he worked, Caesar made him a sandwich, then got him a Coke and in general tried to be helpful. It was good to have him around since Nate needed to clarify a few things. He wanted this report to be tight. The real hell was trying to figure out how much to put in or leave out about his relationship with Caesar. Finally, Nate opted for leaving most of it out of the report making a veiled reference to prior acquaintance.

When everything was neat and presentable, Nate stretched. Everything pinched. He stood and stretched again. How long had he been sitting? God, he really needed to hit the gym and work the kinks out properly, but that didn't seem likely anytime soon. Nate turned to find Caesar dozing on the couch. Crouching next to the sofa, Nate shook the other man lightly. Deep chocolate eyes came to half-mast with a glare. Even sleep-fogged Caesar was damn sexy. If only things were different... Nate couldn't even finish the thought. "Okay, I've got a storage area on the back side of my building. We're going to put the shit you stole there for the time being. Tomorrow, I'll figure a way to transfer it to evidence. Then, you're going to lie low all weekend. Give me your phone number. I've got some calls to make Monday, see if I can't set something up. We have to go real careful on this. Real careful, you understand?"

"I get it." Stifling a yawn, Caesar struggled to sit up. Before Nate could move, Caesar grabbed his arm. "Don't fuck me on this Nate, please."

The plea was genuine. Caesar had to rely on Nate's pull to keep him safe and out of jail. Nate wasn't sure how much of that trust was misplaced. He offered the best reassurance he had, "I'll do what I can."

CHAPTER 11

Al Gregor was always happy to see you. Even at seven a.m. on an already muggy Monday. If Caesar wanted to be cynical, it was because seeing you meant you were in trouble. People in trouble paid to get out of trouble. Attorneys who were paid were happy people. But with Al it was always a pat on your back, how's your mom, type of happy.

Saturday, Caesar'd been working on the TV cabinet when it hit him he should have called Al *first*. Running to Nate was just knee-jerk stupid. Unfortunately it was done, and he'd have to unwind it as best as possible. He'd left a message with Al's service that it was urgent. Of course everything in Al's business was urgent. By Sunday afternoon he had a breakfast meeting with his attorney and a nine o'clock meeting with his attorney and the government.

Caesar tried to remember the first time he'd used Al. It was way too far back, but he was pretty sure he'd found the man's name scribbled next to a pay phone in holding. Below it were a few comments about how good he was. He vaguely remembered some of those because they were funny in an off the cuff sort of way. Stuff like, "it doesn't hurt when he puts his hand in your pocket" and "he could plead an elephant down to a mouse." A criminal defense attorney's best advertising: repeat offenders who liked you. Shit, Caesar wished he'd found Al the first time he'd been popped.

Al rocked back in his green pseudo-leather executive chair and steepled his fingers over the bridge of his sharp nose. Two cups of expensive coffee sat on either side of a scarred fifties-era desk. It was one of those big walnut things that would take six guys to lift. How the hell Al had gotten it up the narrow set of stairs and into his second floor office above a tailor's shop had always confounded Caesar. "You should have called me first, kiddo, you know that." The time, but not the coffee, would show up on his bill. That's the kind of guy Al was.

"I was scared, Al." Caesar hid his embarrassment by grabbing the coffee and slurping it down. To fast, he hissed as it burned his tongue. "It was nasty shit. It freaked me out. I wasn't thinking straight." Setting the paper cup back on the desk, Caesar dropped his hands into his lap and picked at his cuticles.

"Hey, kiddo." Al called everyone kiddo. "We all do stupid stuff. That's what keeps me in business." Even when chiding his clients, Al's gray eyes smiled. "And you think this cop, Nathan Reilly, is straight with you?"

No, I think he's hung a little to the left. Caesar shook the joke out of his head before it had a chance to hit his mouth. Instead he said, "Pretty much. He's got some reasons to keep it pretty low-key, treat me good."

Al shrugged out of his suit jacket and tossed it across the computer stand jammed between the desk and the wall. Everything in Al's office was jammed. Cheap bookcases overflowed with manuals and mementos. Caesar's knees knocked the edge of the desk while his back bumped against books. Al always said it was because most of his work wasn't done at the office. The place was basically a large filing cabinet. Big, fancy lawyer's offices came with big, fancy lawyer's fees. When Al handed you the bill, you knew you weren't paying for the art on the walls.

"Why?" asked Al. "Are you a regular informant of his? Remember kiddo, cops can be mad dogs, bite the hand that feeds them and all that."

For a moment Caesar just stared out the grimy window. A *taquaria*, a coin-op laundry and a bail-bonds place stared back at him. That's how you always knew you were near a courthouse. Law offices, pawnshops and bondsmen were disproportionately represented. Caesar turned his attention back to Al. Gray hair, gray eyes with rumpled skin that matched his rumpled shirt. "You're my attorney, right Al?"

"Yep, kiddo." Al nodded. "You're paying me."

"And so you need to know everything, right?"

Al's eyes narrowed. "Yeah, if it bears on your case, I need to know it."

"I'm gay." Caesar looked out the window again. That was the least awkward of the things he was going to have to tell Al.

"Okay." Al leaned back in his chair again and sipped his coffee. "I assume you'll tell me why that bears on your case."

"So's Officer Reilly." Caesar swallowed "We're involved, sort of." As he spoke he dropped his eyes until he was staring at the toes of his work boots. He really didn't want to see what Al's expression was.

The creak of worn springs told Caesar that Al was no longer in casual, laid-back mode. "By involved, and the fact that you won't look at me, I'm interpreting that as playing mattress bingo?" Caesar risked a glance. Al's elbows were propped on the desk, his fists cradling his chin. When he caught Caesar looking, both eyebrows shot up. "Caesar, kiddo, you don't *sort of* have sex with someone. You guys screwing?"

"Yeah." It came out on a whisper of breath.

"Normally, not my regular line of inquiry, but on a regular basis? Define your relationship with this cop for me."

"Well, when we first met, things happened too fast to talk about...well anything." Caesar risked another swig of coffee. It had cooled a bit. After a few gulps, Caesar realized he was just delaying the inevitable. Deliberately, he set the cup on the edge of the desk. "So it wasn't until a little later that we figured things out. You know, what he does and what I do. But every time we run into each other, we seem to end up in bed." He ended the sentence with a shrug.

"You're," Al seemed to search around his brain for a way to phrase it, "fuck buddies?"

"How 'bout fucked-up buddies?" Caesar rolled his eyes and shook his head. He had no idea what to call it. "I guess that's about as close as you could get."

Massaging the bridge of his nose with his thumb, Al thought for a bit. Then he had another question. "How many times? This is going to go down as one of my weirder consults...not the strangest, but up there."

"Three times."

"That's not bad," Al leaned back in the chair again, and stared up at the ceiling. "Over how many months?"

Caesar fiddled with an imagined spot on his jeans. He cleaned a bit of dirt out from under his nail with his thumb. He ran his hand along the edge of his jaw, toying with the fringe of a goatee. It wasn't until Al coughed impatiently that he answered.

"Two weeks," he mumbled.

A roll of the neck was all it took for those gray eyes to hit Caesar hard. "Ah, to be young and horny, I didn't get that much sex on my second honeymoon. At least there's an excuse for why you ran to a cop. Shit, kiddo, next time, think with this head," the attorney tapped his forehead with his middle finger. A gold and diamond ring flashed in the dim morning light. "And not the one between your legs, okay?" Al went back to reading Caesar's future in the cracks in the ceiling. "Well, that's a decent reason for *him* to keep you out of trouble. But, kiddo, you know it won't be his decision. You're not stupid. It's going to go up the feeding chain, and everyone is going to want to take a bite …outta you."

"I know. That's why I called you when I really thought it through. But I've got to do this Al. It's just so wrong."

Al snorted. "That moral streak is not good for your line of work." Scratching his jaw, just below his ear, he thought on the problem. "Give me something to trade, I may need it."

"What do you mean?"

"They're going to want to hang you. 'Tell us everything and we'll still send you to prison for B&E, thank you so much for being a concerned citizen' and all that rot. They're not going to want to be seen as soft. And you've bit them on the ass, breaking into a cop's house. You've dug up a lot of nastiness and they're going to be defensive about it. You dirty one cop and you've dirtied them all." Al stood and grabbed his jacket. The rest on top of the computer hadn't done it any favors. Wrinkles eased out and new ones formed as he shrugged it on. "Think about it on the ride over. We'll take my car. You can leave your truck here."

Caesar fished in his back pocket as he stood. "Oh, that reminds me. I brought it." When he found the papers he held them out to Al.

"What?"

"The check and title to my truck...for the lien, like we did last time." Al's retainer was pretty reasonable for standard stuff. There was no telling how much time and money this mess would take and he'd want some assurance that the bill would get paid. "You know I ain't got big money up front, but I'm good for the payment plan."

Al took the papers between two fingers. "Well let's both hope I can keep you out of doing time." He laughed, tossed the papers back on his desk and held the door open for Caesar. "Your truck isn't worth the impound and court fees if I actually had to go through executing the lien. We'll take care of the paperwork when we get back." That was classic Al.

Also classic Al was the car he drove. He ushered Caesar to the back lot where a sleek, silver sedan crouched next to his beleaguered truck. Nothing big and flashy, but it wasn't the cheapest model by any means. Caesar settled into the leather bucket seat trying not to think about what was ahead. Al distracted him with war stories as they headed for the freeway. They were meeting at the Northeast Station on San Fernando Road. Al's office was in East L.A. That meant a crawl through the East L.A. interchange on the 5 with a short jog up the 2.

Inching through traffic, Caesar came up with a few offerings. There were some jobs he was suspected on, even been questioned about, but never been charged. Like many burglaries, the police had a decent idea who was responsible but they just couldn't *prove* it was him. Al had once told him that only about thirteen percent of burglaries were ever solved. Caesar liked those odds, although it made him feel real stupid about the times he'd been caught.

Caesar and Al walked into the police station and ran into a wall of suits. Three of them, not counting Al, were waiting in a tiny room. Nate was the only one, besides Caesar, who was in anything less than a jacket and tie. And Nate was spit-and-polish in his blue uniform. Damn did he look good in it, narrow waist circled by a heavy black belt, his arms bulging under navy short sleeves. Somebody needed to take his picture for a recruiting poster. Put a guy like that on the billboard, and there'd be women lined up six deep to apply.

Nate threaded between two men wearing badges and a woman who wasn't. The other cops were a study in opposites. A rail-thin white guy and a heavy-set Asian. Stepping close to Caesar, Nate whispered, "Who's he?"

Al snorted, he'd probably figured out who Nate was the moment he saw the officer. "My lawyer, Al Gregor."

"Why'd you bring a lawyer?" Al had definitely figured it out. If he hadn't, Caesar wouldn't have still been talking with Nate. "You didn't say anything about getting a lawyer."

Sealing Caesar's suspicion, Al leaned in. "Don't say anything you haven't already, okay." He offered a bright smile to Nate but spoke to Caesar. "I'm going to introduce myself to everyone. Stay right here. Don't worry, kiddo, I'll take care of you."

Caesar nodded his understanding. Then he hissed at Nate. "Why wouldn't I bring a lawyer?"

"Don't you trust me?" Nate actually seemed hurt, although he was trying like hell not to show it.

Caesar didn't want to hurt him. "I think I trust Nate." He shrugged. "Officer Nathan Reilly, not so sure about that. The uniform changes things." With a glance about the room, he mumbled out of the side of his mouth. "The rest of them, not as far as I can spit."

The prosecutor was a middle-aged woman with an overabundance of prematurely white hair. Cotton candy nails flashed as she spoke with Al. The two detectives looked grim. They kept sneaking sideways glares in Caesar's direction. Maybe they were offended that he'd dared to bring in legal counsel. Well, it was his skin, not theirs. Fuck 'em if they couldn't take a joke.

Caesar and Nate were left in a corner by themselves. That somehow felt comforting to Caesar. It shouldn't have been. The silence between them was neither pleasant nor friendly. He sure as hell wasn't about to apologize to Nate for bringing in Al, but he could explain it.

"Look Nate," Caesar whispered, trying hard not to look like he was conspiring or anything, "I've been to county, I don't want to go back. And as much as you think you can do right by me, we're both outclassed here."

Nate snorted. Then he shifted. "Maybe." The word came out all growly, as though he hated admitting Caesar might be right.

Anything further was cut off when Al and the lady prosecutor made their way over. "Okay, kiddo." Al's body was loose, but his eyes told Caesar this was serious business. "You think you could live with a couple of charges of criminal trespass?"

Caesar ran his hand through his hair and thought about it. The one thing he didn't want was to go back inside the zoo. "Would I do time?"

The prosecutor tapped her nails against her teeth. "Can't guarantee that you won't." Her voice was low and breathy. Caesar thought she sounded like an aging porn star. He masked his sudden urge to laugh with a cough. She sighed, "I can guarantee the charge bargain, that's between all of us. But any sentencing would have to be approved by a judge."

Caesar risked a quick glance at Al. His attorney nodded. They'd talked about possible pot sweeteners. "What if I threw in who my fence was on those jobs?" That asshole had jerked Caesar over a few months back. Caesar had moved on, but the prospect of sticking it to the jerk to save his own skin had a certain ring of come-uppance to it.

"We still might get stung by the judge, but I can push." She turned to Al, "I'd be guessing we'd be looking at least at some probation."

Al's eyes were locked on Caesar's. He had to have caught the sudden rise of panic at the word because he put his hand on Caesar's shoulder. First a comforting squeeze, then he turned back to the prosecutor. "How long are you thinking about?"

She shrugged, "Standard for a felony is five years formal."

Caesar started to sweat, which was strange because ice had replaced the blood in his veins. Formal probation sucked. It meant random drug tests. Pretty much your rights went *adios*: your house, your car, your body could be searched just because. Monthly meetings with a probation officer were supposed to take fifteen minutes but they cost you all day. If you skipped out, there was this big anvil over your head, waiting to fall the next time you jaywalked or looked wrong at a cop.

"No more than three summary."

"I don't know if I can get a judge to go for low term bench probation on three serious misdemeanors." She rolled her eyes. "He's got a rap sheet. Your boy's no misguided youth…he's a career criminal."

God, they were talking about him in the third person. Caesar hated that. It added another layer of agitation to the whole dance. When you became an abstraction without a name, you got lost in the system. Al looked completely cool and in charge as he dickered. "Restitution would be part of the deal, obviously. We could tack on some community service in lieu of time." Caesar was glad one of them was cool.

"Restitution would definitely have to be a part of it." Her hands waved in the air like she was casting some arcane legal spell over the process. "With community service, a judge might swallow the unsupervised better. I'd recommend that and push for it."

Something really warm and solid pressed against Caesar's back. It took him a moment to realize it was Nate. The cop was angled sideways, so that he bumped without looking like he intended to bump. Caesar guessed it was to hide the move from the detectives across the room. So low that Caesar almost didn't catch it over the attorney's negotiations, Nate hissed, "She'll do what she says, don't worry about it."

"So he'll plead guilty to three counts criminal trespass."

Caesar caught that and broke in. "I want No-lo."

"You realize there's no real difference between a no contest and a guilty plea."

"Look, it's just important that I don't have the guilty stamp on my forehead right now. I just don't want the words there." He swallowed and chewed on his bottom lip. "It's a personal thing. The sentence will still be the same, so it shouldn't be that big of a deal. You'll still clear those cases, you'll get the info on this one and you'll have Chaz."

Al looked at the woman. "What do you say?"

"Like I said, Al, you know I can't guarantee the sentence bargain. But your client will plead no-lo to three misdemeanor counts instead of the felony. He'll give us the info on those and finger the guy who's receiving. Restitution and community service will be part of the bargain. Then, and this is what I'll use to push the judge on sentencing, he'll cooperate fully in the investigation, trial, the whole shebang on the kiddy porn possession matter."

"I think it's more than just possession." Caesar's voice sounded defeated to his own ears. But hearing the terms laid out like that was hard. Fuck, be a good guy, and this is what happened. Maybe he should have just called in an anonymous tip. Way too late for that now, and not like anyone would have taken it seriously anyway.

"Okay, I do, too." For the first time she smiled at Caesar. "But right now what we've got is evidence that he has dirty pics of kids. Usually, guys like that don't stop there, but that's what we'll start with, okay?"

"It's up to you, kiddo."

He risked a quick glance at Nate, still standing behind him being unobtrusive. The cop's right hand was hooked into his duty belt. Just as he was about to turn away, Caesar caught the subtle thumbs-up. "Yeah. It's good."

"Okay, I want it in writing before Mr. Serrano says another word." Al held up his hand. "I know…no guarantees about the sentencing. But I want it in there that it's your recommendation. I'd like the detectives to sign off on it, too. It can't hurt that everyone thinks this is a good idea."

CHAPTER 12

Poncho's little black chin rested on the floor by Caesar's feet. Ass butted up against the sink, Caesar looked down to see large, soulful doggy eyes. They accused him of being stingy. Caesar stopped, a triangle of a microwaved *quesadilla* raised halfway to his mouth. "What?" The starved groan he got in response was utterly pitiful. It was also utterly bullshit. The dog had wolfed down his own food not minutes ago. "No, this is my dinner." Caesar crammed the section into his mouth. "You had yours." It came out mumbled.

Everybody wanted something from him these days. Ponchito wanted his food. Al wanted his money. The cops wanted his ass in a sling. Shit, he'd spent the entire day at the police station. Once the deal had been cut, Nate bailed on him. What more did he expect? Nate had gotten what he wanted and he left Caesar to suffer under the interrogation. Thank God Al had been there with him. Otherwise he would have been left alone with those two asshole detectives. There he was, cooperating, and they still gave him a hard time. Al had to jump in twice and ask the prosecutor to rein them back. If he'd trusted in the power of Nate-all-mighty, Caesar would have been screwed.

Another groan from the floor let him know that Ponchito still wanted Caesar's dinner. The only other life in the house was the canned laughter from the TV in the front room. Layered on top of that was traffic drone from the Pasadena Freeway and the asthmatic wheeze of the bedroom window unit. Hopefully, by the time he was ready to sleep, it would be halfway cool in there. Record temperatures and humidity pounding LA that summer meant it was an unlikely proposition.

Caesar reached back and tore off another section. Poncho followed his every move. Eating at the sink again, just him and his dog. Man, he needed a life. And hell, it wasn't like what he'd agreed to today was going to help with that. Probation and restitution meant coming up with a steady job. And, on top of that, Caesar had hundreds of hours of community service to work off. That pretty much guaranteed that every weekend for the next five years would be spent collecting trash along the side of the freeway. Poncho whined again. Caesar caved. "Pig," he grunted and tossed the last bit to the dog. The *quesadilla* arced through the air to be snapped up before it hit the floor. It was amazing how fast Ponchito could move when he wanted something.

Caesar rinsed the plate and shoved it, still wet, back in the cabinet. Hands dripping, he ran them through his hair and let the water run down his neck. At least that was halfway cool. He was so fucked. And he was so pissed at Nate. How could Nate just abandon him like that? Caesar trusted the guy. One minute he was there giving Caesar high signs and the next he was just gone. No good-bye, no I'll be back to check on you later, nada.

Wandering back into the tiny living room, Caesar stripped off his shirt. It was too hot to be dressed. He flopped onto the couch, bare feet pointed towards the front door. Behind him he could hear Ponchito's paws clicking across the kitchen. Then a whump sounded as he nosed through the tiny doggy-door out into the back yard. Caesar balled his shirt and tossed it past the TV into the open bedroom. The only thing that saved the one bedroom shack from being a complete dump was the workshop in the detached garage.

The heat made him drowsy. Through half-lidded eyes he watched the flickering screen. *Protagonistas de Novela* was on. The soap star wannabees running through stylized tears and out-of-context, insane dialog from the latest *telenovelas* caused him to laugh out loud a few times. They were all so interchangeable he'd forgotten which of last season's contestants had actually won. Thinking about it, the show might not be a re-run. Well, it wasn't like he watched anything with regularity.

Caesar was about to flip to the news when Poncho bolted in from the back. The terrier mix slid to a halt before the front door and let out a single, deep and loud, "Woof." It was always so strange to hear that bark coming from that dog…like Ponchito had stolen the vocal cords from a pit bull. As footsteps sounded out on the concrete stoop, Caesar hit the mute button. Whoever it was tried the dead doorbell. Then the knock came. Poncho turned and sneezed, he'd done his job.

"*¿Quién es?*" Caesar called the question from the couch.

"Caesar, its Nate." The cop's voice sounded agitated. "I need to talk to you."

Halfway off the couch he stopped. Just what he didn't need, Nate. "Go away!" Perfect way to cap a crappy day.

Nate pounded on the security door. Metal mesh clattered harsh against the iron bars. "Caesar, come on! Let me in!"

"No. Go home." Trying to think, Caesar pressed his palms to his forehead. "You got what you wanted."

More pounding rattled both inside and outside Caesar's skull. "Open the fucking door! I wanna talk to you!"

Damn, if Nate didn't stop yelling someone was going to call the cops. The thought almost made him laugh, almost. "But I don't want to talk to you!" Caesar yelled back.

Everything went quiet outside. Then a growl came from the other side of the door. Damn, that man had such a sexy way of expressing his frustrations. It reverberated up and down Caesar's nerves. Low and steady, Nate hit him with a threat. "Want me to start yelling all over the neighborhood about today? Hey, this guy's a stooge, working for the cops."

Cabrone! What an asshole. Jumping from the couch, he made the door in two steps. "You're gonna get me fucking killed, stupid cop!" Caesar yanked the door open to find Nate leaning against the jamb. At least he wasn't such an idiot as to show up in uniform. A tight polo shirt and even tighter jeans hugged his frame. Caesar managed to contain the mental drooling to a minimal level. Keeping the security door securely fastened between them, Caesar spat. "What the hell are you doing here?"

Nate leered. "I want to talk to you."

"Okay." He glared at the self-satisfied bastard. "You're talking to me."

"Inside," Nate commanded.

That cop voice made Caesar all watery inside and not in the way he was used to with cops. No way in hell would he ever admit that to Nate. Sarcasm was his only retreat. "No, I think you're outside," Caesar sniped.

Standing and crossing his arms over his broad chest, Nate dropped the casual act. "Do you really want your neighbors to see me standing here talking to you?" He let the thought sink in for a bit before continuing. "They've seen me in uniform. They might start putting things together themselves."

Caesar twisted the deadbolt and walked away. Nate could let himself in. When he got as far as the arch leading to the kitchen, Caesar turned. It put a decent amount of space between him and the cop. Plus, there was only one place to sit in the living room...the couch. Caesar did not want to sit on the couch with Nate. He shoved his hands in his pockets and glared.

Nate stepped into the room and pulled the door shut behind him. A quick flick of his eyes took in his surroundings. Then he chose to prop himself up on the opposite wall. Nate said, "We need to talk."

Poncho yawned. His gaze flicked between the men. When he saw that neither was going to take the couch, he claimed it. Hopping onto the middle cushion, Poncho rubbed his face against the fabric with satisfied grunts. Then he flopped down, nose hanging off the edge so that he could keep master and visitor both in view.

"About what?" Caesar tried to look everywhere except at Nate. "Do I need to call my lawyer? You know that's going to cost me extra."

Nate dropped his chin and crossed his arms again. "That's what I want to talk to you about." Drumming his fingers against one bulging bicep, Nate seemed lost in thought. Finally, he came up with his question. "Why the fuck did you bring a lawyer in on it?"

How could Nate even ask such a question? "To save my fucking ass!" Packing as much venom as he could manage into the words, Caesar spat the response. "That's why. Are you just a moron?"

"I told you I'd take care of you...didn't you believe me?" Nate sounded hurt.

Caesar sighed. Nate made this so hard on both of them. It had to be that blue-tinted set of contacts permanently implanted over his eyes when he graduated from the academy.

"No, I honestly didn't." Maybe Nate had only been exposed to the good side of the police. Or maybe he wore blinders so that he didn't have to see the shit that cops dished out to people like Caesar.

"Why?"

"You're a fucking cop, Nate. Cops can't be trusted." Shaking his head, Caesar tried to see a way around it. There wasn't. "As much as I like you, that will always be a problem."

Lip out in a near pout, Nate asked, "What reason have I ever given you not to trust *me*?"

"What reason have you ever given me *to* trust you?" Caesar ran his hands across his scalp. "And shit, the moment you got what you wanted out of it, you were out of there." Fingers laced above his head, he started pacing. "Such a good way to take care of your witness."

Nate's head snapped up. "I didn't have any choice!" His arms uncrossed and he took two steps farther into the room. "The detective told me I was no longer needed so it wasn't like I could hang around. I couldn't disobey a superior officer. They pull all the strings. I have to trust that they'll do right by my people."

"And that's," Caesar moved in, hissing, "why I needed someone on my side." His dark eyes searched bright green. "I can't trust that they'd do right by me. And know what, once you were gone, and even with my own attorney right there, they tried to fuck with me, go back on things. To them I'm just another crook." He slammed his palm into Nate's chest and then swept it to the side like he was brushing something foul off the cop. "I'm nothing. *Nada*. Nobody. Get it?"

Chest-to-chest, they stared each other down. Dropping his eyes first, Nate mumbled, "I'm sorry I left you with them. I know better. I just, I just thought it would be different because I told them." The cop hesitated. "I lied and told them you were a friend from way back...you know. 'I haven't seen him in a long time but we go way back.' It's not like I could tell them the truth."

"I don't think that would have made a difference, Nate." Damn it, he actually felt sorry for Nate. Caesar's life was screwed, but he felt sorry for a cop. What the fuck was wrong with him? He bumped that solid shoulder with his fist and snorted, "If you told them you were sleeping with me, it would have been ten times worse. Don't beat yourself up." Caesar stepped away and dropped heavily on one end of the couch. Poncho sidled over and Caesar scratched his ears. "Look, I'm gonna work with you on this. There's levels of wrong and that pretty much tops them all. But don't expect me to live by your," he held out his hands, outlining Nate's form in the air, "cop kinda code. My world, your world, it's like some weird ass sci-fi show...running side-by-side but not really the same place at all."

"Doesn't have to be." Nate dropped down, resting his butt on his heels.

"What?" Caesar kicked his knee with one bare foot. "You're going to turn to a life of crime?"

Nate swatted Caesar's ankle as he tried to keep his balance. "Asshole. I meant you could use this as an opportunity to turn your life around. You can't live like this forever. What happens the next time?" He managed to steady himself with a tight grip on Caesar's thigh. Caesar willed himself to ignore the little sparks that flared under the touch. "One day you'll get caught and you'll do some serious time. You said you didn't want to go back to county...but fuck, what about state? Think about it. That's hard time with fucking scary people: murderers, hard-core bangers. Is that what you want?"

"Gee," leaning in he used a falsetto kid's voice, "Officer Nate, thanks for the scared straight talk." Oh hell, there was that cologne. This close the spicy, musky scent wound around Caesar's brain and made it hard to think. The damn heat didn't help. Caesar swallowed.

Nate didn't back down. "Well, hell you need one. You ain't stupid, Caesar. You have other skills. What you're doing with your life is just throwing it away." The fingers on Caesar's leg tightened. "Shit, somebody should have given you one a long time ago."

Caesar's eyes drifted down, fascinated by the little tuft of hair just visible where Nate's shirt gaped. With distraction like that, Nate's last sentence barely registered. "Somebody should have given me a *what* a long time ago?" He licked his bottom lip before running his teeth over the same spot. It wasn't just the lack of air-conditioning that was making it hot in the room. Every inch of Caesar's body vibrated with how near the cop was.

"You're not paying attention to me," Nate growled.

Oh that sound, that smell, that guy, Caesar inched forward and whispered, "I am paying so much attention to you." Damn, playing with fire and wanting to get burned. He wrapped his hand over Nate's fingers and squeezed. It sent blood surging up his thigh and down his cock.

"Shit." Nate's response was breathy, like he'd just got the wind knocked out of him.

Tugging at the V of Nate's Polo, Caesar mimicked the sentiment. "Shit, yeah." He brushed Nate's lips with his own and earned a low moan. Everyone else had gotten what they wanted out of Caesar today. It was time to get a little back. He pressed the kiss hard, waiting for Nate to draw away. Instead he pushed back melting into Caesar's mouth. Caesar let go of Nate's hand and moved to cup Nate's crotch. God, he was all hot and hard and trapped under the denim. Caesar's dick throbbed in response.

Nate groaned and scrabbled, pushed and writhed until they fell back onto the couch. All the time Caesar fought with the buttons on Nate's jeans. A startled yelp from Poncho sounded as the dog abandoned the sofa. He barked and then ran into the kitchen. Neither man paid any attention.

Nate's fingers wound into Caesar's hair, pulling and tugging. Caesar sucked on Nate's tongue and they both moaned. Finally the last button came free and Caesar slid his hand inside. Solid and hot beneath the cotton of his briefs, Nate's cock pulsed against Caesar's palm. Caesar rode Nate's thigh, grinding his own aching prick against hard muscle.

He pushed Nate back and up and fumbled with the snap and zipper on his own pants. Damn, Nate was so good looking. Shirt hitched up, Caesar could almost count the ripples in his abs. And how he wriggled as he shoved his jeans and shorts down…it was desperate and seductive all at once. Caesar had to stop and breathe when Nate's prick jumped free. So thick and beautiful, he knew he'd never get enough of that cock. He was addicted to this green-eyed, blond cop. Like all addictions, it was so bad for him, but he couldn't stop.

The claw of the zipper tore into his senses. Caesar pushed down his own jeans. Nate reached down and ran his palm against Caesar's prick. The thief almost died with that powerful touch rubbing his skin.

"Oh God, Caesar, so fucking hot." Nate's voice smoldered. "Fuck getting everything together. I want you now." One set of strong fingers hooked into his waistband, sliding the briefs off his hips. He hissed as the elastic caught and tugged on his prick. Then he moaned when he sprang free. Nate's other hand slithered behind his head as he leaned in. Hell, it was like being a teenager again, rolling around half naked on the couch. But the moment Caesar's cock brushed against Nate's, it didn't matter. His lips sought out that wonderful mouth again. He buried his hands in the soft curls on Nate's chest, loving how that skin felt under his touch.

A slick sheen of sweat covered them. It added delicious friction to where their bodies slid together. Nate smelled so good, so male like this. When Nate's smell merged with the scent of Caesar's own need, it almost overwhelmed his senses. Their hips rolled together again and again, stirring the heat between them. And the sense of being bound at the knees by his jeans was incredibly erotic. He was free and trapped all at the same time, Caesar's balls burned with feeling.

Caesar licked at the salt coating Nate's jaw. "Yeah, oh fuck yeah." Nate babbled exposing his throat to Caesar's kisses. Nate's fingers tore at his back. The taste, the touch, the smell of Nate was nearly more then he could handle. It was perfect, so, so perfect. "You're so fucking hot. I need it." Nate's hips bucked, driving him into the cushions. Caesar was thrusting up against him. Powerful hands slid down to grab Caesar's ass and pull him hard against the man above him. "Give it to me." When Nate let go, he was absolutely shameless. It drove Caesar crazy with his own want.

Nate began to tremble. It shot shivers into Caesar's skin. Nate's voice was hot above him, "I'm gonna cum. Caesar, I can't take it…can't hold it."

Caesar sped up the pace. Nate's cock was burning alongside his own. It tensed, growing so hard, and then Nate was jerking against him. Gasps from Nate tickled down Caesar's spine. Liquid fire ran between them. They were so sticky-slick now. It wrapped his cock in shocks each time he moved. Caesar was burning and freezing at the same time. The shudders started just behind his balls and screamed down his cock. "Fuck! Nate!" Was all he managed before he added his cum to the slick between them.

Nate dropped, exhausted against his body. It was all Caesar could do to remember to breathe. He was so sensitive just after. Everything about Nate was magnified times ten. The soft cotton of his T-shirt bunched along Caesar's cheek. Nate's nipple tickled the corner of Caesar's mouth and his silky hair brushed along his jaw and neck. The sound of Nate's heart thundered in time with his own. Caesar drew lazy patterns on the inside of Nate's hip, making the man twitch.

Finally, Caesar sighed. "We gotta stop doing this, Nate."

"I know." Nate's voice sounded satisfied, not contrite. "When?"

Caesar chuckled. "Don't know, got any good twelve-step programs?" He should get up. He should move. Caesar ignored both impulses.

"Or we could go on one of those daytime talk shows." Nate's fingers were playing in his hair again. Caesar wondered if Nate realized that doing that would re-start the motor. "What would the title be? I'm gay, I'm a cop and I sleep with a felon. That'd be a ratings grabber."

"You're evil, Nate." Caesar's tongue snaked out and teased that tempting bit of flesh. Nate sucked in his breath. Somebody else was sensitive just after, too. "Evil and addictive."

Wriggling down Caesar's body until their eyes met, Nate snarled. "Ditto."

CHAPTER 13

Nate woke sandwiched between two bodies. One was only about two feet long, compact and nestled against his thigh. The other was much more intriguing, and naked under the sheets with Nate. Black hair drifted along the edge of a sharp cheekbone and spilled across Caesar's shoulders. There was a comforting weight in having Caesar's body pressed that close. And he smelled of musky spice. Warm and lean with one brown arm slung over Nate's chest, Caesar was all sorts of wonderful first thing in the morning.

Caesar snored softly; his head snuggled in the crook of Nate's right arm. Fingers of his left hand hooked over the top of a seventies-era headboard, Nate stretched as much as he could without disturbing Caesar. Ponchito snored, too. Of the two, the dog was louder. The off-key symphony grated on his not quite awake nerves. One way to kill the serenade, Nate cocked his leg and shoved the dog off the bed.

With a grunt Poncho hit the floor. Scrabbles sounded. Then a black nose appeared over the tangle of blankets at the end of the mattress. Poncho put his forefeet up on the edge and glared at Nate. Mismatched sheets bunched under his paws. Nate shot the look right back and added a low growl. They locked eyes. Cop and dog stared each other down. Poncho broke first. Snorting, he dropped to the floor and trotted off to do whatever it was dogs did first thing in the morning. That left the bed to the boys.

With the distraction gone, Nate could concentrate on what was important. He let go of the headboard and ran his hand between his legs. Shit, first thing in the morning and he was already horny. Nate was going to need therapy after this investigation. It was crazy. Worse than crazy, it was hazardous to his professional health. Not only was Caesar a crook, he was a confidential informant on an investigation Nate was assigned to. If that wasn't a train wreck waiting to happen, Nate didn't know what was.

Twirling his fingers through a longish strand of Caesar's hair, Nate tried to think things through. IA had told him about the assignment yesterday. They hadn't pulled him from his beat. But he was at their beck and call. They needed officers with discretion, men they could trust. Since he'd been the one to bring it to them, he was already as involved as they came. He was probably more involved than they'd ever want to know.

Caesar shifted, rubbing up against Nate. Oh hell, Caesar was hard in that early morning kinda way. Although Nate hadn't woken with a full-blown hard-on, he was getting there fast. He shifted and Caesar breathed in deep. Then Nate was staring into a set of sleep-filled, coffee-colored eyes. The most he could manage was a soft, "Hey."

"Hey, yourself." Caesar mumbled, blinking. "Where's Ponchito?"

"Wait." Nate tugged on the hair still wrapped around his hand. "I'm here in bed with you and the first thing you ask is where the fuck is your dog?" He shifted, drawing up his knee to tent the sheets, trying to conceal what else was trying to tent them.

Caesar's hand slid from Nate's chest to between his legs. Nate groaned clutching his sac as Caesar's touch danced along his prick. "Well yeah," Caesar muttered the words against Nate's jaw. "'Cause if he's around, he gets upset if I pet anyone else."

"Oh, wow." Nate lifted his hips into the touch. Early morning fire was building in his hips. "I'm going to get petted?"

Caesar sucked on Nate's neck just behind his ear. A firm grip circled his cock. Caesar whispered, "Or stroked." The statement was punctuated by Caesar's hand sliding along his shaft.

"I like stroked." Nate groaned. It was hard to get the words out.

Propping himself up on his elbow, Caesar looked down and laughed. "Inside or outside?"

Nate swallowed. God, he was such a slut for this guy. Hopefully there was a chapter of Hooked on Felons Anonymous out there somewhere. They were going to end up with a new member since he couldn't shake Caesar out of his thoughts on his own. He ran his hands up Caesar's arms, tracing the muscles underneath skin. First thing in the morning was no time to try and ditch an addiction. "How 'bout both?"

"I can so do both." Caesar growled, leaning in to kiss him. That sound shot shivers all through Nate. He closed his eyes and gave in to the kiss. Caesar's mouth was soft and warm, just drifting and touching and kissing; all of it was so nice. Waking wrapped up with Caesar was much better this time around. Man, if he hadn't gotten called into work that morning…well, he had it now. And damn, what he had. Sexy, considerate, but still demanding and hot in bed, too bad there wasn't a way to make it actually work. Fuck it all. Nate gave in and allowed himself the illusion of possibility.

Caesar's weight shifted. Nate could hear him fighting with the drawer of the ancient night stand. With a grunt and a crash, the drawer flew open. Caesar broke the kiss and lifted himself up on his hands. His face said that the world was trying to ruin the moment. "Hold on a second, Nate." Rolling his eyes, he shook his head and leaned off the bed. The position gave Nate a nice view of Caesar's ass, dark skin barely covered with a floral sheet. As Caesar rummage through the contents spilled on the floor, Nate pushed the sheet down, exposing more cheek. Damn, Caesar's ass was so tight, the man had butt divots. "What are you doing?" Caesar's voice drifted up from the direction of the floor.

"Whetting my appetite."

Caesar hauled his torso back onto the mattress, "Really?" Amusement sparked in his brown eyes as he edged over to Nate. "For what?"

"You," Nate pulled him close against his chest, "what else."

"Damn, Nate," Caesar's fist settled near Nate's hip. The chill touch of plastic slid along Nate's skin when Caesar opened his fingers. "You're so bad for me."

He could feel Caesar fumbling with things. Nate probably should have helped, but he was getting into early morning slut mode. Get fucked, have someone feed you breakfast in bed; Nate chuckled to himself. The most he offered was spreading his legs to give Caesar better access to what they both wanted. "We're bad for each other." Nate moaned as Caesar's finger worked inside his hole. He lifted his hips, trying to ride the touch. Slick and hot and so good, Nate couldn't wait for it to get better.

Cuddled up against Nate's side, lips against Nate's bicep, Caesar laughed. "I like bad." He punctuated it by slipping another gel-coated finger inside Nate's body. Nate moaned. Caesar's other hand was busy with his own preparations.

"I'm coming around," Nate could barely get out the words, "to the whole bad boy appeal."

Caesar pulled Nate's thigh over his hip. "I intend to have you 'coming'." Fingers were gone, sending anticipation shivering through Nate's frame. It got ten times worse when he felt Caesar's cock sliding in the crack of his ass. Nate's legs spread wide and open; Caesar pushed into his hole. It filled him so nice. Biting his lip, Nate pushed his head back against Caesar's shoulder. With Caesar's prick deep inside and his hands roaming all over Nate's body, Nate could barely think. His thoughts and his feelings always got all jumbled at times like this. Not that he needed to think much. And he knew he had a tendency to spew all sorts of sweet nonsense during sex. He didn't want any of it to be something he'd regret later.

Kisses landed on his neck and jaw and cheek. As his lips worked over Nate's skin, Caesar whispered, "Talk to me, I like it when you talk to me."

Nate stroked himself in time to Caesar's thrusts. He rolled his hips so that they'd have just the right angle. Caesar shifted and nailed him just right. "Fuck, it's so good!" Nate's whole body jerked as the feeling tore through him.

"Yeah?" The low throb in Caesar's voice told Nate the reaction was exactly what Caesar wanted.

He rocked back trying to find it again. "So hot and thick inside me." It was hard finding words that worked. Hell, it was hard just getting his brain to connect with his tongue. The friction on his dick didn't match the heat burning up his channel.

Caesar rammed into Nate's ass, both of them riding the heat of morning sex. Nate met him stroke for stroke. Reaching back, Nate yearned for a taste of Caesar's lips. Like he'd read Nate's mind, Caesar was there giving Nate everything he needed. The gentle tasting and touching was so intense when overlaid across hard thrusts. *"Media naranja."* Nate almost lost Caesar's words within their kiss. The most his mind could wrap around was orange and he had no idea why he'd be half of one. He wished Caesar would speak Spanish to him more often. Nate loved the way it sounded. But it seemed in bad taste to ask for it. Instead he just lived for the few times it happened.

"God, Caesar!" Nate shook. It never took him long in the morning. Maybe because he was already so relaxed when it started. His hand trembled so bad he almost couldn't keep his grip to finish. Then Caesar's touch was there, sending him up and over.

A few breaths later his brain started firing. Sated, Nate could concentrate on his lover. He rocked his hips and tightened his thighs. Caesar moaned and shuddered. Who said you couldn't top from the bottom? One arm wrapped tight over Nate's chest, the other around his hips as Caesar pressed his forehead between Nate's shoulder blades. Such control and abandon all at once, he loved how Caesar moved. He loved that he was making Caesar lose himself. Caesar jerked him tight with one word, "Nate!" and then he was overflowing with heat. These were the times that Nate wished they didn't live in a world where they had to worry about safe sex.

Panting, they lay wrapped together. It felt so good to wake up with someone, be with someone. And it was going to hurt like hell when it finally came to an end. There was just no way this was going to not end. Finally, Nate tried to distract himself with a positive thought. "Know what the best thing about morning sex is?"

Caesar snorted and pinched Nate's hip. "Sex?"

"No," Nate laughed, "nobody has to sleep on the wet spot." The joke earned him a growl and a lighthearted tussle that carried him through the rest of the morning.

CHAPTER 14

He hit the station locker room still smelling slightly of sex, covered in a film of sweat from the gym, and wearing one of Caesar's shirts. Working for a living had its down side. He would have much rather stayed at Caesar's and continued wrestling between the sheets. Although Caesar did make him breakfast, and even brought it to him in bed. Frosted flakes and coffee could be damn romantic with the right person.

He managed roll-call without any comments. After that, the Sergeant pulled him aside and told him to report to the Turney Street address. The warrant was in the process of being served. As a critical part of the investigation, the IA detectives wanted him on scene. Of course critical to the investigation meant standing at the front door acting like a uniformed bouncer. If they'd given him a velvet rope and a pair of sunglasses it would have been exactly like a club. Only the cool kids could get in. If you weren't on the list, you didn't have access.

It gave Nate a lot of time to think about Caesar. Nate so didn't want to be thinking about Caesar. Every time he did, everything became tight and hard. A cop with a hard-on guarding the door, just what the LAPD didn't want. Good sense and Nate weren't close friends right now. That was blatantly obvious. And he knew he should let his Sarge know how involved he was…but he just couldn't bring himself to. That would wreck his relationship and his career.

Finally, the sweltering day managed to distract him. Summer in Los Angeles made it hell to be wearing navy. This year was particularly brutal: record temperatures and humidity blanketed the valleys. At least he had short sleeves, but the thick cotton and polyester held the heat on his skin. What little shade Nate found on the porch didn't stop the sweat from sliding down his back.

Nate was trying to create a false breeze by puckering the back of his shirt when an unremarkable American-made four-door rolled up to the curb. Unremarkable and American-made pegged it as a detective's car. A man got out of the passenger side of the unmarked and got out and got out. Nate blinked. Damn that guy was big…like professional football player big. A mustache and a buzz cut marked him as LAPD old school. Nate stopped trying to cool down and crossed his arms over his chest while another man exited the driver's door. Almost as tall, he lacked the beefy substance of the older detective. Even at this distance Nate could tell his dark brown skin was pocked. Restless eyes darted over the house, Nate and the other police officer as they headed towards the house.

Nate stepped to the edge of the small porch. Tight, but polite, he asked, "Can I help you gentlemen?" God, he felt like he should be asking them if they wanted fries with their burgers.

"Hey son," the big man flashed a fatherly grin, "what's going on? This is Syd Price's house."

"Yes, sir." Nate smiled back, but didn't uncross his arms. Something about these two jarred him. "I'm sorry I can't tell you what's going on."

Apparently taking that to mean Nate didn't know, the detective laughed. "S'okay, we'll just go in and talk to the Dick in charge." He started to move around Nate.

Countering by stepping back and then sideways, Nate shook his head. His feet were splayed in a wide I-don't-take-no-shit stance. "Sorry, no, sir, can't let you in." This time he dropped the nice tone in his voice. The guy may have outweighed him, but Nate bet he had twice the muscle.

"Excuse me." It was the other detective that spoke. It was like he couldn't believe a uniformed officer would ever stand up to him.

Nate guessed that few would. "I have my orders, Detectives. No one goes in without prior okay from the lead Dick."

"Who's that?" The big man mimicked Nate's arms over chest and spread legs. He glared down his nose.

Nate cocked one eyebrow. No one intimidated him. If he'd been easy to intimidate, Nate would have quit the force two weeks after he started. "Renee Chavez."

"Homicide?"

The other cop leaned in and whispered in a low voice usually reserved for when people were talking about the dead or drug lords. "Internal Affairs. Was a junior during the Rampart investigation." He shook his head and palmed a face covered in stubble. "Ran across him during the aftermath of a freeway chase I was involved in. Real jackass."

"IA?" The big man's stance eased some. "So what's this all about?"

"Can't tell you that." Nate didn't relax. "You'd have to speak with Detective Chavez."

Another look down his nose and the man licked his lip. "We will," as much threat as could be packed into those words came across, "later. Maybe. Come on, Frank." It was the first time either had used a name. "Let blue boy baby-sit. We got work to do." Nate didn't let his breath out until the pair were back in their car and headed down the street.

The rest of Nate's day was spent watching the correct people go in and the correct people come out carrying sealed bags of evidence. The only other spot of excitement was watching the news vans show up and record the rote, "No comment," spouted by the detectives. During a short break, he phoned Carol and left a message that, if she was lucky, she might catch a glimpse of him on TV. One of their jokes…his sis complained that she hated to watch the news because she knew that one day she was going to see something horrid. And that something would involve Nate. So, he teased her with warnings. Ah, the glamorous life of a beat cop. His dad used to say that it was like the old line, always a bridesmaid and never a bride. You got invited to all the big parties only to find out they wanted you to serve drinks.

Nate wouldn't trade it for all the glamour in the world.

After hours of waiting, standing, watching and waiting some more, his shift was over. Eight hours of guard duty. There were worse things. As Nate checked back in at the station, he heard the buzz of a radio from someone's desk. "Police are being notoriously tightlipped about a search warrant served at the house of veteran LAPD Sergeant Syd Price." It was amazing how fast the news vultures caught wind of things, it hadn't taken more than an hour for the news vans to converge on the scene. Probably, someone tipped them off from inside. The detectives were playing this one as close to the vest as they could, but word always managed to get out.

Nate shook his head as he trundled into the general confusion of the locker room. His shift was going off while another was coming on. The chaos always reminded him of high school. A lot of back slapping, a lot of catching up with people you only saw during transition. Nate often used it to fill in whoever had his beat with the details of his shift, things that seemed off, parties that might get out of hand. Tonight he didn't have to seek out his relief. What he'd been involved in was over and done for the time being.

He swapped jokes with a couple of old timers and took a moment to give a rookie he knew a piece of advice. But he kept it pretty brief. All he really cared about now was a shower, dinner and the drive home. Nate yanked open his locker, shooting a jibe back into the showers. A single piece of paper drifted down. Looking around, everyone was wrapped up in their own on-duty/off-duty worlds.

Nate stooped and picked up the paper. Scribbles crawled across a page torn from a notebook. The words dropped ice into his gut.

> *Dear cock-sucking, shit-dick scum*
>
> *I hope you choke on the glass of your lover's enema water. I would watch my step, fag, there are a lot more bigger and badder people out there than us and you are doing a good job of pissing them off. I'd hope you get AIDS, but that ain't quick enough.*
>
> *Keep your shit-stained nose out of issues you don't understand. We know you're going to go crying to that whinny gay boy cop group. But remember we know who you are, you don't know who we are.*

The note was littered with misspellings and signed simply *us*.

Nate could barely do more than just stare at the paper in his hands. It hurt to breathe. He wanted to fight, he wanted to fight and rip into whoever thought this sick joke was worth putting on paper. He slumped down onto a bench and tried to think.

CHAPTER 15

Flipping channels between sitcom drivel and *Noticias*, the Spanish News, Caesar tried to make sense of where his life was headed. Actually he knew…his life was going to hell. No doubts about that. For a guy who spent his life trying to stay below radar, he'd sure popped up and painted a target on his back.

Maybe after all this shit died down he'd move back to Texas. Put this all behind him and start over. It would take a while to find a fence he could trust. Until then there was construction. There was no way he was going to get a legitimate job…even if he wanted to. His old bust was hard enough to deal with. The new stuff, there was no way he could spin that on an application. Al said he'd work a deal, but Caesar had no illusions about that. If he was lucky, the guy would get him out of doing time. There was just no way he was going to come out of this with a clean slate though. And nobody, nobody, wanted to hire a thief.

Caesar flopped back on the couch, heat sticking to his bare skin. It was so awful, he'd stripped to just his jeans. The heat hadn't been this bad in LA for ages. All his fan did was push hot air around to a tonal buzz. It irritated him more than it should. Some of that could be traced to a virtual house arrest and the accompanying boredom. Go home, don't get in any trouble, and stay where we can find you. It felt like he was a teenager being lectured by his aunt. Except that his aunt didn't have blond hair and six-pack abs.

What was he going to do about Nate? Waking up yesterday with Officer Nathan Reilly, the buffed out boy in blue, Caesar just wasn't used to those kinds of relationships. He'd made Nate breakfast for God's sake. It was no testament to his cooking skills, but he hadn't done that for anyone in ages. For the first time ever somebody he'd slept with knew exactly what he did. And it was a problem, for both of them.

Caesar couldn't believe he'd been with Nate four times. That was one time longer than his last two boyfriends. He wasn't really sure he could count Nate as a boyfriend…fuck buddy, maybe. Sex friend? We're both desperate and horny so let's screw acquaintances? None of those labels fit well. It was way too confusing to try and sort out, but he needed to. It was messy. It was complicated. Caesar hated both messy and complicated.

Damn it all, he was starting to really like Mr. Goody-Two-Shoes. And not just because of the sex. Something about that boyish smile just rocked him to the core. He was honest with Caesar. Nate hadn't promised him anything he couldn't guarantee. That was one of the things Caesar really cherished when he found it in someone. It was rare.

Poncho's growl from the back yard clued him in to visitors before the knock even sounded on the door. Probably Jehovah's Witnesses, they were always bugging people. Seconds later an annoyed bark and metallic scrabbling on the rear screen reminded Caesar he'd locked Ponchito out earlier. Even his dog managed to get on his nerves these days.

Caesar flipped off the TV, then tossed the remote on the couch. Yuck, the weave of the sofa was patterned into his skin. Hot, sticky, and tattooed with herringbone, it was a miserable afternoon all the way around. With a "shush" through the screen to Ponchito, he turned the two deadbolts and opened the front door. The wrought iron security door stayed locked between Caesar and his visitors. Just in case, Caesar kept an old broom handle right next to the door. This was gang territory after all.

"Caesar Serrano?" A big man stood on the concrete step. All Caesar could process at first was just how damn big the guy was. It wasn't just that he was heavy, but he must have stood close to six-nine and filled almost the entire view through the screen outside with his bulk. As if to counter that, his face was friendly, sporting a handlebar mustache above a soft mouth. He reeked of cop.

"Yeah." Even with the barrier between them, Caesar was grateful for the two and a half feet between the frame and where he stood holding the front door.

The man's eyes flitted back and forth scanning the room behind Caesar. "I need to talk to you about the incident you reported."

Incident he'd reported. He loved how cops phrased things, like it was some guy pissing on the sidewalk. And of course they needed to talk to him. Cops always needed to talk things to death. When Nate and his supervisors and the prosecutor and Al had all gotten together, it took them forever of talking just to get to the point of the whole meeting. Caesar was almost ready to be locked up just to get some quiet. So, now that he was cooperating, they were going to talk him to death. "Okay, what about?" He crossed his arms and leaned against the edge of the door. Viewed through the mesh on the security screen, the man seemed to have a weird skin condition.

"Can I come inside?"

"Can I see your badge?" When the big man flashed it, Caesar asked, "Why do you need to come inside?"

"It's just routine follow up. And it's miserable standing out here."

Caesar shrugged. "It's miserable in here."

"Look, do you really want your neighbors knowing your working with the cops?" If anything the man's smile got bigger. Shit, that was the same line Nate had used. They must teach it in cop school. "And," the cop continued, "Your buddy Nathan Reilly sent me some stuff for you to look over." *Chingaso*, why, at every turn did he have to be reminded that Nate was one of *them*? Why couldn't he come out and do his own dirty work? Typical cop, passing the buck to someone else to handle. Caesar kicked himself for letting Nate into his life the other night. Stupid, stupid, stupid!

When Caesar didn't respond the cop reached under his jacket and showed the edge of a manila envelope. "Look, some of the stuff I'm supposed to show you came out of the house." Caesar's stomach dropped. It had to be more photos in that pack. He really didn't want to see any more photos out of that house. "I'm not sure I would want one of your neighbors accidentally seeing this." Caesar didn't want to be seeing what he was pretty certain the cop would show him. "Or," the smile narrowed to a thin line, "I could take you back to the station if you want."

Turning the deadbolt on the security door, *"Chíngame!"* Caesar hissed in defeat. He pushed the door open and turned to walk back to the couch.

The security door banged against the house…louder than it should have. Caesar spun to see two men shoving in from behind the big man. Where the fuck had they come from? The first was short; his rounded, bald head was stark counterpoint to an otherwise sharp face. Almost on his heels was a tall black man. A five o-clock shadow crawled across his pock-marked chin.

"You freaking lying, piece of shit!" The first blow came from nowhere and spun him, knocked him back into the room. "You planted that crap!" Caesar stumbled backward, landing a punch of his own. The big man stepped inside, grabbed him up under the armpits and held him while the black guy punched him in the gut. Caesar brought his knees up and lashed out with his foot. A grunt from the black guy said he'd connected solid.

He used the momentum to throw himself sideways. He tore free of big man's grip and stumbled towards the kitchen. Caesar threw windmill punches as he spun away from his attackers. A hand landed on his neck. Twisting, Caesar pitched them both into the wall. Baldy wrestled him into a head lock, pounding his skull. Using the weight of his body, Caesar pushed them up against the wall. He cocked his fist back and slammed it into that ugly, shaved head. Thick, wet slaps rang out as their fists found flesh. Then someone grabbed his leg and flipped him to the ground

Struggling, Caesar tried to get up from his hands and knees. Down was not a place to be in a fight. The big man hit him on the elbow with the broom handle and Caesar fell on his face. Pain ran through his arm like claws shredding his skin. One guy jumped on Caesar's butt, while another yanked him up by the hair. A denim-covered knee caught him under the chin. He felt more than heard the crack as bone connected with bone.

Ponchito, bless him, was scrabbling at the kitchen screen and barking up a storm in that big dog voice of his. Three more random blows caught him across the back and side. Caesar was on his stomach. With a heave he threw the black man off and tried to scramble for the door. *Get out! Get out now!* His brain screamed.

The big man kicked his arm out from under him. "How dare you, scum, it's political we know it!" One grabbed him by the leg the other caught him by his neck carrying him farther into the kitchen. Big man swung the handle like a bat, catching him up under the ribs, lifting him off the floor. Caesar gasped. He couldn't breathe.

Caesar stumbled, dropped back to his knees. "Come on Bert, take him down! Finish it!" Another blow landed on his hip. There was too much pain. It all melded into one throbbing mass in his stomach.

Trying to cover his face, he felt the wood land hard on his arm and heard the crack as the stick broke. Splinters drove through his skin. "Whoever paid you to do it better come scrape you off the floor, spick!"

A kick landed in his kidneys, pitching him forward again. Cesar took a breath and dove for the screen. Again someone hit him across the shoulders. He was falling. He slammed through the screen, sliding across the dirt on his face. Ponchito was all over, snapping, barking and growling at the attackers who'd followed him out of the house. It sounded like there were children screaming. His eyes could barely focus through the pain. Swings spun abandoned on the swing set in the yard behind his.

Kicks to his knee and chest and ass and thighs hardly registered. Cries of, "*¡Ayuda!*" were dim behind the taunting of his assailants. As Caesar tried to rise, a knee caught him in the gut lifting him up. "Hey! Hey!" The words sounded far away. It was hard to hear them over the ringing in his ears.

"*Ese!* Leave him alone asshole!" People were running toward him. One more kick and his attackers were running away from him. Caesar rolled onto his back and groaned. The world spun above him and he closed his eyes to stop it. Poncho was whining, licking his ear.

Strong hands moved along his arms. A soft voice, a woman's voice sounded somewhere above him. If he concentrated, Caesar could probably figure out what she was saying. But he couldn't concentrate. Someone else spoke right down near his face. "Don't move man." Caesar had no intention of moving any more then he absolutely had to. "We called the police."

Caesar started to laugh. Oh God, it hurt to laugh. "Fuck," he coughed, "they were the police."

CHAPTER 16

The major excitement was over for now. The whole case was heading down that slow slope to justice. Nate was a little disappointed. It had been a break from the routine of DUIs, shoplifting and domestic disturbances. Now he was back on the beat. Tuesday's note still scrambled his thoughts. His gut ached every time he remembered the words. Like a good cop, he'd turned it into his superiors. Normally, he would run to the union rep, but there was a good chance it was connected to the Price case. Someone had to know. If it hadn't been wrapped up with everything else, Nate wasn't sure what he would have done. The case made the decision easy. It didn't make the hurt, fear and betrayal go away.

As he drove through the twisted streets of Highland Park, the call came across about a fight. Every sense revved. Calls did that to officers. Who knew what Nate would find when he got there. It could just be an argument that got too loud for the neighbors to stand. Or it could be an all out gang jump in. He was amped and ready when he screeched to a halt at the address.

Stress was an inherent part of his job. They called it hyper-vigilance. Sort of a low level state of readiness pervaded every waking moment. Even when he wasn't on duty it didn't turn off. Patrolling, monitoring calls and constantly scanning people and cars for potential trouble left him brain dead by the end of most shifts. Then, all the way home Nate would be waiting for a call while he scrutinized every car he passed.

Two young women, one bouncing a baby on her hip, were in the yard. Both wore tank tops, tight shorts and cheap plastic flip-flops. Both looked at him like he was a little nuts to be laying rubber in their street. The neighborhood seemed familiar to Nate, but he couldn't place whyj. It was more than just familiarity with his beat. Something bugged him about the area. As he got out of the car, he smiled. *"¿Señoritas,"* neither of them looked old enough to be the baby's mother, *"Ustedes llamó la policia?"*

The one with the baby and sporting blond streaks in her hair answered. *"Si. Un batella."*

There was a fight. That much he'd gotten off the radio. There didn't seem to be much going on. Well, whatever had called him out was pretty much at the mop up stage now. He took a wild guess as the girls weren't volunteering much in the way of information. *"¿Doméstica?"* Both shook their heads in the negative. Well, not a husband and wife brawl. God he hated those. Talk about a call that had the potential to go wonky at any moment.

This time the other girl answered. *"Tres hombres, rayar a alguien un muchacho."* Three guys beat the shit out of another guy. Good, another old fashion dog-pile. *"Dos gringos y un negrito."* Now that was odd. Two white guys and a black man beating someone up in Highland Park. Usually those were the victims.

"¿A donde? ¿Aqui?" He emphasized the question by pointing at their feet.

"No." The older one shook her head motioning behind the house. *"A la otra yarda."*

The other yard... maybe she meant the house behind hers. *"¿Detrás?"*

"Si, la casa detrás." Passing the baby to the other girl, she motioned for him to follow. *"Venga, venga."*

Nate keyed the mike on his shoulder and relayed the information as he walked. They passed through a rickety gate and into the back yard. Pointing towards the back fence, *"Aya."* Cheap chain link separated their property from that behind. As they wound their way through a minefield of broken toys and potholes the she yelled, *"Papa! La Policia!"*

With a metallic scrunch, Nate hopped the chain fence. Like the aftermath of most fights, the scene was chaotic. Several people were hovering around one guy lying prone in the beaten dirt yard. A woman in scrubs knelt next to the man. When the girl had shouted, a heavy man in a wife-beater tee and swim trunks looked up. He bent to say something to the woman. She nodded and he trundled over to Nate.

"*Hola Señor.*" Nate shaded his eyes against the late evening sun. "*¿Un batella?*"

"Yeah." Jerking his head back towards the group, "Gloria, from up the street, she a nurse at county." The man's accent was almost thick enough to make his otherwise passable English incomprehensible. "She say he beat pretty bad."

Nate radioed for an update on the ambulance. Cops were usually the first on the scene for a fight. They had to ensure everything was calmed down before the EMTs got there. Sometimes that meant triage on Nate's part. He was never terribly comfortable with that. At least this time there was medical help on the scene so he could do *his* job. As he fell in step with the man, he flipped open his pad. "Did you see the fight?"

"No, some. I see he come running out his door." A thick fingered hand shot out to indicate a door at the side of the house. Just beyond that was a detached garage. How familiar it all was nibbled at the back of Nate's brain. "And three guys they come out after him."

They reached the small group clustered about the prone man. "Okay, don't go too far. I'm going to need you to tell me what they looked like." People parted as Nate shoved his way forward. A little black dog lay next to the prone figure. It whimpered, turning sad eyes up to him. He knew that dog. Oh shit, he knew this house. "Caesar?"

Blood had barely dried over Caesar's mouth and chin. The nurse pressed a filthy rag against his nose to staunch the bleeding. A laugh turned into a fit of coughing. "Fuck, Nate."

As the world clamped down around his lungs, Nate dropped to his knees. "Okay, okay." He took two deep breaths trying to calm himself. He was here. He was in charge. Everything was going to be fine. God, that was the spiel he always gave the family of victims. "Look, the ambulance is on its way. Stay calm. This nice young lady is going to take good care of you, but I need to talk to her for a minute okay? Don't go anywhere."

Caesar shot him a glare that would peel paint. Nate ignored him. Managing to stand even though his knees felt like jelly, he motioned for the nurse to step to the side. When they were out of immediate earshot, "What do you think?"

"I don't do trauma...." She hugged herself, "I'm in the maternity ward. But I don't think anything's broken. Doesn't look like any internal bleeding, at least not as far as I can tell. He seems lucid enough. You'll want to get him to a hospital for x-rays and the like."

"EMT is on its way." Nate tried to think. It was so hard when people you knew, maybe even cared about, were involved. "Think there's any problem with me talking to him about this?"

Both eyebrows shot up. "What, I'm a doctor now?"

"Yeah," Nate flashed a nervous smile back at her, "and I'm a detective. You and me, we're the closest he's got."

"Should be okay." Gloria's voice made it apparent that she wasn't terribly comfortable being the medical guru. After thinking on it more, she chewed on her bottom lip and nodded. "He took some blows to the head, so we want to keep him awake anyway. If you talk to him that'll help. You know him, right? You knew his name."

That was a tricky question. He had no idea how much of Caesar's activities his neighbors knew about, and he definitely wasn't comfortable letting on that the thief was involved with the police. Nate's expression went tight as he scraped the bare ground with his heel. "Kinda, long time ago. See each other around some times."

The answer seemed to be enough. "Know his family? Someone should call them."

"No." Nate could be truthful there. "I don't know him that well."

"Okay. We can ask him who we should call." The nurse headed back, Nate only a moment behind her. With every step she seemed to gain that indefinable nurse confidence. Probably a pretty close kin to police officer confidence; always act like you are in complete charge even if you're ready to piss your pants.

Someone had propped Caesar's head with an old blanket. Most of the others were standing back a ways, almost to a person with the same body language and expression. Resigned and mildly bored would be Nate's guess. Both he and the nurse knelt, and Gloria pulled the rag away from Caesar's nose. Blood still oozed, but not as thick or as fast as it likely had earlier. "Caesar, that's your name?" Caesar grunted in response. "I'm here with you until the paramedics arrive, okay? *Tu amigo*, the officer, needs to talk to you okay? Think you can handle that?" Caesar scrunched his eyes and nodded.

"Hey, how you doing?" Nate used the most soothing tone in his repertoire and tried to ignore how his hands shook.

Caesar opened one eye and glared. "Take a wild fucking guess." The last word ended as a hiss.

Patting his shoulder made Caesar wince. Someone had worked him over good. "Well, if you feel half as bad as you look…I'd say you feel like you've been hit by a Mack Truck."

"Close." That got him half a laugh.

"Tell me what happened, Caesar."

"Why?" He groaned. "You're the one who got me into this shit."

The wail of the arriving ambulance brought Nate back to his job. He picked out a random woman and gave an order. *"Señora, el frente y trae aquí."* Trusting that she'd do what he said and direct the EMTs to the back yard, Nate turned his attention back to Caesar. "What do you mean?"

"They were cops, Nate." Caesar's tone was filled with venom, distrust, everything that said *I knew I shouldn't have gotten involved.* "Pretty silver and gold badges and everything." Poncho butted Caesar's hand, trying to worm under an arm. Nate grabbed the dog. Scratching Poncho's ears and holding the wiggling mutt, he let Caesar continue at his own pace. "They were screaming that I was part of a set up." Caesar drew in a ragged breath and ended up coughing again. Gloria leaned in to help him sit up some. "Nate... they were gonna kill me. It would have gone that far if I didn't get outside. I don't want to do this anymore, Nate. Let me out of it." With the look Gloria gave Nate, she was thinking this was a lot of the police's fault. She didn't seem pleased that he'd been so cagey. "Lock me up. I'll be safer there."

Throwing in as much sarcasm as he dared, Nate spat. "You think?" Nate leaned in. Gloria would hear, but the rest needed to be kept out of it. "Bullshit," he hissed, "You know better.

You can't back out now." The dog squirmed trying to get close to Caesar's face. Behind them the metallic scrunch of chain link announced the arrival of the paramedics. "It's gone too far. You've got to trust me. I'll take care of you...I promise."

"Nate?"

"Trust me. You don't have to think about anybody else. I won't let you get hurt again." He had to move to let the EMTs do their work. Poncho barked and struggled trying to get to his master. Shushing him, Nate tried to think. The Sarge needed to know. If he called for anyone else, it would trip alarm bells for the perpetrators. He miked in to the station asking for a message relay to his Sergeant and asking for a call back by phone. It was done in 10-code and he debated whether to add an emergency designation. Nate decided against it.

The guys who knocked Caesar around would understand the transmission, but it wouldn't be out of the ordinary and hopefully not suspicious. He'd fill in the Sergeant and let him rally the troops and get the detectives up to date about their witness. Wow, he was already thinking about Caesar as *their* witness. While it may have been true, Caesar was *his* responsibility. There was no way he'd shirk that. He'd stick with Caesar at the hospital until his safety net was in place, Nate was pretty sure the Sarge would go for that.

Moments later the code came back for Nate to call in. That was fairly S.O.P. If you wanted to use a land line, you could do it on your own dime. He shifted Poncho to his other arm and dug for his cell. The mutt yelped and snapped at him. Holy shit, what was he going to do with the dog?

CHAPTER 17

Nate managed to find a small space to work on his reports from the night before. About halfway through, he felt a looming presence behind him. Turning, he found himself confronted by a wide expanse of chest clothed in navy blue. Nate's eyes crawled up to the grim, sun-worn face and hard hazel eyes. "Reilly, I need to talk to you." The man rumbled. "Come in here for a bit." The Sergeant moved toward one of the interview rooms. H.M. Robinson, as uptight and by the book as you could get. Nate swallowed. He never really trusted people who had initials instead of names. You always had to wonder why. Still, his Sergeant had never treated him bad.

The tiny box Nate stepped into held a couple of plastic chairs and a small table. Acoustic tile flaked off the walls and the place smelled vaguely of piss. A one-way mirror looked out into the hall beyond. "Have a seat Reilly." Robinson spun one of the chairs so it faced away from the mirror, pointing at it and indicating that was where he wanted Nate to park. Nate wasn't sure what was up. It was an odd place to hold a mini-meeting. Usually, if it was serious, the Sarge would do it in an office. If it wasn't, he'd catch you in the locker room for a quick chat. "Look we've had a complaint."

"A complaint?" Awkward and uncomfortable, he settled into his seat.

Robinson took a deep breath. "Yeah, that you made some inappropriate remarks to a rookie."

"Like what?" Nate was off balance, thrown. Inappropriate? In what way? Mentally he rifled through the past few weeks. There wasn't anything he could recall that would be complaint worthy. "What did I say? Get off your sorry ass and act like a cop? Done that a couple of times."

"No, Reilly, serious stuff." Robinson leaned against the table and crossed his arms. "This kid says you offered to show him how to search for a concealed weapon. You'd give him some *personal* tutoring in pat downs and all the places guys are reluctant to search another guy." Taking another deep breath the Sergeant continued. "And that you were touching yourself when you said it."

It took a moment for things to sink in. When they did, they hit hard. "That's bullshit!" Nate's eyes nearly bugged out of his skull as he shot out of his seat. "You know its bullshit, Sergeant!"

"Sit down and shut up Reilly." The Sergeant's face was stone. Nate dropped back into his chair. "You know how I feel about you. You're a great cop. If I was out on the street, there's no one, and I mean no one, I'd rather have out there with me. But for every one guy like me, there're two out there who've got a problem that you're gay. And you've gotten in on the ground floor of an investigation that's rocking a lot of boats. So, yeah, it's complete and utter bullshit, and we've got to treat it like it ain't. So I'm going to, officially, ask you to take a few days off."

"No, that's just…."

"Hold on." Although his face remained impassive, the Sergeant's eyes flicked up to the mirror. Nate bet there were twenty guys standing around watching him get chewed. Thank God they couldn't hear what was going on. "That's the *official* story, at least for now. I've talked with the detectives, the Captain and IA and we all agree that our star witness needs to go lie low for a while. And he needs protection because next time they might just end up shutting him up for good. So you're taking him and skedaddling until we can get Mr. Serrano, in one piece, to the Grand Jury. So that's your orders. I've written them down for you. You can pick them up in my office on your way out."

A ruse? The import trickled into Nate's brain. "Nobody writes that kind of stuff down." He tried to keep his volume and tone at the same level as before. While nobody would be able to catch the words, you could tell when people were arguing in one of these little pens.

"I know." The Sergeant's voice managed to convey that he was glad Nate had caught on. "But I want you to know I'm not going to screw you, Reilly. When you get back, you already have the piece of paper that explains it. You can have it put in your file. That way, if any of us let you down, you're covered. No one can back out of the deal. You okay with that?"

Nate let his shoulders slump in mock resignation. It wasn't that hard to pull off with the bombshell his Sergeant had just dropped. "Yeah, I guess." What was he going to do with Caesar? Things had already gone so far with him. Nate swallowed and ran his bottom lip under his teeth as he tried to think.

He must have come off as reluctant or nervous or both, considering Robinson's reaction. Eyes narrowed, Robinson stared down at Nate. "There's something you need to tell me?" Nate's eyes jerked up to fix on those of his Sergeant. Oh shit, did Robinson know? Had he guessed? He must have put too much resignation into his body language. That really would tank his career. Nate didn't say anything. "Look, the guy's a con and I'm asking you to baby-sit him, take him off all alone somewhere for a few days." He and Caesar all alone somewhere, Nate shifted hoping he didn't come off as hot and bothered as that statement made him feel. "If you've got a problem with it, IA can find someone. It's their bag after all. I just thought it might solve two issues."

Nate took a deep breath. "I'm good with it, Sarge. You can count on me."

"Don't worry Reilly, you're a good cop, I won't let you down, either. We all know where this flack is coming from. They're targeting who they think is in the weakest position. It's wrong. But obviously these guys don't care much about what's right. So, I'm going to give you my cell number I've got the lead Dick's as well for you. We're the *only* two who you tell where you're at. Got it?"

"Yeah, I got it." Nate nodded.

"Okay, get out of your blues. You don't have to say anything to anyone. Act like you would if you'd been hit by this, okay?" The Sergeant stepped up to Nate and put his hand on his shoulder. To everyone watching, it would look like he was trying to reassure one of his boys. "Go pick him up from County-USC. I've had the docs delay release so you could go. I wouldn't do more than grab some clothes and bolt."

Trying to keep his expression somewhere between appropriately chastised and more than a little pissed off, Nate followed the Sergeant out of the interview room. When the door opened, a sudden rush of activity, all within viewing distance of the one-way, confirmed everyone in the squad room had been watching. After that Nate didn't have to work at the pissed off part. Someone had set him up to bring him down in front of the people he worked with, the people he trusted.

Nate glared out into the room. More than half the officers wouldn't meet his eyes. Rumors must already be spreading. Even with admin on his side, those rumors would be enough to damage his standing in a lot of guys' eyes. Fuck them all. He stalked to the locker room. Only three other officers made a point to swing by and tell him how wrong it was. Another woman caught him on the long walk from the Sergeant's desk out to his car. There were likely a few who sympathized, but didn't want to be seen coming forward. That pissed him off even more.

Thoroughly irritated, Nate trudged to his car. He shot another glare at two plainclothes officers, one of whom was leaning against his Taurus. Not like they deserved it, but Nate was in the mood to throw some misery around. Both returned the nasty look before moving off. What the hell were they doing hanging around the parking lot anyway? Most importantly, what were they doing hanging around his car?

Nate did a walk-round inspection. No scratches to the paint and the tires all had air. Popping the flap, he checked the gas cap. Still firmly in place and locked down. Given where he lived, the key lock security cap insured no sugar in the tank or any of that nastiness. He popped the hood to find everything in place... as much as he could determine in place in the solid mass of aluminum comprising the engine. Still, there were no obvious puddles of brake or other fluids on the ground. None of the doors or the trunk was jimmied. Finally he checked his plates. Yep, both the month and year registration stickers were in place. It didn't feel like coincidence, two cops loitering by his car, but it obviously had to be.

The more he thought about the whole situation, the angrier he got. He twisted the key in the ignition, backed out of his space and tore into the streets of Los Angeles. Fuck them all. Trying to trash his career to save that of a fucking pervert... it was so wrong. If he ever found that son-of-a-bitch, the number his buds did on Caesar would seem like a walk in the park. Nate hit the 2 already doing seventy and dodged through midday traffic transitioning onto the 5.

Thoughts of Caesar backed him down a bit. What was he going to do with that guy? Caesar's house was no good. The bad guys knew exactly where that was. His apartment wasn't much better. There'd be people who, while they wouldn't do it in public, might drop by to commiserate on his administrative fuck-over. Explaining who the hell Caesar was and coming up with an excuse as to why he was kicking it with a felon... not doable. Or at least it wasn't convincingly doable.

Nate didn't come up with a suitable plan in the short drive to County-USC. The wedding cake-shaped monstrosity jutted out of the Boyle Heights barrio, its random levels and additions surprisingly elegant instead of jarring. Still, hospitals gave Nate the willies. There was really no sane reason for it. The antiseptic smell was a little too creepy. It always reminded him of his few visits to the morgue.

All his investigative skills were needed to find Caesar's room in the various towers and halls. Between County administration, the hush-hush layer the department had thrown down over the thief's whereabouts, and the general sprawl of the building it was like negotiating a labyrinth. The damn place was larger than the Pentagon and not as well laid out.

Finally, with a bit of luck and a lot of perseverance, Nate stumbled across the room he wanted. Caesar sat stiffly on a metal hospital bed. A gash above Caesar's eyebrow was held together by a smear of superglue and a butterfly bandage. Under the sleeve of his T-shirt, a livid bruise crawled from his shoulder to his elbow. Another bloomed along his jaw. Nate figured there'd be matching ones on his ribs and thigh. A large abrasion covered his right cheek and blood from his nose had dried just along the inside of his nostrils. He looked like shit. Hell, he probably felt like shit.

Spanish language programming buzzed on an ancient set bolted to the wall. The two other occupants of the room were either unconscious or dozing. It was hard to tell which. The department had been lucky enough to wrangle this bed out of County. A private room would have been an impossibility.

Nate leaned against the door. "How you doing?"

"I've had the shit kicked out of me." Dark eyes slid toward Nate. Red, swollen skin around the right eye spoke to a solidly connected punch. Bluish circles under both indicated a sleepless night. "You go ahead and guess how I'm doing."

Reminding himself that it could have been worse, Nate walked over to Caesar and bumped his shoulder with one fist. "They treat you okay? Room alright?"

"You mean other than I spent nine hours in the ER waiting to be seen before I even got here." Caesar swung his legs off the edge and groaned. "That was like four this morning, it's *mediodía* now. For ten hours I've tried to sleep, but they keep busting in and waking me up. So I gave up and tried to watch TV, but the signal's crap. I'd say I've been better."

"Well, paperwork's supposedly done." Nate held out his hand to help Caesar off the bed. "You are now under police protection…that means me." Hissing as he slid off the edge, Caesar ignored Nate's offer. "Okay, let's run by your place and you can pick up some stuff. Then you're coming with me."

"Where?"

"Don't know yet. But that's not something you need to worry about."

"Where's Ponchito?"

"He's fine, sucking up to Carol in Burbank. I'm going to go find a nurse and we'll get you out of here."

Sergeant Robinson shouldn't have worried about delaying things. It took Nate almost twenty minutes to track down a nurse and another hour and a half before a doctor arrived to sign Caesar out. While Nate secured his release, Caesar napped. He continued to doze fitfully during the drive to his home. Nate let him sleep in the passenger seat of the Taurus as he slipped into Caesar's house and collected what he might need. It felt odd to Nate to be in another person's house, rushing and ransacking through their stuff. He wondered if Caesar felt like this when he was robbing homes.

A gym bag, shorts, T-shirts, underwear and toiletries, Nate tried to get enough for a good week's worth. He also snagged a button down shirt and slacks out of the closet. Caesar would need clothes to testify in. Then Nate locked the house up and headed back to the car. Chucking Caesar's stuff next to his warbag before climbing into the car, he realized Caesar had barely moved. The guy had to be just dead on his feet. Nate didn't even play the radio on the drive up to Chatsworth. Caesar needed the rest.

When they finally reached Nate's place, it took a few shakes to rouse the man. "Come on." Nate smiled and tried to look reassuring. "You can go back to bed inside. More comfortable there." Every move Caesar made as he followed Nate into the apartment was stiff. Nate figured he was sore as all get out on top of being exhausted. He headed for the bedroom straight off. Nate would get Caesar settled before dealing with everything else.

There was too much to plan. Nate had no clue what to do next, he'd never had an assignment that came close to this. Usually someone higher up the chain made decisions on where to stash witnesses and the like. For the moment, his apartment was the best he could think of. Right now, his thoughts spun off in a thousand different directions...mostly in the, "What next?" line. A stop at home where he could be quiet and concentrate should be okay. There would be lag time before word got out of Caesar's release. By then they'd be somewhere else.

Caesar limped through the house and into the bedroom behind Nate. "What the hell is that a picture of?"

Nate turned. "John Constantine." Framed in the doorway, Caesar stared at the poster like he thought it might come off the wall and bite him. Nate took a second look at the picture above his bed. Really, it was one of the tamer ones. No creatures spitting blood or possessing mortals. Returning his gaze to his guest, he shrugged. "*Hellblazer.*"

Those dark eyes slid to his own. "Who?" Putting an exaggerated amount of distance between them, Caesar moved around Nate and toward the bed. A hiss slid between his lips as he settled on the edge.

Poor guy, Nate had taken some beatings when he played football in high school. Caesar looked like he'd been playing football without the padding. Probably hurt in all sorts of places, places you never thought you could hurt. "It's from the series *Hellblazer*." Nate waved towards the poster as he sat down next to Caesar. "John Constantine is the main character. He's this really fucked up guy who fights demons…started out in *Swamp Thing*."

Slowly, Caesar dropped back on top of the covers. Another hiss and Caesar closed his eyes. Pain ate across his face. Voice tight, he asked, "Wasn't *Swamp Thing* a comic book?"

"Want me to get you some more painkillers now?" When Caesar shook his head no, Nate went back to the other topic. "So's *Hellblazer*."

One eye cracked open. "You read comics?"

"Well, they're not like for kids or anything."

"You read comics?" Caesar snorted. "Wait, wait, you don't just read comics, you have a fucking comic poster on your wall." His voice teased. "Did I miss something? Are you fifteen and hide it well?"

"Fuck off." Nate threw a punch towards Caesar's shoulder, pulling back at the last minute so that it just bumped him. "You watch those crappy Mexican soaps, don't you start in on my tastes in entertainment."

"Hey!" Caesar grabbed his wrist and jerked.

"What's that one you were watching at the hospital?" Nate pretended to fall, catching himself inches above Caesar's prone form. His hands were on either side of Caesar's chest, holding him up. Pelvis snug against Caesar's hip, he stared down. Both of those deep, dark eyes were open now. Teasing Caesar back with his tone, he added, "The one about the four sisters who share everything, including their boyfriends, because nobody can tell them apart. Hell, the actresses don't even look like each other."

"*Las Vidas de Hermanas Gemelas.*" Caesar smiled, pain seemingly forgotten. His eyes narrowed. "Wait how do you know that plot?"

He was busted. "There's this old lady that lives on the corner of Fig." Nate laughed. "We used to get calls all the time that someone was breaking in or some shit. What it really was is she doesn't have anyone anymore. So if I've got some time, I drop by there, visit with her. That way she doesn't have to call. She watches all those weird ass shows. She tells me all about them like they're real people."

Caesar sighed. The sound was somewhere between drugged and contented. Or maybe it was contented because he was drugged. "You know, you shouldn't be this close to me."

"Why?" Even as fucked up as he was, Caesar was still damn good looking. It had to be those big, dark eyes.

"God, cause I need to sleep." Caesar's finger traced Nate's ribs through his shirt. "But you're making me think about all kinds of things that have nothing to do with sleeping."

Nate leaned in. "Like this?" He whispered the question against Caesar's lips.

"Oh yeah," Caesar's fingers drifted lower, teasing Nate's belly, "like that."

"I think you'd," kissing again and again, Nate managed to get all of it out, "fall asleep on me if we tried anything."

"Yeah, probably." Caesar's tongue traced patterns of heat behind Nate's ear. "Could use some other types of relaxation right now. Doctor says it's good for me."

Nate slid down next to Caesar on the bed. "You're so full of shit." He smiled as he said it. "You couldn't get it up if your life depended on it." That earned him a snort and then a deeper, harder kiss.

Nate loved the taste of Caesar's mouth. He worked his tongue between willing lips again. It was so good exploring like this. Their mouths moving against each other, Nate couldn't believe how wonderful it was just making out with no thought of going farther. He'd always thought of dating as an insert tab A into slot B proposition. Everything else was just foreplay delaying the main action. But with Caesar, it wasn't like that. This type of sharing was incredible in and of itself.

Drowning in the gentle touches, Nate forgot to care about what this could do to his career. The looming possibilities of Board of Rights hearings and IA inquiries vanished when Caesar brushed his cheek or his pec or his wrist. Each kiss blew a little bit more of *the cop* from his soul, leaving him just Nate.

Nate Reilly, who was pretty much loosing his mind for a guy he shouldn't.

They lay there for a while, wrapped up against each other, not doing more than kissing. Finally, Nate nuzzled into Caesar's neck and then pulled back. He stared down at a banged up, but still damn sexy face. "Bet you're tired now." All he got in response was a drowsy chuckle. "S'kay," he ran his knuckles over Caesar's sternum, "go to sleep. I'm going to head into the other room for a bit. I've got things to do." When he looked at Caesar, all bruised and battered, the mixed up feelings swirling about his brain made a little more sense. This wasn't his job, this was personal. You always lost focus when it was personal. "You take it easy. Catch some sleep if you can."

"No problem, *papi*." Caesar's voice sounded like he was ninety percent gone already.

Nate rolled over and clambered off the bed. Caesar was already out. Nate had to stop himself from laughing. Mouth half-open and feet hanging off the edge, Caesar looked like a passed out drunk. Passed out, definitely. Nate shook his head before grabbing Caesar's ankles and hauling him properly onto the mattress. Caesar didn't even stir. He couldn't be hurt by it, though. Caesar had been through too much in the past twenty-four hours to hold exhaustion against him. As gently as possible, Nate adjusted Caesar's position. Then he fished an extra blanket out of the closet and threw it over the sleeping man.

While Caesar slept, Nate walked out into the living room. After shutting the bedroom door, he slumped on the couch. What the fuck was he going to do about this? There was no way one cop could hold back the tide of the LAPD in vengeance mode. Sooner or later, someone would put two and two together and figure Nate's leave of absence was far too convenient to Caesar dropping off the radar.

And Goddamn it, when he'd seen Caesar all busted up at County, all he wanted to do was bust a few heads himself. It wasn't the obnoxious moral streak that led to his wanting to join the force in the first place, the one Carol always teased him about. The sight hit him deep and personal. He wanted to kill somebody and make them pay with their skin. Only the years of on-duty training in maintaining his cool kept him from screaming and ripping the hospital door off the hinges. Carol would say he was becoming *attached* and somewhere, deep down inside, Nate suspected she might be right.

Nate grabbed the phone and punched in his sister's number. On the second ring she answered. She had caller ID. "Hey sissy," he used the name to needle her. "Got a moment?" Inspiration had struck.

"As long as you don't call me sissy again." In the background Nate could hear Poncho woofing at something interesting.

"No problem." Trying to keep his voice as positive and upbeat as possible, "Look, some things have happened. You still got the keys to the beach house? It's not rented out right now, is it?"

"No." Carol hesitated. Then she yelped and muttered, "Damn dog." There was shuffling and grunting on the other end of the line. Nate wished he knew what the hell was going on. Finally, "Just sit you damn mutt. God, he just has to be in your lap all the time." Like master, like dog. "With the plumbing fiasco and having to re-do the floor I didn't schedule it to list vacant until August. Why?"

"I need to take a few days off. Some shit's happening and I'm going to disappear for a bit."

"Are you okay, Nate?" Panic thrummed just under her voice. It was the same kind of panic their mom used to get when she took a call from dad.

"I'm fine." He paused. There wasn't any reason to hide it from his twin. "Caesar's not." He felt like a failure admitting that, like he should have been there. He should have stopped it.

"Oh my God, what happened?"

"He's got some info on a cop who may be real dirty. He brought it to me. I took it up the chain. Then good ol' blue brotherhood went into lock-step and some guys beat the shit out of him." He didn't know how much he should tell her. It was best she didn't know most of it. Still, she was going to have to know why he wanted the keys. "I need to get him out of sight for a while. So, I was thinking about taking him up to the beach house. It's still in mom's name. If somebody had a lot of time and energy they could track it. But we only need a few days."

"Yeah, okay." Then silence dropped on the line. Finally Carol spoke again. She seemed much calmer this time and a little teasing crept into her tone. "So, you're taking Caesar to the beach house for a few days?"

"This is business, Carol." She always knew just how to nail him.

"Yeah, but business mixed with pleasure is always so much more fun."

They'd already had that. "No -- no fun." Even in his own ears his voice sounded guilty as all sin.

Nate had to pull the phone back from his ear when she burst into hysterical giggles. Counting to ten before putting it back against his ear, he caught, "Don't tell me you're not even considering it."

"I'm not even considering it."

"You lie." She was still giggling, just not as loud. Then she stopped. "Wait, you're going to take the dog right?"

"I hadn't thought that through but yeah, Caesar would want his dog with him."

"Good, 'cause he's tearing apart my apartment." Now her tone was exasperated.

It was Nate's turn to tease. "How bad do you want to get him out?"

"Like yesterday."

"Good, Caesar's crashed and I don't want to leave him by himself." He chuckled. "You can bring the dog and the keys."

"Nathan Reilly you are such a shit!" Her yell carried over the line.

"I'm your twin brother," he shot back into the receiver, "it's my prerogative."

CHAPTER 18

The trip up the Ventura freeway was tedious. Before the 405 interchange, they never made more than twenty miles per hour. The better part of the ride was all stop and go. Once they passed the magic mark, the freeway opened up to a more reasonable flow. Still it was congested. It was always congested. That first half-hour Poncho had bounced all over the Taurus' interior. Finally the dog had settled into Caesar's lap, occasionally popping up to look at traffic.

Pain meds and his dog on his lap made Caesar drowsy. He had no sense that he'd drifted off until he felt the car hit the off-ramp. He blinked and shook his head. Nate was humming along to some God awful pop song on the radio. His fingers kept time with the beat, tapping against the steering wheel. When he noticed that Caesar was awake, he flashed his brilliant smile.

"Good nap?" Nate's tone was forced, like he was worried. Caesar considered it and dismissed the possibility almost immediately. Nate was a cop, they never worried.

"Yeah," Caesar yawned, "I didn't know I was that tired." It surprised him that he was able to sleep at all because, unlike Nate, Caesar was scared shitless. It was only paranoia if people didn't really want you dead.

"Healing up takes a lot out of you. I wouldn't be surprised if you spend a lot of time just napping on the deck." Nate laughed. "It's what my dad used to do when we'd come out during the summer. Mom would putter around the house, Carol and I would spend all day on the sand and dad would just crash. I could never figure it out. Then, my third year on the force, I came up with Carol and some of her friends. I slept the entire time." The patter soothed Caesar's nerves. Talking about normal lives, vacations, those sorts of things, took the edge off his fear.

Strip malls gave way to residential streets as they drove into Oxnard proper. "What did your dad do?" Other than the sky was blue instead of brown, it looked pretty much like any other Southern California city.

"He was a cop." Bitterness crept under the words.

Caesar snorted. "Following in your father's footsteps, huh?" Just like Nate. Good little daddy's boy…good looking big old hunk o' daddy's boy. Caesar shook the thought out of his head.

"Yeah, although he tried to talk me out of joining up."

"Why?"

Nate seemed to think for a moment and then barked a laugh. Poncho's ears pricked up at the sound. "Because I'm gay, and he knows it. He told me, 'if you really have a death wish, let me just take you up to the roof of the Bonaventure and throw you off. It'll be quicker and cleaner that way.'"

"Obviously you didn't pay much attention."

"Nope, I'm just a pig-headed son-of-a-bitch. Just like my old man." Nate pulled up to a gray cinderblock wall abutting a one-car garage. The only two breaks in the flat façade were a small wood gate and the garage door. Both were painted white. Just over the top Caesar could see the peak of an asphalt shingled roof. Multi-level condos rose on either side, imprisoning the little house on its narrow lot. Jumping out to open the garage, Nate left the car in idle. Poncho wiggled and panted, wanting out, and Caesar had to hold the terrier mix tight.

When Nate slid back into the driver's seat, he smiled. "Just a little bit more and you can get out of this hot car." Caesar knew he was talking to the dog, but it was still comforting to know. They pulled into the shadow of the garage. Nate killed the engine and jumped back out to close the street access. At the thump of the door hitting the pavement, Caesar let Ponchito go. He grunted as paws dug into the bruise on his side. One bound and the dog was out Nate's door. It took slightly more effort for Caesar to extricate himself. It was going to be ages before he felt right again.

"Oh, you," Nate knelt by the side door, cradling Poncho's muzzle in his right hand and letting himself be licked in the face. "It was such an awful long car ride, huh? Poor puppy." Nate twisted the doorknob with his left and pulled the door open. Poncho jumped through and then stopped. Tail wagging, he dipped and barked. His attention was solely focused on Nate. The brief time in Nate's care had apparently secured Ponchito a new best friend. It didn't look like Nate had suffered from it either.

Whores, the both of them.

"Go play," Nate laughed as he stood and the dog was off. Then, smiling, Nate turned back toward Caesar. "Come on, let's get inside. I'll come get the rest of the stuff later."

Caesar walked grudgingly around the car. Damn he was stiff from the trip. He leaned on the hood of the Taurus and stretched. Sore joints and ribs made him wince. When Nate tried to give him a hand, Caesar shrugged him off with a glare. "Remember, you're just keeping me out of sight for a while. You don't have to pretend to be nice to me." He was hurt, but he wasn't an invalid.

Nate shrugged. "Your choice." Then he walked away into the sunlight. It shot red and gold highlights through his hair and danced across his broad shoulders. Instantly, Poncho was back with an old tennis ball. The dog dropped it at Nate's feet and the cop bent to retrieve it. When he did, his butt flexed under his slacks. Suddenly another part of Caesar's body was aching. He shifted and silently cursed Nate for being so damn good looking. Then he limped from the garage.

The front yard wasn't much more than a concrete walkway leading from street to front door. A few planters, overflowing with geraniums, saved the space from being absolutely barren. From somewhere just beyond the house, Caesar could hear the shush of waves hitting the beach. A gull cried and then went silent. That and the wind were the only noises. For a city boy, it was a little disconcerting.

Poncho danced at Nate's feet as the cop walked to the front door, almost tripping him more than once. The dog was definitely a whore. They were going to have a long master-to-doggy talk later about loyalty. As the door swung open, the mutt skittered onto a tiled entry. Nate turned, waiting for Caesar to catch up. "It ain't the Ritz, but it will do." When Caesar stepped up, Nate put his hand on Caesar's arm. "Look, there's only one bedroom. It's yours while you're here." His voice was almost wistful. "This is business after all."

Again, Caesar reluctantly shook off the touch. "Yeah, your business, my fucking life ruined."

"You're doing a good thing, Caesar, doing what's right." Nate's voice and eyes said he really believed it. Just like a cop to be all gung-ho and moralistic. "Remember that."

"Tell that to the assholes who beat the shit outta me."

Nate sighed. "I don't know what to tell you about that. There's good and bad everywhere." He stuck his hands in his pockets and stared at his feet. "If we didn't have bad cops we wouldn't need Internal Affairs." Then he fell silent for a bit. Caesar waited. Finally, Nate looked up. His bright smile was back. "Come on, let me give you the five cent tour."

Nate led him into a single floor shack on the beach. If the house had been in Highland Park it would have been called a dump. Up in Oxnard, with the surf hitting the shore just outside your back door, it was prime real estate. It was the kind of place Caesar had seen as he walked through the public beach accesses with his uncles. Back then he'd seen them as toys of the supremely wealthy. You couldn't be poor to live here…a cracker box on the strand would run you a million easy. Still, many were rented out to vacationers just to make ends meet. Which meant easily replaced furnishings and apartment white paint.

Set up in a straight line, the hall along the left led from the front door all the way back. Caesar could just catch a glimpse of the ocean through the sliding glass doors at the far end. The first door on the right opened onto a tiny bedroom. It wasn't much more than a bed, nightstand and a 13" TV on a small table in the far corner. A roll-down blind covered the only window. Caesar guessed that it was more to hide the view of the neighbor's fence than to prevent anyone from seeing in. "It's a little stuffy." Nate commented as he walked around the full-sized bed. Poncho followed, bounding from the floor and landing on the sailboat-themed spread. As Nate cracked the window, letting in the beach air, Caesar leaned in. Several shell prints hung on the wall above the rattan headboard. The door to the closet was just on the other side.

Poncho dropped onto the bed and rolled over, begging for a rub. Nate sat on the corner and obliged him with a tummy scratch. The dog groaned with pleasure. "I don't get why you, a burglar, own such a dinky dog." Nate's hand covered almost all of Ponchito's belly.

Caesar propped himself against the doorframe. "Ponchito's a dinky dog with a big bark."

"But he wouldn't scare a five year old." With a final pat, Nate stood, then slid past Caesar and wandered down the hall. "How can that thing protect anyone? Didn't help you much."

"Sure he did." Caesar followed, passing the small bath before stepping out of the hall into the kitchen/living area. "His barking is what brought the neighbors and got those guys out before they killed me."

Nate yanked the dowel from the track of the sliding door. "Yeah, but if he'd been a big ol' pit bull or something..." He pulled it open letting the breeze drift in from the beach. Poncho shot through Nate's legs before he could close the screen. "Oh shit!"

"Ah, don't worry about him. I'm here, you're here, food's here. He'll come back when he's hungry. Dog ain't so stupid as to try and head back to Highland Park." The den was somewhere between trailer park and homey. One of those old seventies-era plaid couches sat behind a coffee table made from driftwood. Caesar bypassed that and settled into a wicker chair. A blue rug broke up the expanse of cream tile flooring the entire house. Ugly, but most likely practical for a beach house. "You gotta understand something about dogs. The first time I got popped, I was fifteen and I called the cops myself." Nate's little slice of family history somehow tempted him to give a bit of his own background. "I broke into this asshole's house. Like an idiot I didn't case it a day before to back up the stuff I'd figured out earlier. If I had, I'd have known he bought himself a guard dog."

Nate snorted as he sprawled onto the couch and kicked off his shoes. It was strange to see the cop relaxing like that, even if it did seem a bit forced. The times they'd been together had all been either business or let's get naked quick scenarios. Nate on the sofa, Poncho playing in the yard, suddenly Caesar flashed to the possibility of *a future*. He swallowed. Caesar was a little worried that he was enjoying this. They were on the run, hiding from someone who'd tried to kill him. There was no way he should be having a good time.

Well, except for the fact that he still hurt like hell. That sucked rocks. "So I get in, the dog takes after me, I managed to lock myself in the bathroom—and of course I chose the one with this tiny little window I couldn't get through. Spent a couple hours sitting on the can realizing I was a total idiot. The dog's still going nuts when the owner gets home." Caesar laughed at the memory. Years after it was funny. At the time, it was anything but.

"He tries to pull it off the door. Dog's pissed he can't get me, turned around and mauled the owner. I had to pull off the towel rod, beat the shit outta the dog with it and call 911 to sew that guy's arm back on. I managed to get the dog off of him and into the bathroom." Caesar pushed back his sleeve showing off a set of scars on his forearm. They'd faded considerably over the years but were still visible. "I got bit twice and the cops got there before I could get out. Luckily dude had the shot records. Turns out he'd bought the damn thing for protection but had no idea how to control it. Honestly, big or little doesn't matter. If there's a dog that's gonna bark I'll usually pass up the house. Too much risk and it attracts too much attention. Last thing a burglar wants is attention."

Nate's head was pillowed on his arm, his smile sleepy. "I can see that." With a grunt he rolled to sitting. "Know what, before I get too comfortable," Nate bent over to retrieve his shoes, "I should run to the store and grab some food. I wasn't planning on using the place as a safe house. We don't keep it stocked, although there might be a case of soda in the garage if you get thirsty." As he tied the laces, Nate grinned. "Make yourself at home. I won't be long."

"Okay." Caesar struggled out of the chair and wandered over to the TV. It was ensconced in a cheap, white-washed entertainment center. "I'll probably just watch the tube for awhile." He scrounged among beach themed knickknacks for the remote.

Nate coughed and he turned. The remote was swallowed in Nate's grip. With an electric pop the screen activated. Nate tossed the remote onto the coffee table as he stood. "You're stuck with regular programming. Although, I think there's some old tapes for the VCR over there." Walking toward the front door, he shot over his shoulder, "Maybe I'll pick up a movie while I'm out. You want drama, comedy or porn?" Nate ducked out the door before Caesar could answer.

For a while, Caesar flipped through the channels. He really needed to get his mind on something other than Nate. *Chingaso*, that cop just pushed all sorts of buttons Caesar considered safely switched off. A future, he'd actually thought about a future...with Nate. He shuddered. Even if it was the tiniest second of a thought, it scared him worse than the idiots who wanted to see him dead.

News was the only thing that came in clear and he wasn't up to watching that. It reminded him how deep in the muck he was. Killing the TV, Caesar wandered out onto the deck. A weathered fence of broad, gray boards marked where the Reilly property ended and public beach began. Caesar looked across the sand as he sat on the steps. Poncho was happily rolling in piles of kelp washed up on the beach. Caesar groaned. What was it with little dogs and the need to find the smelliest shit in the world to play around in? He whistled and Poncho jumped to his feet and sneezed. Then the terrier mix bounded across the sand to play attention-slut at his feet.

God, Poncho stank! Caesar could barely breathe with the smell of fish and garbage. He darted back into the house and found some dish-soap and an old towel under the sink. Not great, but it would do. When he came back out, Caesar had to chase down his dog. Psychic canine senses must have warned Ponchito he was about to get a bath. Finally the mutt was corralled and soaked under the spigot at the side of the house. They were both dripping by the end of it all. One hand latched on the terrier's collar; he struggled to get his shirt off. Not only was it wet, it was sandy and soapy. He pitched it up onto a deck chair to dry and then toed out of his shoes. They, and his socks, would have to dry out as well. Still, Caesar figured it was a good thing the house was tiled as he carried the wet dog back inside.

Nate looked up over the counter between the kitchen and living room. He shoved a box of cereal into the cupboard. "You know there's probably a suit in the closet if you really wanted to swim that badly."

Glaring, Caesar slid the screen shut behind him and dropped Ponchito to the floor. "He found something nasty to play in. I had to give him a bath." The dog promptly shook off the remaining water and trotted into the kitchen. Caesar followed, using the towel to dry his hair, the rest of his body would just have to air dry.

"Good," Nate drawled. "Now you both smell like wet dog."

When Caesar pulled the towel off his head, he realized Nate had changed. Instead of Polo and Dockers, Nate was wearing an old flannel shirt with the sleeves ripped out and a pair of cutoff jean shorts. Caesar swallowed. The ragged shorts had more holes than fabric. The rents teased him with glimpses of toned ass. Nate's flat stomach flexed as he swung to grab a can, and then stretched to put it above the stove. It was unbelievably cruel that a cop was that sexy. It was hell that Caesar was stuck in a beach house, with no TV, and a cop that was that sexy. They should have killed him, 'cause he was going to die from this.

White plastic bags littered the counter. Caesar dug into the nearest, trying to distract himself. The first thing he pulled out was a tin of dog food. "What the fuck kinda dog food did you buy?" Caesar turned the little gold tin over in his hands. A miniature, inbred, somethingorother stared with sappy eyes from the pull back lid. "Chicken and veal... hell, I don't eat this good."

"What?" Ponchito danced about Nate's legs as the man pretended to ignore him. Caesar took a long, hard look. Ponchito never got that worked up over anybody but him. Hmph, half the time, the mutt didn't get that worked up *for* him. Slut. Nate shrugged, digging in the fridge. "It's dog food."

Caesar rested his butt against the counter, "No it's like little-expensive-pooches-with-froofy-names-wearing-booties kinda dog food." The terrier mix skittered back and forth across the kitchen. One man held the golden tin. The other was still rummaging in the fridge. He was obviously having problems deciding which possibility held more promise.

Nate bent down farther, giving Caesar a clear view of his upturned ass. "I don't know," Nate mumbled, searching, "I went to the pet store and bought dog food. What the hell do you feed him?" That ass was enough to make Caesar not really care if Nate spoiled his dog. He was more than welcome to spoil both of them...often.

"At a pet store?" He shook his head, glaring at Nate's back. "You bought the food at a pet store? You just fucking made of money?"

Beers laced through his fingers, Nate turned. He held them out. "Where the hell else do you buy dog food?"

Popping the tin, Caesar didn't even listen much to the reply as he dropped the can on the floor. The sound of the tin did it. Ponchito was like a set of springs on uppers at his feet. Then the dog did a nosedive into the food, pushing the tin with metallic scrapes across the floor. "You've seen the store with the big ass red K." Beer was good. Nate was so much better. He stepped in and took one of the bottles. He used it as a pointer. "Ponchito here, he's a street dog." The cap came free with a pop and a hiss. "He gets whatever the fuck is on sale. And if he's really nice, maybe I give him a hot dog." Growling, he added "If you're really good, maybe I'll give you a hot dog."

CHAPTER 19

Nate dumped charcoal on the hibachi and wondered what he was going to do. The single hottest guy he had ever met was prepping chips and dip in his kitchen while he struggled to strike a match. Here they were, hiding out, and he was playing like they were taking a vacation at the beach. Reality was going to bite him in the ass big time. Nate couldn't help it. If he thought too much about the truth, fear might paralyze him. A cop who second-guessed himself was, in his dad's words, 'good for nothing and no good at all.'

On the third try he got a match going long enough to light the paper and start the coals. Nate tossed the matches on the table and leaned against the deck rail. A few days alone with Caesar and Nate wasn't sure what would happen.

Shit, when Caesar had wandered in, shirtless and his pants soaked through, Nate had thought he was going to die. Warm, brown skin and toned body, Caesar had everything he wanted. And it wasn't gym queen, but a hard muscled frame from lifting boards and swinging a hammer. Damn Caesar for being so sexy. He'd had to dive into the refrigerator just to keep from jumping Caesar.

Of course, when Caesar made the hot dog comment, Nate had busted up. It was like a line from a bad porn flick. Caesar had glared and then stalked off to the bedroom to change. While Nate had collected the hotdogs, buns and condiments on a tray, he kept inventing excuses as to why he needed something out of the bedroom. Only serious unwillingness to let Caesar know he'd gotten under Nate's skin kept him in the other half of the house.

Forcing himself outside to cook, Nate wondered how he was going to make it through the night. Four times Caesar had swayed him and Nate had given in. Well two were before he knew what Caesar was, but the other times, they counted. That was just weak. Problem was, where Caesar was concerned, Nate was always going to be weak. That dark skin and those deep eyes just revved Nate up in ways he wasn't used to. Part of it was that most of the guys he'd been with were just so…gay. Like bad sitcom gay.

Caesar was just a guy. Throwing four dogs on the grill, Nate figured that had to be the *thing*. Caesar was a guy who liked drinking beer and watching the tube. The soap opera addiction was weird, but at least it was TV. He built things and worked with his hands. While Caesar didn't have steady employment, outside of stealing shit, it was a regular type of job. No fancy I-have-more-education-than-you or a fake-studio-smiles kind of man that drove Nate absolutely nuts. It was so nice not to feel like a damn prop.

And Caesar dressed like your average Joe: nothing fancy, nothing designer, just clothes. Caesar was all common sense and down to earth. There was nothing pretentious about his life. Well the dog was a little shi-shi. But that was only because Ponchito was small. Otherwise he was just a guy's dog, a good ol' mutt. He hadn't asked *shall I make hors devours*? Caesar had shouted from the kitchen, "What kind of crappy-ass salsa did you buy and where the hell are the tortilla chips?" Everything he showed you was unvarnished Caesar.

Nate liked that rough-shod guy. A lot more than he wanted to admit. And it scared the shit out of him. Nate needed to maintain a detachment, keep a professional distance from Caesar and his emotions. Unfortunately, he knew he'd passed that point over coffee in bed almost a week earlier. Personal involvement just skewed his whole world view and made it hard to think like a cop. Right now Caesar needed him to think like a cop, not some love-struck boy-toy.

Nate turned when he heard the screen slide back. Caesar had switched into a pair of low-slung cargo shorts. A blue bowling shirt gaped open across his chest. The tight cut of his abs drew Nate's stare down. Just below Caesar's belly button a thin line of dark hair peeked over the edge of his shorts. Why did he have to tell Sarge he was okay with this gig? He didn't want to have to worry about things. He didn't want to be scared that he couldn't make everything right. All Nate wanted was to wrap Caesar in a bear hug and make the rest of the world leave them the fuck alone.

Mismatched bowls of chips and salsa landed on the plastic table with twin thumps, breaking Nate out of his thoughts. Caesar grabbed a chip, dragging it through the salsa before shoving it into his mouth. "Ow, shit. It hurts to chew, I feel like someone tried to make me swallow a basketball."

"You're lucky they didn't break your jaw with what you told me." He shook his head. The only reason Nate didn't have a good view of the bruise on Caesar's chin was the little fringe of goatee covering it.

"What's for dinner?" Caesar dropped into one of the patio chairs, feet kicked out across the deck.

"Hot dogs." Caesar stared at him like he wasn't certain if Nate was being serious. Nate jerked his thumb towards the grill as he wandered to the table. "Go see."

"You're warped." The dark eyed man growled before wolfing down another chip.

"No, I'm Nate." He grinned like a kid. "You're the one who suggested it, not me. But, hey, sometimes you just got to go with the flow."

Caesar flipped him off. "Fuckhead."

"Jackhole," Nate shot back as he settled into his own chair.

Poncho trotted out the door, his nails clicking on the deck. Scanning the men, then the table and finally the hibachi, Poncho sat back on his haunches. It wasn't a begging stance. His demeanor was more of an 'I'm here, being entertaining but unobtrusive.' In the first hour at Nate's place, Poncho had figured out that Nate didn't hold with slavish begging. Subtle worked better. And the dog played it like a well-worn violin. Poncho really was a smart little cuss, and cute on top of that. Even Carol, who was so not a dog person, had fallen for the little mixed breed.

Finding that the begging-without-begging wasn't working, Poncho dropped and strutted about the perimeter. Nate could just see the wheels turning in that doggy head. This was his domain, his guy, including the guy with the sexy dog food and he was going to protect them. Let anyone try and pull something and he'd bark 'em to death. Or maybe piss on their feet so that they'd slip and break their necks. Taking a final sniff off the edge of the patio, Poncho apparently decided everything was okay by him. He walked over, woofed at Caesar and then jumped into Nate's lap.

Caesar's hand stopped, chip raised half way to his mouth. He licked his lips, apparently thinking about things. "It is not right that my dog likes you more than me." The glare said he was serious about that.

"Naw." Nate raised his hands, denying any evil designs on Caesar's dog. "It's like kids with their grandparents. I'm special and new. After a while he won't want me anymore. I mean, you're his person."

"It's because you feed him expensive goddamn dog food. You're spoiling him." Caesar finished the last word with a crunch into the chip.

Well, Nate had to admit to himself, it was only because he couldn't spoil Poncho's master. He'd much rather be in Caesar's lap than have the dog in his. The thought of running his hands over that flat, warm belly made him want to forget about dinner. Especially in this heat, who wanted to eat in weather like this? It was almost seven and still close to eighty degrees, even with the breeze off the ocean. Nate threw his head back and blew out the breath he'd been holding.

"You hot?" Caesar grabbed the edges of his shirt and fanned himself. "I am."

Nate had to agree with that statement. He watched as a line of sweat beaded at the hollow of Caesar's neck then made a slow descent around the edge of his pec and moved to pool at his navel. That started him panting heavier than the damn mutt. And, fuck, his shorts were way too tight. The kind of tight that broadcasted clearly where his thoughts had drifted.

A sizzle-pop from the grill reminded Nate that he had food cooking. Pushing Poncho off his lap, he stood and wandered over to check the hotdogs. The mutt immediately jumped into Caesar's lap. What a slut. "Well, the dogs won't take much longer." He pushed them around with a fork. The surf hitting the strand sounded inviting. Smiling, he turned back toward the table. Caesar was rubbing Poncho's ears and making kissy faces. He stopped the moment he realized Nate was watching. Nate laughed, "We could eat and then hit the water. Just because we're on official business doesn't mean we can't enjoy ourselves a little." Nate knew it was an excuse to pretend that things were normal, that they could be normal and together.

"We could." Caesar glared at Nate and then looked out at the ocean. The tide was heading in, it would be at its highest point an hour or so before midnight. "Ah, Nate, I don't swim very good."

"Really? Well, okay." Sometimes it was hard to remember that not everyone had the opportunity to learn. "We won't go out far. Waist deep is good enough to get cool, isn't it?"

"I guess so." Caesar smiled. This time it was all for Nate. "Give me a wiener, I'm starved." Nate had to bite his tongue at that line.

The food was downed with beer and a comfortable silence. About a third went under the table for Poncho's benefit. Neither man wanted to admit he was slipping bits to the dog. For his part, Poncho wore a groove between their feet. By the time they finished eating Poncho had given up and was sprawled on his back asleep. Nate pushed back from the table. "I think we killed him."

"Naw, he's fine." Caesar bumped him with his foot. Ponchito opened one eye then let it drift shut again. "Although I think he ate more than we did."

"Probably." Smiling, Nate stood. "Come on, race you to the water." He was already halfway off the deck.

"Race? Wait, okay, not fair!"

He could hear the thump of Caesar's feet behind him. Two steps into the surf and Nate slowed. Caesar splashed in after him. Nate gauged it, waited. When he felt the spray from the other man's steps, Nate stopped, turned, grabbed Caesar's arms and tossed him into the waves.

"*Chingado!*" Caesar came up sputtering and cursing in Spanish. Dark eyes flashed with murder. "*Pendeja! Chinga pendao te' chucha!*" Wow, he was on a roll. He was also dripping. Salt water beaded on his skin and caught the last of the fading sun. "Oh shit!" Caesar held his body stiff, and hissed. "That stings in the cuts!"

With a laugh, Nate dropped to his knees. Damn, the water felt good…almost twenty degrees cooler than the air. Sand tickled as it trickled from under his legs as the surf rolled back.

For a moment he forgot just why they were in Oxnard. "See I told you, no more than waist deep."

"You are an asshole, Nathan Reilly." Caesar pushed the hair back from his face. Still, a smile flashed just under that feather-light mustache. Then his eyes went wide. "Oh shit!" A black bomb hit his chest, knocking him back into an incoming wave.

Wriggling and barking, Poncho half-paddled half-ran toward Nate. The dog seemed pleased that both men had decided to brave the surf. "You evil little thing." Nate hauled Poncho out of the water and was rewarded with doggy kisses. Tucking the terrier mix under his arm, he offered the other hand to Caesar. "Cool enough?"

Caesar ignored his hand and crawled forward. The shirt was almost transparent and plastered to his skin. "You would know evil." Nate held his breath. Caesar was close enough to kiss. Instead, he got a question. "So you used to spend a lot of time here as a kid?"

Damn. "Yeah. My grandparents bought it in the fifties, back when everyone thought this was the middle of nowhere." Nate struggled to stand. It was rough going. The beach rolled under his feet and Poncho twisted in his grip. "I hated it, because there was nothing to do up here. But then, in high school, Carol and I were suddenly the cool kids 'cause we had a beach house to party at. Not that we could get away with anything... my dad knew all the cops up here, but the idea of it was great." Stepping up to the tide line, Nate dropped the dog on the sand. Poncho shook off the water and then bounded off toward the house. Thank God for tile floors. He looked back to catch Caesar stifling a yawn. "You're still not a hundred percent. Let's head in. We can swim more tomorrow."

As they walked back toward the house, Caesar's hand thumped him in the back of the head. Then a light touch snaked down his back. Without thinking Nate moved to pull Caesar in close. Before his hand could touch that brown hip, he caught himself. No, no, and no again. He'd been playing with himself, pretending, but Caesar wasn't his boyfriend. This was a job. Nate jumped over the steps and landed on the deck. "Come on let's get out of these wet clothes. Then you can hit the hay."

Tossing his shirt on the deck chair before stepping in to the living room, Nate popped the buttons on his shorts. "Leave the wet clothes outside." Caesar's shirt from earlier in the day was already out there. The deck was starting to look like a high school boy's room. "I'll wash the salt out tomorrow." Nate's cutoffs followed. The wet slaps of his feet sounded as Nate hustled to the bath. He returned with two towels in his hands and one about his waist.

Caesar was easing himself out of his own shorts. Nate felt a twinge of guilt. Roughhousing was probably not the best thing for Caesar's recovery. It was all Nate could do not to stare. Bruises bloomed dark purple on his skin and the split on his lip had opened, oozing blood. God, Caesar had to be stiffer and sorer than all hell. Even looking like he'd been hit by a Mack Truck, Caesar was incredible. Strands of thick black hair clung to his cheeks. That heavy cock nestled between his legs. Nate wanted to drop to the floor and devour it.

Caesar looked up, hand held out for a towel. "What the hell are you staring at?" When Nate passed it over, Caesar snapped it out and then began drying his hair.

"Nothing." Nate lied.

"Bullshit." Caesar lifted one edge of the cloth so he could glare at Nate.

"Ah, come on." Nate swallowed. Caesar had him dead to rights. To hide it, Nate went after Poncho with the remaining towel. Black ears pricked up. Then the dog shot toward the front of the house. Nate protested as he headed down the hall after the retreating mutt. "Not like I ain't seen what you've got." Catching him in the bedroom, seconds before Poncho hit the bed, Nate swaddled the dog in the towel. Happy grunts told him that Ponchito was as much in denial about wanting a rubdown as Nate was about wanting his master.

"You," Caesar's voice came from the doorway. Nate glanced up from where he knelt next to the dog. White terrycloth draped over Caesar's dark shoulder, leaving everything mouthwateringly on display. One finger gently flicked Caesar's thick cock, "just want what I got."

There was no way Nate was going to be able to keep up the pretense. "Well, yeah." He shrugged. "Who wouldn't?"

Caesar laughed. "You're just trying to trick me into thinking you're a nice guy." Stepping around dog and man, Caesar dropped his own towel on Nate's head. "That way I won't make you sleep on the couch."

"My house," Nate grumbled, dragging the cloth off his hair. Ponchito was as dry as he was going to get. Nate turned, balled both towels and tossed them in the hall. He'd do a general pick-up round later. "I could make you sleep on the couch."

"You already said the bedroom was mine." Springs groaned as Caesar flopped down on the bed as if to prove ownership.

"Shit, I did, didn't I?" Damn dog was burrowing into the laundry, nesting. Strange things that little dogs did...Nate was going to have to find him a blanket or something. Although he wouldn't admit to Caesar that he'd let Ponchito sleep on his bed at the apartment the night Caesar'd been beaten.

Caesar spoke up from behind him. "Nate, you don't have to sleep on the couch."

Nate twisted. There was Caesar on the bed, naked and toned and oh so sexy. One of his legs was bent at the knee and he pillowed his head on an arm. His free hand was making lazy circles around his stomach. Each pass stroked against his cock. It was so hard. Thick and big and as dark as the rest of him, it jumped as Caesar moved. The red head of his prick begged to be licked.

Swallowing, Nate stood. He licked his lips before breathing, "We shouldn't." Nate's own dick ached. He grabbed himself, pushing against his own palm for some relief. It only made the want worse.

"We shouldn't..." Caesar's eyes smoked. Nate was drawn to them, moving toward the bed without consciously thinking about it. "...have any of the other times either."

The remaining towel hit the floor. "True." Nate bent down over Caesar. Their cocks brushed together and sent shivers through Nate's hips. Caesar's touch was like magic. "Ah, damn Caesar, what the hell do you do to me?"

"Me, *ese*?" A strong hand wrapped across the back of Nate's neck, pulling him down. Before their lips touched, Caesar whispered, "You're one big ol' mass of blond-haired, green-eyed muscle and you ask what I do to you?" Then they were kissing and Nate was melting from the inside out.

When they came up for air, Nate was panting. "Okay, how 'bout, you can do anything you want to me?"

He earned a growl for that. "I'll take that." The sound shot down Nate's spine and through his balls.

Caesar's fingers drifted across his ribs and he shuddered. It felt so good. Nate pushed his hips against Caesar's. He wound his fingers into Caesar's hair and stared down into those chocolate eyes. Caesar's tongue ran along that full bottom lip, inviting, teasing. Oh, yeah, Nate could take him up on that invitation. He bent down and gently brushed Caesar's mouth with his own.

A wet nose caught Nate in the small of his back. He jumped against Caesar, yelling, "What the fuck?" Twisting, he found Poncho sitting on the covers with his tongue hanging out. "Okay, no." Wide eyed he turned back to Caesar. "I'll stay but the dog has *got* to go." Poncho looked hurt by Nate's rejection.

Caesar scrambled under and across Nate's body, snatching up Poncho by the middle. "Sorry Ponchito, you're so out of here right now." The terrier writhed in his grip. "*Papi* has someone else to pay attention to for a bit." Caesar dropped him in the hall and slammed the door. Incessant scrabbles on the tile told them Poncho was not pleased. The dog could just deal for a little bit.

Nate rolled over and leaned off the edge of the mattress. Quickly digging in his duffle, Nate came up with condoms and lube. He hadn't actually consciously thought about packing them. If he had, he wouldn't have. But in the back of his brain, in his subconscious, he must have known they'd find themselves in this situation. Thank God for impulses because he didn't keep a handy supply at the beach house.

As Caesar stepped back to the bed, Nate sat up. He wrapped his arms around those lean hips and licked across the flat of Caesar's stomach.

"Aye, Nate," Caesar hissed, running his fingers hard across Nate's scalp, "you're like an addiction."

That throbbing cock bumped against Nate's chin. He moved to taste it with his tongue. Caesar's taste was incredible: dark, sweet and musky. Nate knew he'd never get enough of that flavor. It was a mutual addiction…that much was certain. "I want you to fuck me, hard." Nate mumbled against velvet skin.

"Hard?"

"Uh-huh." Nate ran his tongue just under the flared head. "Real hard."

"Goddamn." Caesar pushed his arms away and clambered up onto the bed. "Get on your knees then."

Rolling onto his stomach, Nate drew his knees up under his body. Caesar spread his cheeks wide. Nate pushed back into the touch, thrusting his ass against Caesar's hands. Such strong hands, it felt so good. Nate clutched the pillow tight against his chest. He felt so vulnerable like this: legs spread open, ass up in the air, tight balls and throbbing cock on display for his lover. Everything ached for Caesar's touch.

He looked back over his shoulder. Caesar knelt behind him, licking his lips. Dark brown eyes roamed all over his body. Nate could feel them on his skin. Caesar's prick pulsed in time with his heart. It was like that long, thick rod was begging to be put inside him. Nate wanted it inside him. He could already feel it.

Caesar leaned in and nipped his ass. Nate shuddered as Caesar's tongue traced patterns of heat on his skin. The touch traveled closer and closer to his hole. When Caesar's tongue found it, Nate's eyes rolled back in his head, "Oh, God, tongue-fuck me." Each swirl around that oh so sensitive spot traveled down his dick and vibrated in the tip. "You're so good to me. So good."

"You bet I am." Caesar's tongue was joined by his fingers, spreading Nate, opening him up. Caesar's other hand slipped down to stroke Nate's burning prick.

It felt so incredible. Everything Caesar did felt unbelievable. Nate writhed under the onslaught. "Like that, like that." Shivering as the slick explorations worked him, Nate moaned and babbled. "Please, Caesar, fuck me, do me. I want it." God he was such a cock slut. "Fucking stick that dick in my hole and make me scream."

Lips moving up Nate's back, Caesar whispered, "You're so demanding. I like it."

"Ah, please!" was all Nate could manage as the fingers disappeared and the thick head of Caesar's cock bumped his hole. Slowly, Caesar pushed. Nate felt the slight sting as his body resisted. Then his breath caught as it gave and Caesar slid inside. "Damn, you're so big, so fucking big inside me!" He shoved his hips back demanding, taking more.

As Caesar thrust, his hand slid along Nate's cock. "You don't do anything but ride and talk to me." His palm twisted along the length and Nate groaned.

Slow and easy and deep, Caesar fucked him. Nate dropped his head between his arms. He could look back under his body and see those brown fingers teasing his dick. He could feel and watch Caesar's heavy balls bumping against his own tight sac. Caesar drew back, almost all the way out, and shifted his weight onto his less-abused leg. His free hand settled into the small of Nate's back pushing him down. The other let go of Nate's prick and slid to grip his hip. "Oh, God!" Nate breathed as a knee grazed his thigh. He had a few seconds to prepare and then Caesar drove in deep and hard.

Caesar's thrusts drove him down against the bed. Nate's cock was tangled in the covers. Each thrust hit so right. "Shitfuckingyeah!" Coherent speech was an impossibility. It was all Nate could do to ride out the pleasure screaming through his body. "Sheets, fuck, sheets!" The cloth stroked his prick hard, the friction sucking up into his balls. Caesar's cock pounded him so good, spreading him wide. His lover's fingers dug into his skin and Nate felt Caesar shudder. Wild thrusts pushed him harder and harder into the covers. Nate's balls tensed so tight it was painful and then heat and ecstasy was pouring out of him. "Goddamn, yeah!" spilled over his lips, as cum spilled into the sheets.

They both collapsed onto the bed. Caesar's weight felt good on his body. Finally, Caesar pulled out and rolled next to Nate. Nate shuddered with aftershocks as Caesar slid one arm across his shoulders. Nate turned his chin and stared into a satisfied set of brown eyes. Their faces were inches apart. This was good. Caesar moved closer, pressing up against Nate's skin.

Lips teasing the line of his jaw, Caesar worked his way up to where he was next to Nate's ear. "I think," he whispered it soft and low, "we're in such trouble together."

CHAPTER 20

Caesar stretched and yawned, every muscle screamed in protest. Ah shit, was he stiff. It felt way too early to be up and about. The first thing he noticed was Ponchito's warm body balled against his legs. Nate must have let him in the room. The second thing was that Nate wasn't balled up anywhere near him. Hopefully that meant coffee was in the works. Sleep fading, the sound of heavy breathing and regular thumps on the floor seeped into Caesar's brain. Curiosity finally moved him. Caesar rolled to the edge of the bed and glared over the side.

Back on the floor, hands linked behind his head, knees bent and spread for balance, Nate hauled himself up. His elbows bumped the opposing knees and then the cop dropped back to the floor. Caesar watched as Nate repeated the sit-up. He was counting under his breath, although too low for Caesar to catch. It was just plain evil to see anyone that motivated just after waking up. "What the hell are you doing, Nate?" He grumbled.

Without pausing, "Sit-ups, what does it look like I'm doing?"

"Whatever it is," Caesar rested his chin on one arm and watched, "It's way too early in the morning to be doing it." After a few more repetitions, he asked, "Why?"

"Why what?" Nate panted the question as he did another rep.

It was exhausting watching Nate. "Why are you on the floor doing sit-ups at this time of the morning?"

Nate dropped back to the floor and stared up at Caesar. "I've got to stay in shape."

"Nate." Caesar slowly slid his gaze over that toned body. "If you were any more in shape your six-pack would have six-packs." That earned him a laugh. It felt nice to be teasing like this with Nate, it almost made him forget why they were together. Although, he wished he were a little more awake. He yawned through his next question. "Not that I don't admire the results, but are you really that into yourself?"

"Into myself?" Nate rolled, propping himself up on one arm. "You think I'm vain?

Caesar shrugged. "Okay, if it's not that, what is it?"

"Alright, it's a little bit of that." The shy smile Nate flashed melted into Caesar's thighs. Damn, Nate was sexy like that: a little sweaty, posing without posing in his tight boxer-style briefs. Caesar's thoughts were drifting towards a different kind of work out. Nate continued, "It's not bad getting attention."

Caesar slid off the bed. Unlike Nate, Caesar was still naked. "Ah, ha." He crawled toward Nate. "See I knew it." Caesar ran one hand up a hard, muscled leg. Nate shivered.

Sitting up, Nate's own hands wandered over Caesar's arms. The shorts did nothing to hide his rising desire. Nate leaned in, licking his lips. "But, it also gets rid of a different kind of attention."

Early morning wants, what could be better? Caesar scooted closer as his free hand drifted down between his own legs. Things were getting harder by the second. "What do you mean?"

"I don't hide the fact that I'm gay." Nate's touch joined Caesar's and he sucked in his breath. "I don't go waving it around in people's faces, either. There are still a lot of guys on the force who don't like it." Slowly, like they had all the time in the world, Nate stroked him. "While I'm pretty sure there's people making shitty comments behind my back... when you look like you can put some guy's head through the wall, people don't mess with you."

"I guess any excuse will do, huh?" Caesar slid his fingers across the back of Nate's neck. "Come here." Gentle pressure added to the command.

Grinning, Nate let himself be pulled in close. "What?" He teased.

"Well..." Caesar let go of his own cock so he could rub Nate's prick through his shorts. Nate groaned and pushed into the touch. "Seeing you down on the floor, on your back, knees up, made me want to mess with you."

Nate was already twitching. "I could live with that kind of messing."

"I bet you could." Caesar growled before kissing Nate hard. He opened his mouth, inviting Nate's tongue inside. When

Nate obliged by slipping it between his teeth, Caesar began to suck. Nate moaned. Caesar worked his hand under the band of Nate's shorts. Nate's prick was so thick. Warm and silky, the sensation of his rough hand around that solid dick sent shivers up his arm. Caesar twisted the cock in his palm and sucked the tongue in his mouth until Nate was almost whimpering. What a sexy sound. It was almost as good as the babbling.

Sliding his fingers under Nate's heavy balls, Caesar used his wrist to push the fabric down. He shuffled and twisted until Nate was in his lap. Shorts slung under Nate's sac, Caesar pushed his cock between Nate's legs. His prick slid from fabric to skin, making him shudder. Nate rubbed against his belly. As their tongues tangled, Caesar's hand slithered through the leg of Nate's briefs and pulled his cheeks apart. With one finger he circled, teased and tormented Nate's hole. The cop rolled his hips angling for the touch. Finally, Caesar pushed into Nate. So hot, Nate's body sucked him in as Nate dropped his head back and moaned. Caesar latched onto the hollow where Nate's neck met his shoulder and sucked on his skin.

Caesar's cock bumped against Nate's balls, rolling them with hard touches. Warm, fuzzy skin molding itself around his prick felt so good, solid and soft all at the same time. Nate's fingers dug into his shoulders as Nate leaned back giving Caesar all new places to explore. Green eyes locked on him. The hunger behind them tore into Caesar's soul. Nate was always so responsive. It blew Caesar away that a man like Nate could be into him at all.

"Fuck, Caesar, yeah…." Nate moaned thrusting in his own slickness along Caesar's belly. Caesar looked down to watch. A purple-white head teased him as it lay against his stomach. Then Nate pulled back. Sparks followed the trail of moisture.

Caesar's finger worked deep inside Nate, exploring until he found that spot. Nate moaned and drove his mouth onto Caesar's. The kiss was blistering. It robbed Caesar of everything but the desire to take Nate over. Fuck himself. All he wanted was for Nate to have it all. They bucked and drove their pricks together.

Caesar bit his lip to back it down. He couldn't stop. Everything was just too good. "Nate, I'm coming, Nate." He hissed against a hard shoulder. Nate reached between them, wrapped his hand around Caesar's prick and pulled. It didn't take more than three strokes and Caesar creamed Nate's hand. With a groan he pulled Nate against him and returned the favor. His tongue pillaged Nate's mouth as he caressed the hard flesh. Still working the pleasure inside Nate's body, Caesar stroked him inside and out. Nate moaned, long and low and hard. He shuddered, body tightening around Caesar's finger before coating both their bellies with cum.

Satisfied, Caesar pulled back and purred. "That's more like a proper morning workout."

"Shit, yeah." Nate seemed just as pleased. As he slid his arms behind Caesar's neck, Nate hit him with a question. "Why do you do it?"

"Do what?" Caesar had an idea what Nate was asking. He just didn't want to ruin the mood.

"Steal shit." Nate leaned back against the bed. "How did you start?"

Damn post-sex confessional. At this point he'd have told most guys to fuck off. Because it was Nate, Caesar answered. "Mostly? I was bored. I had nobody to talk to. My dad got hurt when I was a teen and they shipped me off to my aunt, who I'd never met. I left all my friends behind." Grunting he wriggled out from the tangle of legs and crawled back onto the bed. Nate twisted, crossing his arms on top of the mattress. When Caesar bent down for a kiss, Nate clambered up next to him. They both lay back, Caesar tickling Nate's hip as he continued. "And I don't have nothing at that point. So first I started picking up stuff at job sites. And the money wasn't great, but it wasn't bad. But I got a real rush. And then I just started looking for a better rush. Now it's what I know how to do."

Nate twitched and grabbed Caesar's wrist to stop the tickling. "Why don't you give it up?"

"You say that like it's so easy." He flopped back, arms behind his head, and stared at the ceiling. "What else am I going to do, Nate? At least I don't sell drugs, man."

Propping himself up onto one elbow, Nate glared down at him. "Okay, wait, selling drugs is bad. But, breaking into peoples' houses, destroying their sense of security in their own home and taking shit they broke their backs to earn... that's okay?"

"You're just a dumb cop, right?" A playful shove against Nate's chest took the sting out of his words. "I don't know how to do anything else."

"I saw you building furniture." There was a lot of respect in Nate's tone. Caesar wasn't used to that. "You work construction. Those are things you could do."

"It's not that easy." Trying to deny Nate's praise, he countered, giving himself an excuse not to succeed. "The last time I was out on probation I damn near starved because I couldn't make enough money. No one would hire me in a regular job when they found out why I'd been to prison."

"Get a contractors' license." Nate was just one for coming up with pie in the sky plans apparently.

"First, not sure I can with a felony record." Caesar knew all the excuses by heart. Secretly, he believed most of them. "Second, I know you have to be able to prove that you've worked in construction for four years. Hell, I don't even know who I worked for last week, much less a year ago. I get paid cash, under the table.

His boy in blue responded confidently. "We can figure something out."

"We?"

"I can't date a crook." Nate thumped him in the chest. Caesar winced. Hell, he was bruised even where he didn't have bruises.

"Well, too bad," he glared. For some reason he was a little scared that Nate was this upbeat. He tried to come up with another negative. "This is going to fuck me. I had a real good chance at something." Not that he would have taken the chance. "And the plea bargain is going to blow it to hell."

"Why?"

"Ah, my little brother got me hooked up with some people." Caesar tugged at Nate's nipple and got his hand slapped. "And they're interested in me. But it wouldn't work."

"What are they interested in you for?" Damn, now Nate was interested.

Caesar sighed. "One of those documentary things. Kinda a home-improvement show, I guess."

"You'd be Bob Villa?" Nate sat up and stared down at him. Disbelief shone in his green eyes.

"No…the show, it's not building stuff." Caesar sat up and waived it off. "It's called *Housebreaker.* Basically I'd get paid to break into peoples' houses and then there's a retired Burglary Detective who's the security guru and we go back through and tell them where the problems are."

"Holy shit!" Now Nate was excited. "You're going to jump on it, right?"

"I don't think I can get bonded." Why couldn't Nate see how many problems there were? Why it wouldn't work. "And TV hosts. They're all these good-looking guys and gals. I'm just nobody. I tried to tell those people that, but they kept after me. That's why I was at that party. Angel talked me into going so that I could talk to them. I've got half a dozen messages on my cell from the guy."

For awhile, Nate sat silent. Then he asked, "Why aren't you calling him back?"

"I don't know how to deal with that kind of people. How do I know he doesn't just want to get into my pants?"

"Carol." The one word was said like it was a magic phrase.

Caesar's eyes narrowed. He couldn't have heard right. "What?"

"Carol can take care of it for you. We'll call her."

That wasn't the issue. Nate just didn't understand. "Nate, people like me don't do those kinds of things."

"Who says?" Nate sounded annoyed that people would be that truthful.

Why couldn't Nate just understand that it would never work? "Everybody!" Caesar spat and started to roll off the bed. He needed a shower and the conversation was going nowhere. Nate wasn't in touch with reality enough to understand the problems.

"They lie." Nate grabbed his arm and pulled him back onto the bed. He searched Caesar's face earnestly. "You can do it. I know you can."

Caesar swallowed. Something in his voice, his eyes, said Nate really believed it. No one had believed those kinds of things about Caesar for as long as he could remember. "You think?" He could barely whisper the question. If he tried it and couldn't do it, that would be so much worse than not trying at all.

"I know it." Nate brushed Caesar's hair back off his forehead. The tenderness of the touch was more disconcerting then the unbridled confidence. "Let me call Carol for you. She'll take care of it for you. You won't have to do anything."

"I don't…" Caesar was stopped by Nate's hand over his mouth.

"I'm not going to let you talk unless you say yes."

Caesar nodded and Nate pulled back. "Okay, you can call Carol."

CHAPTER 21

After an hour on the phone with Carol, Caesar decided to take a walk. Poncho needed to get out and he needed to think. Everything was so confusing. She'd spouted off about agents, contracts and labor codes. His head swam with references to client lists and commitment to integrity…hell, he'd never been committed to anything. Artistic freedom? Merchandizing agreements? Royalty statements? All he wanted was a paycheck. When she'd asked if he had an attorney he wanted to look over things, the only name he had to give was Al Gregor. Carol said she'd take care of everything and get the paperwork over to Al first thing.

He left a quick message for Al. Hopefully what he left on the machine was an explanation and not insane ravings. When Caesar asked if Nate wanted to join him, the cop begged off, reminding them both that he had to check in with his Sergeant. As scrupulously as possible, IA was combing through the list of Price's associates to see who fit the description of the cops who'd attacked Caesar. If they found likely suspects they'd need to arrange Caesar's viewing. Then there were details of when Caesar would testify before the Grand Jury awaiting confirmation. Nate looked as disgusted as Caesar felt, reminding them that this wasn't playtime.

Maybe to take the edge off things, Nate hinted he was planning something special for lunch to celebrate. After the calls was headed to the store again. Chocolate syrup spread all over that man's naked body would be special. Somehow he figured Nate had more traditional fare in mind. Oh well, there was always *after* lunch for the naked Nathan Reilly type of celebration.

Caesar hit the beach. Poncho bounded off chasing surf. Just beyond the haze, Caesar could make out the bulk of the Channel Islands. The water was so blue up here. Near Santa Monica, the only beach Caesar had really been to; the ocean was a murky green-brown. Palms jutted out of the dunes, adding a gentle rustle to the wind. Clean, white sand stretched miles in either direction. It was peaceful, quiet. Surf and gulls were about the only real noise. Not many places in the metro hell could qualify for that.

Maybe, if things went right, Carol could get him an advisory position on the show. That would work. He was nowhere near qualified to host the damn thing. What's-his-name just wanted in his pants and was trying to stroke him with that offer. Caesar was sure of that. They'd get some good-looking actor to be the mouthpiece. But he could do some advising, sort of like the stunt guys. Let someone else look pretty and Caesar would do the actual work. Angel said that's how it always was on those reality gigs. If things went good, he could buy his mom a new TV. She'd like that.

And then, maybe, he might work on Nate. The screwing around was good. It was damn great as far as it went. But dating, a normal life, it kinda sounded nice. Boring, but nice. He was getting old enough that boring held some interest. Nate seemed hot for Caesar. Caesar was definitely hot for Nate. Working it into something more... he hadn't let himself hope for that type of thing in ages.

A bark caught his attention. Ponchito was playing the slut again, drumming his paws and wiggling his whole body in that notice me way. When he saw Caesar watching, the dog darted into the surf. Laughing, Caesar grabbed a bit of driftwood and tossed it toward the water. Ponchito sent up spray as he chased after it. It'd been a long time since he'd had the time to play with Ponchito. If he weren't still so damn stiff, Caesar might have started a game of chase. Instead he let Ponchito entertain him with his antics and just walked and thought about the investigation, *Housebreaker,* and the general bizarreness of his life recently.

Mostly, he thought about Nate.

He thought about green eyes and blond hair. It bordered on obsessive, how much he dwelled on those features. But Nate was too much of everything he liked. His poke at Nate's vanity had been pretty hollow. Caesar liked guys with muscle, always had. Most of the time those bodies came without body hair, another of his *things*. Not that he was into bears or anything, but a little bit was really good. Gym queens seemed compulsive over shaving every last bit off. The contrast between the soft down over the chiseled chest… that Nate was built and a little furry, rocked Caesar's world.

Added onto that, Nate was a nice guy, but not a push-over. Caesar could totally see Officer Reilly rescuing some little girl's kitty and then turning around and busting a guy up. Again a hard core under a soft exterior, it got Caesar every time. Although he still had to figure out what Nate saw in him. Good looking? Well, yeah, he'd been told he was. But Nate didn't seem the type that would stick around on the basis of a pretty face and decent-sized cock.

The fact that he was having those kinds of thoughts at all scared the shit out of Caesar.

Finally, he headed back to the house. Time for lunch. Or time to convince Nate to skip lunch and go right to desert…with chocolate syrup. As he approached the house, Caesar sensed something was wrong. Two men stood on the deck. Sitting in one of the deck chairs, Nate's arms were crossed defensively over his chest. The taller of the pair had sandy red hair and a sun-burnt complexion. His companion was a fatherly looking Hispanic man. Both the men were older and, although casually dressed in jeans and polos, not dressed for the beach. The way they held their bodies and their constantly scanning eyes, made them reek of cop.

Caesar paused. Nate had said no one knew they were in Oxnard. His Sergeant and the lead detective from Internal Affairs were the only two who had that information. So what were cops doing here? Until he knew otherwise, Caesar decided to play it safe. Moving just to within earshot and playing like your average beachgoer, Caesar plopped down onto the sand. He could keep an eye on Nate, but not be obvious. And if it was cool, if things were okay, Nate could call him over. Poncho was still chasing waves, which was good. They didn't need the dog shooting up onto the deck and giving everything away.

"Come on, Reilly." At the edge of his peripheral vision he could see the red-haired man getting flustered. He was damn near shouting at Nate. And his jaw was tight, like he was reining himself back from bigger outbursts.

The older man leaned against the porch rail. "You know it's not right." Voice soft and smooth it carried the hint of an accent Caesar had grown up with. "You got enough problems." He was much more calm and reserved. Caesar strained to catch what he said. "Why are you making waves for yourself, Reilly?" His tone was fatherly, his words anything but. "Don't act like some stupid fucking rookie."

"Life's got to be hard enough on you, Nate." Under control again, the other officer chimed in. "Look at your dad. How the hell does he take it?"

Caesar knew exactly what the *it* the moron was referring to. "Let's see…" Nate shot back. "It's my life so he lives with it. If you actually knew David Reilly, you'd know that."

"Make it easy on yourself." The guy tried to cover by acting smooth, giving Nate an out. "We know this is just a big mistake. That con is just trying to screw you so he can get off. You know it's a set up. It's got to be."

"Think what you want." Nate's growl sent the hairs on Caesar's neck crawling. "I'm just doing my job."

"Look, life could get a lot worse for you."

"Are you threatening me?" Chair legs scraped as Nate stood. Caesar suddenly understood what Nate had meant about his body being a shield. Both men took an involuntary step back when confronted by that mass of muscle. Nate's voice went low and dangerous. "I don't think you want to be threatening me." Eyes narrow, shoulders tight, Nate stepped forward. "Look, I'm chilling out here, trying to get over how someone tried to frag my career. And I've been pretty pissed about it all day. Now you assholes are here and I don't have anyone else to take it out on." He laced his fingers together and then cracked his knuckles. "You'll do fine."

The red haired man blanched, but the other cop just chuckled. "You're not that stupid, Reilly." Heading to the stairs, he turned. His companion passed him up and walked out onto the sand. The Hispanic cop looked at the sky then looked at Nate. "Just think about what we said."

"I have." Nate shoved his hands into his pockets and glared. "I don't like it."

"Your choice." He shrugged as if it really didn't matter. With another chuckle he followed the other officer. As he made his way past Caesar, the cop looked down. Caesar got a good, hard once over. The thief tried to look as unconcerned as possible, meeting the guy's stare before shrugging and scanning the beach for his dog. Over his shoulder Caesar could feel the weight of that calculating glare. Then it was gone and the guy's footsteps sounded in the sand. Caesar waited long past when he thought they'd be gone before calling for Ponchito and heading into the house.

Through the sliding door, Caesar could see Nate pacing the living room. He was nodding, talking into his cell phone as he measured off the distance between the walls. The click of the lock must have startled him because Nate spun. Panic crawled behind his eyes, and then he backed it down to police officer calm. He let out his breath, smiled and shook his head as Caesar eased the door open. Before Caesar could catch anything, Nate shut off the phone and dropped it into his pocket.

"What was that all about?" Caesar asked as he slipped into the house. Poncho skittered past his feet, heading for the bedroom most likely. Wet and sandy; the perfect condition to roll around on the bed. They needed to change the sheets after last night anyway. They'd gotten it sticky enough that both of them had been stuck with the dreaded wet spot. Share the heat...share the misery.

"They're trying to get me to back off the investigation." Nate ran his hands through his short, spiky hair, Acting like two other cops hadn't been out to roust him. "Mostly because they think I can intimidate you into recanting."

"I heard some of what they told you." Again the fear rose in those green eyes. As quickly as it came, Nate shoved it down. Caesar shook his head wishing he knew how to tell Nate it was okay to be scared. Hell, he was so freaked he wasn't sure he could piss straight. "That's fucked up."

"It is way fucked up." Nate palmed his face and sighed. "I don't know how they found me here. Especially so quickly. That's just bizarre. No one is supposed to know we're here. And what's really weird is they didn't seem to know you were here. I don't get it."

The light, airy beach house suddenly felt claustrophobic. "Do you think it's safe to stay?"

"I don't know." Nate's jaw tightened as he scanned the room. Then he shrugged. "I mean, do I think they'd try another go at me anytime soon? Probably not. But they'll be back and sooner or later someone will realize you're around." He laced his fingers over his head, pressing palms against temples. Blowing out his breath, he added, "We'll wait until evening and then we'll probably take off. I had a quick chat with the IA detective. He's setting us up with a place and is going to call me back. Not that we think anything bad is going to happen." Nate didn't sound convinced by his own words. "We just need to go lie low somewhere else. We don't want you or the investigation compromised."

Figuring Nate was worried about the *you* part and the detective was more concerned with the *investigation* part, Caesar flopped onto the sofa. He kicked his feet onto the coffee table. Things were aching again. The doctor told him to take it easy. He never had been good at following orders. As he stretched out, Caesar groaned. Thank God he could take a bit of a break before they hit the road. *La vida loca*—Caesar had never wanted that life. Most likely, Nate hadn't either. "You don't have to do this, Nate."

"What?" Nate dropped heavily onto the corner of the couch. His fingers walked up Caesar's shin, sending shivers along his nerves.

"Protect me from the cops." Involuntary twitches momentarily stole his ability to speak.

"You think that's what I'm doing?" Twisting until he was looking straight into Caesar's eyes, Nate teased, "I thought I was taking unfair advantage of an invalid."

Caesar ran his hand down Nate's chest. Just below the T-shirt he could feel the corded muscles tense. "I'm sorry this whole thing is screwing up your life. I wish I'd never found that crap."

"I'm glad you did find those pictures. It needed to happen." A tight, but genuine, smile confirmed what Nate said, but maybe not for the reasons Caesar thought. "And you are doing anything but screwing up my life."

Caesar moved one hand to mess the blond high and tight. The weight of Nate's skull as he pushed against the touch was electric. "If you hadn't met me..."

"Don't even think about that." Green eyes drifted shut. The smile relaxed. "I wouldn't change a thing about us." A small contented laugh drifted from between Nate's lips. "Okay, I think you should get a real job. I'd like to not be playing this hidey-hole shit. But you, me, I like it like it is."

"Yeah?" Caesar pulled Nate close. He wanted the weight against him, needed to feel Nate's presence in a very physical way.

Nate's hands shot out to latch onto the back of the couch, bearing his weight. Still his legs pressed into Caesar's thigh. There was something to be said for keeping Nate off balance. "Yeah." Nate breathed, moving the last few inches to brush his lips against Caesar's own.

Warm and relaxed they settled into a kiss. Again that gentle exploration, like the first time they'd tasted each other's mouths. Tongues only teased. Lips lingered. Slowly desire crawled through Caesar's skin. The day was melding into a lazy summer Sunday feel. It shouldn't have. They should be worried. They should be figuring a strategy and getting the hell out. Instead everything was narrowing to heat, and sun and Nate. He whispered, "Well, since we have some time to kill." Fingers worked at exposing the skin under Nate's T-shirt. As he moved, he danced his touch just above the skin.

Nate squirmed and laughed, "Killing time, huh?" He sat back, yanking the shirt over his head. While he struggled with the cotton, Caesar popped the buttons on Nate's shorts. "I like the way your mind works."

"Ain't my mind working." Caesar slid his hand under the fabric, cupping Nate's dick in his palm. The soft weight of it felt so good. And rolling Nate's prick around through his briefs, making him hard, the control stoked Caesar.

"Okay," Nate tossed his shirt to the floor. "I like the way that works, too."

They both chuckled as Nate pushed his hips into the caress. Caesar's body was responding almost as fast as Nate's. Of course, he was still trapped in his shorts. And that wouldn't last long the way Nate was feeling him up. God, he had a strong grip. Caesar hissed and ground into Nate's hand. Lazy was quickly giving way to need. "Shit, we don't have anything."

"Anything?" Nate nuzzled into his neck, lighting fires under Caesar's skin. After a bit, what Caesar meant must have sunk in. Pulling back, Nate stared down with lust fogged green eyes. "Oh, yeah, anything."

Caesar reached up and twisted one nipple. Nate jumped. "I should teach Ponchito to fetch."

"You're evil." Nate grabbed his wrist, shoving it against the wall above Caesar's head. The tongue tickling the sensitive skin in his armpit made Caesar struggle. It was too intense there. He writhed between the teasing dance under his arm and the rough kneading of his cock. That and the feel of Nate in his own hand had Caesar reeling. When Caesar was almost shaking, Nate drew back. "Don't move." Rough and needy, Nate kissed him. He could taste his own sweat on Nate's lips. "I'll be back." He bumped the bridge of Caesar's nose with the knuckles of the hand that wasn't pinning Caesar to the couch.

Caesar hadn't let go of Nate's throbbing cock. "Ruins the mood." He squeezed, hard. Nate groaned and shuddered.

"Doesn't have to." Nate pried Caesar's fingers from his prick. Settling both hands on Caesar's cock, Nate squeezed his hand over Caesar's and Caesar's hand over his prick. When he let go, Caesar tried to as well. Nate pushed his hand back down. "Close your eyes, put your fingers here and stroke. Just imagine it's me."

"That's just jacking off through my clothes."

"Okay, then get out of your clothes." Nate snickered and crawled off the couch. As he stood, he said, "Think of it as getting prepared to be ridden."

"What?" Damn Nate looked fine, bare-chested with his shorts hanging open. The hard outline of his cock strained under cotton briefs. And that trail of blond that crawled from his navel and fanned out across his pecs made Caesar suck in his breath. "We gonna play cowboy?" He panted, struggling with the snap and zipper of his own shorts.

"Yee-haw." Nate teased, drawing out the word. "Don't move."

Struggling to push his shorts down, Caesar snorted. "Aye *chingaso*, I ain't goin' nowhere."

"Good. Close your eyes. Two shakes."

"Of what?"

"My ass," Nate growled.

"Not moving, waiting." Caesar dropped his head on the back of the sofa. Closing his eyes he imagined Nate's hand toying with his cock. Broad, rough fingers slid along his sensitive skin. Nate's calluses weren't as pronounced as those on his own hand, but Caesar kept the fantasy going. He circled his fingers tight below the head, pulling the skin up and over. As he played, Caesar licked his lips. Nate was so freaking tight. The feel of that body all over him... he could die a happy man. His free hand wandered down, cupping his own balls and squeezing lightly. Caesar liked things a little rough. Gentle touches were for pansies who did dinner parties with matching silverware and cheeses you couldn't pronounce the names of. He tugged at his balls and ran his tight fist over his prick. The illusion of Nate's fingers doing that to him made Caesar moan.

Nate's voice came from the direction of the kitchen. "That's damn nice."

Caesar cracked open his eyes. Nate was naked, his cock slapping against his belly as he walked. Caesar liked seeing Nate naked. "Get that ass over here, Nate."

Nate stretched. "Oh, a man who gives a cop orders. That can be hazardous to your health." As he ambled over, Nate tore into the condom wrapper and fished out the pale bit of latex. "Want me to put it on you?"

"Are you serious?"

Nate's tongue pushed out, stroked his teeth. "Yeah, I'm serious."

Dropping to his knees on the floor in front of Caesar, Nate stuck the condom between his lips. Caesar tried not to laugh, but it looked like Nate was holding some weird ass sucker in his mouth. Nate shot him a glare and leaned forward. When he wrapped one solid hand around the base of Caesar's cock, Caesar hissed. The grip was firm as he pulled Caesar's skin back. Then he was bending over and sucking Caesar into his hot mouth. Caesar could feel Nate's tongue pressing the latex against his head. Then Nate was moving down, his lips pushing the condom over Caesar's dick.

"Fuck." Caesar panted. "That's a pretty slick trick."

Nate pulled back and smiled. "I've got all sorts of talents." He stood before climbing onto the couch, knees to either side of Caesar's hips. Nate's prick bumped against Caesar's abs leaving little damp kisses behind. His prick was hard, rearing out of all that blond fur. The head was so swollen it was damn near white. The heavy veins painted a beautiful map on his skin. Caesar promised to memorize every single inch of that map.

As Nate wriggled into place, Caesar reached for the lube. Even through the barrier it was cold on his dick and he shuddered. Coating his cock, he ribbed Nate with his tone. "Nah, you're just a one trick pony." Then, his own prick gripped with one hand, Caesar used the head to toy with Nate's body. Nate's balls rolled over his slick, sheathed skin. The touch was just enough to tease them both.

"I thought you were the pony." Nate smiled, adding the sway of his own body. Sliding over Caesar's cock, he licked his lips. "You ready?"

Caesar snorted. "Just hung like one." They both chuckled as Nate knocked Caesar's forehead with his own. If he'd actually believed that about himself it wouldn't have been funny. Still, there was no question about the want. "Always ready for you."

Nate reached back and grabbed Caesar's dick. He gave it a few strokes before settling himself down. The tight hole kissed Caesar's head and he slid his hands over Nate's hips to help steady him. When he looked back up, Nate's gaze was eating him alive. That wide-eyed, totally open expression on Nate's face, Caesar knew he'd never get enough of that. It was a look that said 'I belong to you. I'm giving you everything I've got and then some.' He wrapped his hand behind Nate's neck and pulled him down for a kiss. As his tongue slid between Nate's lips, Caesar's prick pushed up against the tight hole. There was resistance at first, and then Nate's ass gave way to his cock. Each layer of muscle slowly opened. He hissed against Nate's lips as the heat swallowed him. Short, sweet pumps had

Caesar's breath hitching while Nate eased himself onto Caesar's prick: hot and tight and so good.

Nate shifted, riding Caesar slow and easy. He was almost moaning. "This is what I wanted this morning." An inch at a time, Nate was killing him with the pace. When Nate rolled his hips, Caesar's fingers spasmed, digging into that hard body. Nate laughed and the sound sent shockwaves down Caesar's prick. *Chingaso*, but Nate knew he was in complete control.

"Why..." Caesar ran his hand up Nate's chest, tugging on the soft curls there. Staring up as Nate stared down, "didn't you say something?"

Nate didn't answer right away. Instead he worked the cock in his hole. Easing down, then pulling almost all the way off, his green eyes drifted out of focus. Caesar slid his hand along the curve of Nate's hip to find his cock. Fingers shifting the silky skin, he teased Nate with tenuous touches. Nate may have been more into that end of things, but he was no passive fuck. Nate would let Caesar know when he was ready for more. Right now they were both into the slow ride.

Steadying himself on the back of the couch, Nate leaned in. He kissed and pulled back. Then he did it again. Each time he tightened his body, squeezing Caesar's prick. The next time he moved in for a kiss, he stopped just short of contact. "Figured you might not be up to it."

"I'm always up for you." Caesar finished the kiss. Tongue darting past teeth, he tasted Nate deeply. Their tongues fought in slow motion. Agonizingly sweet, they rocked together. Fast wasn't always good. This, in Caesar's opinion, was damn near perfect. It was going beyond the ability to think much less talk. He used his hands to tell Nate how much he was falling for the cop. Caesar met Nate's rhythm, thrusting deeper and deeper into that tight channel. Steady strokes worked Nate's prick. Little by little the pace increased. Neither seemed conscious of it. They only followed what their bodies asked for.

Nate pulled away, arms still to either side of Caesar's shoulders, knees still imprisoning his hips. Throwing his head back, he began to slam himself on Caesar's cock. Nonsense spilled out of his mouth. It had to be nonsense. Caesar couldn't, wouldn't believe that the *want yous, need yous* and *don't want to loose yous* were anything more than that.

Caesar jerked Nate's prick, tightening his fist, giving Nate everything through his touch. Hard as it was, Caesar held himself back. It was ten times worse when Nate's hold bore down, squeezing his prick so tight. Cum bubbled through Caesar's grip. Exhausted, Nate dropped his head on Caesar's shoulder. Caesar drew his lover close, sliding his ass towards the edge of the couch. When he was almost off the edge he pulled Nate down onto him. It angled him just right to slam deep inside. Mercilessly, he pounded Nate's still tight hole. Rewarded again by babbles, Caesar lost himself in the heat pouring through his cock.

He floated in ecstasy until an annoying tone at his feet drew him back to reality. "What the fuck is that?" He mumbled. Nate lay against him, their bodies bathed in sweat.

Nate's reply was almost intelligible. "I think it's my phone. Probably IA."

"Technology, in this situation," he groused, "always seems to ruin the moment."

Nate kissed his neck, ignoring the phone for the moment. "I've noticed that."

CHAPTER 22

Back roads between Ventura and Palmdale cut through strawberry fields. Monster wheeled lines of pipe inched over rows of strawberries, spitting spray. Eventually, the tongue of civilization licked the edge of old California. Street after street of half-built cookie-cutter houses sprouted around every foothill curve. Those gave way to graded ground before fading into winding canyon roads. As the Taurus crested the ridgeline, high desert winds hit. Three hundred and sixty days a year, winds ranging between a stiff breeze and a full force gale scoured the backside of the mountains.

Poncho lolled in the back of the Taurus. Every few minutes he'd poke his head between the seats. Bouncing over both men, Poncho did a circuit of the car before settling back into his spot. Caesar stared off at the road as they descended into the city. Nate scanned his handwritten directions. Intermittent black swipes of asphalt, identified by letters instead of names, broke through oatmeal colored dunes. Nate ticked them off in his head looking for the right one.

They needed to find the hotel and then he was going to lock himself in the bathroom for a good half an hour and lose it. The strain of pretending that everything was okay was killing him. They were being followed, or maybe, they'd put a watch on the beach house. He was a fool to think that place was safe. Enough of the old guard was friends with David Reilly to know about it. Hell, he'd probably mentioned the house in Oxnard half a dozen times.

Finally he found the correct street and turned into an area full of industrial parks. That gave way to the city proper. Four lanes lined on either side by fast food joints and discount marts. After an afternoon of driving, they ended up at a hotel that looked vaguely like a Swiss chalet. It was built in a U and you had to drive under one leg to reach the parking lot. Nate pulled around the corner of the building, just in case the management had a no pets rule. He slid out of his seat, pushing Poncho back into Caesar's arms.

"You two stay here. I'll go check us in." Scanning over a plain parking lot interrupted by pre-fab construction and swatches of tumbleweeds, he sighed and leaned back into the car. Poncho wiggled in Caesar's grip. "Pop the trunk. There's probably some rope back there you can use for a leash. I'll be back in a few."

"Okay." Caesar flashed a smile. The strain of the past few days was showing in the blue circles under his eyes. "He's got to be bursting by now."

"So am I, but I'll wait until we get to the room. Don't go too far." With a snort, Nate slammed the door and headed toward check in. As he walked, he flipped open his phone and dialed his Sergeant. H.M.'s voicemail picked up so Nate left a quick message that they made it and he'd check in tomorrow morning. Details, details, details—they kept reminding him how screwed up the situation was.

A wall of refrigerated air hit Nate as he yanked open the lobby door. The place was tiny and dim, even at mid-afternoon. Nate barely merited a flick of the eyes from the guy at the front desk. Dark-skinned and sharp-featured from God knew which MiddleEastern country, he gnawed indifferently on a candy bar. His Bust-Inspector T-shirt was in sync with his surroundings. A nametag pinned crooked on his shirt said *Sherif*. As soon as Nate passed whatever creep meter the clerk had running, the man's gaze settled back on a tiny TV set by the door. Judge Judy screamed at a couple of losers in the background.

Dime store patriotic prints pretended to be art. The counter's American flag and country paint job pushed the theme over the top. Nate propped his elbows on the scarred surface. That got him another quick glance before Sherif's attention reverted back to daytime drama. Good to know that LA County wasn't blowing its budget on high-service safe houses.

After another few seconds of being ignored, Nate coughed. Now he rated a glare. "I could use a room."

Dropping his snack on a pile of paperwork, Sherif wiped his nose with the back of one hand. "Single, queen or two full?"

Without looking away from the TV he fished a form out of a drawer and slid it towards Nate.

Nate held his hand out for a pen. None was forthcoming. With a grunt, Nate leaned over the counter and grabbed one out of a cup. "Two full." Nate growled as he scribbled in his basic information.

Keyboard clicks indicated the man behind the desk actually worked. Eyes still fixated on the TV set, he mumbled, "Name and I need a card and ID."

It took Nate a moment to fish his credit card and driver's license from his back pocket. "Nathan Reilly." Nate spelled it as the clerk typed.

"How long?" A brown hand snaked out, grabbing the form and cards.

The guy had to be psychic, because Nate would swear he never looked away from the screen. "Just one night." It better be just one night. The I.A. Dick had promised to find them something better in the morning. And it had better be someplace as tight as Fort Knox.

Card keys appeared from the drawer and slid into the slots to be imprinted. For the first time, something other than the TV had Sherif's attention. Lifting himself half off his seat, the clerk handed Nate his cards. Reaching over, he caught a paper sliding out of the printer. "Initial here, sign here." He jabbed the form with a nail bitten finger. While Nate scrawled his name, the man typed something and then looked up. "Okay, room 325 is yours." He ripped off a sheet of paper, circled a room, then passed the map over the counter

Nate paused, hand on the keys. The room was on the front corner of the hotel facing away from the entrance. "That's on the third floor?"

"Yeah."

"Shit." Smiling, he slid the cards toward the clerk. "Look, I've got equipment in my car I want to keep my eye on. You got anything on the first floor, facing the lot?"

Sherif sucked on his tongue. Nate shrugged. With a sigh and more keyboard noise, the clerk scanned the computer. "Nope. Room 260 is available you can see the lot okay, but it's a single queen."

"Whatever." He tried to play it off like it didn't matter all that much. The old keys went under the counter and new ones were imprinted to replace them. As Nate took the cards, "You need me to sign a new form?"

"Not unless you care. It's in the computer."

Nate tucked the keys into his shorts. "Naw, I'm good." He hadn't even made the door before the clerk was again riveted to the TV.

Rounding the corner, Nate blinked from the glare off the high desert. It took a moment to regain focus. When his vision cleared, Nate smiled in relief. Five minutes out of his sight and he was worried that something happened. Cop paranoia was running full steam ahead.

Caesar leaned against the Taurus, Poncho folded and panting at his feet. Yellow nylon rope was tied to the dog's collar and wound through Caesar's fingers. One hand shading his dark eyes, Caesar grinned back. "*Hola*, get a room?"

"Yep." Poncho barked in greeting and lunged to the end of his tether. Obliging, Nate gave his ears a scratch. "We have to share a bed though."

"Oh, the hardships of a public servant." Caesar didn't seem put out by the arrangement.

Jerking open the driver's door, Nate clambered into the car. Poncho shot over his lap and he grabbed the lead so Caesar could jog around to the passenger side. When both doors clicked shut, he teased, "Well, I didn't plan it, but I can't say I'm heartbroken by the arrangement." He'd mostly wanted the two beds in case anyone else saw the receipt.

Nate pulled his car around into the guest parking lot. Tan stucco rose from concrete walks. Their room was at the back, almost at the end of the building. Unfortunately, the nearest space was in the middle of the lot. Nate still felt safer being able to watch who came and went. While Caesar wrestled with his dog, Nate pulled their things out of the back. After a moment's debate, he decided to leave his warbag in the trunk. His piece, however, was headed up to the room with them. He slung the two duffels over his shoulder before slamming the trunk closed and trudging up the stairs and into the room behind Caesar.

The bags landed on the alleged kitchen counter to the right of the door. Mini fridge and microwave; at least if they had to stay more than one night they wouldn't bust the bank eating out. The left wall opened into the bath. Nate pulled his sidearm out of the bag, un-holstered it, and checked to make sure it was loaded. He knew it was, but he checked anyway before setting his pistol on the dresser where he could grab it if he needed to.

The space was pretty Spartan. Hell, there wasn't even a real closet. A shelf-cum-coat rack was screwed to the wall next to the bed. Blond laminate furniture did nothing to lighten the room. Poncho enthroned himself in one of two blue chairs. Both looked like they'd been stolen out of a doctors' lobby.

Caesar grabbed the remote and came up short. A length of chain tethered it to the nightstand. With a grunt, he dropped on the pseudo-patchwork quilt of American flags. Then he jabbed the power button. Static flickered to life on a TV bolted to the dresser. Rapid jumping through the channels proved nothing was worth watching. Parking it on a news program, Caesar tossed the remote back on the table. "How long are we here for?"

The room was depressingly dim. Nate flicked the switch and brass sconces hung on either side of the bed sprang to life. It was still depressingly dim. Nate reminded himself that it was only for one night. "Just tonight." He growled, stalking to the far end of the room. There were two options for securing the room…slim and none, and Nate didn't like it one bit.

A cookie-cutter anchorman droned about the latest happenings in the Sergeant Syd Scandal. You'd think the press could come up with a better handle than that. Nate snorted as he yanked the curtains open. They were the same patriotic print as the bed. There was something to be said for taking a theme too far. A balcony, hardly wide enough for a man to stand on, jutted out over the lot. At least the room had a decent, if angled, view of the parking entrance. It might be safe enough. Nate turned when he felt Caesar behind him.

"TV sucks, it's just reminding me of all the crap I don't want to think about." A lopsided grin cracked his warm features. "You hungry? While I was walking Ponchito, I saw a decent looking Chinese joint."

"Maybe later." The sun drifted through the window. Late afternoon shadows caught the dust hanging in the air. Goddamn, Caesar looked good in a tight white T-shirt, cargo shorts and work boots. Things other than eating roamed about in Nate's head.

Hands stuck in his pockets, Caesar shrugged. "Missed lunch. Thought you might be."

Nate stepped in, running his knuckles down Caesar's sternum. "I can wait to eat." That hard body felt good under his hand. The thought of blowing out a bit of his tension held a lot of appeal. Nate's touch drifted lower. "I'm more interested in other things right now." He was such a slut for this guy. And it might all be over all too soon. Carol would do what she could. It was the best shot Caesar had to make a change. Otherwise, Nate had little doubt Caesar would go right back to his old life. He was determined to make the most of what he could get while he could.

Just in case there wasn't anything more.

"Really?" Caesar moaned as Nate squeezed the head of his cock through his shorts.

Nate laughed and moved in close. "Yep."

Poncho chose that moment to get jealous. He darted between their feet. With a push and then a nip, the dog tried to separate them. Nate wasn't about to let him. It was like some weird-ass dance routine, trying to move and move around the dog at the same time. When Caesar missed and stepped on the mutt's tail, Ponchito yelped. Then he shot off to the far corner of the room.

That was fine with Nate. He'd offer apologies with Mu-Shu pork and a belly rub later.

They staggered back toward the bed, fumbling with each other's clothes and mouths. Caesar dropped onto the covers and pushed his shorts down. Crawling up on the bed next to him, Nate managed to get his own fly undone. Then he bent over and found the best part of Caesar.

That heavy prick throbbed against his cheek. Thick veins and burning skin, all bursting out of thick black hair, there was nothing better. Nate ran his tongue over Caesar's sac, rolling the heavy weights with his tongue. Caesar smelled so good. He tasted so good. Warm and soft, Nate could do this forever. He sucked one ball into his mouth. One hand wrapped around Caesar's thigh, the other pumped his prick as Nate kept sucking on velvet skin.

"Fucking damn, Nate. Suck me hard." He shivered as Caesar twisted. Then a hot mouth slipped over Nate's prick, licking and kissing the swollen head. Giving and getting without even taking the time to get all undressed. Intense didn't even begin to describe it. Nate's tongue slid over every inch of skin before he opened and swallowed Caesar down. He pulled back as Caesar sucked him. Nate hissed. Damn, Caesar could suck so good.

Nate's hand cupped Caesar's balls and he squeezed. Caesar groaned against Nate's thigh. "Oh, hell!" Caesar pulled back slowly and wrapped a hand around the base of Nate's cock. Everything was going all mixed up and jumbled. Nate probed the tip of Caesar's prick with his tongue. Then he drew the head back into his mouth for a slow, sucking kiss. Caesar reached up with his other hand and gripped Nate's hip, encouraging him to fuck Caesar's mouth. Thought was gone.

Caesar's mouth was on fire, burning his dick. His lover's cock hardened with every pull. Nate moaned as his hips started to buck. Lips sliding up and down Caesar's cock, he kept the suction strong and steady. Shudders started and crawled up his spine. He pulled off and moaned, "Ah fuck!" as he came. Caesar worked his still sensitive prick until Nate was trembling.

After a few moments, Nate could breathe again. He pulled Caesar into his mouth and sucked hard. It felt so good to have Caesar filling him like that. Caesar's hips came off the bed. He jerked. Hot and sweet, Caesar exploded.

When they both came down, Caesar twisted to lay his head on Nate's stomach. Nate brushed thick black hair away. Dark and satisfied, Caesar chuckled, "We need to stop meeting like this."

"Asshole." God, this had been some screwed up flight-or-fight response messing with his nerves. When in life threatening danger…fuck like bunnies. Nate couldn't believe how out of whack his responses to the situation were.

"What?" Lacing his fingers through Nate's, Caesar pushed. "You don't think there's a problem with us getting involved?"

"Right now, I'm thinking that I'm not going to worry about it."

"Okay, I can live with that." The bed shifted as Poncho jumped on the edge. Mincing over, he licked Caesar's nose. Caesar batted him away before adjusting himself. When he'd finished, Caesar grabbed the little dog and pulled him close. "You're just jealous...you little whore, you." Caesar rubbed Ponchito's belly, earning grunts of satisfaction. Nate joined in and Ponchito sighed in ecstasy.

Finally, Nate pushed Caesar's shoulder. "Okay, let me get dressed, and we'll go find some food." Nate rolled off the bed. Sliding his pistol into the waistband of his chinos, he caught sight of himself in the crummy little mirror above the dresser. The almost universal cop-casual; for Nate that meant a western-style short-sleeved shirt, untucked, and not-quite-dress slacks. Of course, a concealed weapon in his shorts was about as smart as putting a ferret down his pants, but no way was he going anywhere unarmed. "Alright," he teased, "I'm dressed. Ready?"

Caesar shoved Ponchito off his lap. With an apologetic tousle of the dog's ears, he slid off the bed. "Be good and I'll bring you something." Then Caesar sidled up to Nate. For a moment they just stood together, close but not touching. "Know what?"

"What?"

Strong, brown arms wrapped around Nate's middle. "I don't regret it."

"Regret it?"

"Yeah, all of it. No matter how fucked up it is." Caesar waved toward the general direction of the TV. "I get to be with you. Fuck, even though we've never even been on a real date or anything. But, I mean, I've never felt like I was getting this close to anyone. Even the guys I went on *real dates* with." Caesar paused for a moment. "I'm really getting kinda stuck on you, you stupid cop."

Stuck on him? Nate smiled, what an understatement that was. He was so far beyond just stuck on Caesar it wasn't even funny. "Well," Nate pushed a strand of hair back out of Caesar's eyes, "why don't we have a date now?"

"What the hell are you talking about?"

"You and me." Pulling back, Nate stared into Caesar's chocolate-colored eyes. "Let's go grab Chinese. We'll sit down in a real restaurant, have a beer or two, order whatever the couple's special is and read each other's fortune cookies." A shit-eating grin was tearing his features, Nate could feel the strain in his cheeks. He didn't care how silly it looked. "Of course, with the way you look, everybody will think I beat you or something." All he cared about was that Caesar might, just might, feel the same way he did. "So, will you go out with me tonight?"

"If you're asking, you paying?" Caesar bumped Nate's nose with his own. The arms around Nate's waist tightened playfully.

"Nope...City of LA's treating tonight."

"Good." Pulling away, Caesar's smile mirrored his own. "I may be easy, but I'm no cheap date."

CHAPTER 23

They sat outside, on the patio of a converted California bungalow, drinking Tsingtao beer. It felt good to just talk about not much of anything and feed each other bits of Cheng Du. It almost pushed away the lingering dread that followed them. His mama always said, 'act like things are good, and sooner or later they will be.'

Caesar stole the last spring roll off Nate's plate. "For a guy who grew up in Southern California," Caesar teased, "you sure suck with chopsticks." Dots of red-brown chili sauce decorated the otherwise white tablecloth.

"Fuck you." Nate laughed. "I have many other talents you don't know about."

Caesar rocked his chair back. "Yeah, planning on showing me some?"

A piece of chicken nearly slipped from between the chopsticks. Nate caught it with his tongue seconds before disaster. "Maybe." He sucked in his breath from the heat before chewing, then took a swig of beer. "Course, don't know what you're going to do with proper techniques for kicking in a door."

"Don't know either." Caesar downed the last of his bottle. "But it could come in handy in my line of work." Nate glared at him for that comment.

"You done?" When Caesar nodded, Nate double checked the tab and he pulled out his wallet. He threw down a few rumpled bills. "Not your line of work anymore," he corrected.

Cartons left by the waitress already held the remnants of shrimp and rice for Poncho's dinner. "That's not a hundred percent yet." Caesar dumped the last of the chicken into the mix as he stood. Ponchito would burst if they let him have all this. They'd probably need gas masks as well. Making a mental note not to give the dog everything at once, Caesar folded down the tabs. "We both know it. Don't get your hopes up, Nate."

"Make it a hundred percent. Commit to it." Chair legs grated on the decking. Caesar looked up into the most earnest set of green eyes he'd ever known. There was nothing that would ever shake Nate's faith in his sister or the world. That shone clear and Caesar couldn't face it. Instead he just shrugged and walked off onto the now dark street, carton dangling from one finger. Dots of light lit up every few feet.

Nate caught up with him, draping a strong arm across his shoulders. Caesar snuck a look and caught Nate with a relaxed, contented smile. When Nate glanced over and found Caesar staring, his smile got even broader. Tentatively, Caesar slipped his arm around that tight middle, his hand just resting on Nate's hip. From under Nate's shirt, the butt of the pistol rubbed against his forearm. After a few steps he realized Nate wasn't going to shrug him off. "You don't mind walking with me like this?"

"No." Nate laughed. "Why should I?"

It took a moment for Caesar to think it through. "Never quite figured you for a PDA kinda guy."

"Well," Nate paused, hand sliding under Caesar's hair. One finger tracked down his spine sending tiny shivers through his back. "I ain't going to snog you shitless on the street, but I like this. I really, really like this." A car slowed and Nate went tense. He didn't relax until it turned into a parking lot and passed them by. "After all of this is over, I'd like to see if we can't have a little more of it. You know, when we don't have a big freaking anvil hovering over our heads."

"I wouldn't be opposed to that plan." What surprised Caesar more than Nate's admission was that he really wouldn't be opposed to it. No matter what else was going on, being with the big, optimistic cop made his life better than Caesar ever considered it could be. Hell, he was already trying to figure out how to introduce Nate to his mom. Of course, that might actually require telling her he was gay first.

They wandered under the hotel's entrance and crossed the lot, still holding each other. A big, American-made sedan was parked next to the Taurus. Almost simultaneously, they both pulled up short. With the extra antenna and the circled E on the license plate there was no doubt in Caesar's mind that it was an unmarked police car. "Shit." It came out as a sibilant hiss. Suddenly very nervous, Caesar stepped away from Nate. His gaze jerked about the building and caught a movement at the corner stairs. Swallowing, he stepped into deeper shadow and whispered, "Shit, that's one of the guys." Thank God the lot wasn't properly lit.

Nate followed, reaching behind his back, under his shirt. The dull metal of his sidearm caught the dim light, and Caesar swallowed. Nate checked the safety then shoved the pistol into the front of his pants. "Which guys?"

Caesar grabbed Nate's chin and turned it towards the glass-enclosed stair well. Two men, one the size of a linebacker, the other African-American, jogged up the first flight of stairs. "Those are two of the assholes who beat me up."

Nate jerked away from Caesar's grip. "Those detectives? Damn, I met them at Syd Price's house. They tried to bullshit their way into the scene." Like he was trying to wipe away the image, Nate palmed his face. "How the fuck did they find us? Somebody's gotta be following us. Or maybe there's a leak in IA, they set this place up." Nate slammed his fist against the side of the building. "Fuck!"

The men paused on the second floor landing. After an unheard discussion, the bigger cop bounded up the next flight. Caesar was confused. "Why is he headed to the third floor?" Their room was on the second floor.

For a moment Nate was silent then he snorted. "Shit, they probably just looked at the hard-copy of the registration. The clerk was originally going to give us a room on the third floor."

Caesar did not want to stick around to find out what they were after. Besides, he had a pretty good idea. That idea ended up with him on the ground and sporting more bruises or worse. "Well, we can't go up with the guy on the stairs. We've got to get Ponchito and get the fuck out of here."

"No, we just need to bolt." Nate grabbed Caesar's arm. "We'll come back later for him."

Yanking his arm out of Nate's grip, he spat. "I'm not leaving my dog."

"How the fuck are you going to get the dog?"

Really, how was he going to get Ponchito? Caesar forced himself to slow down and breathe. Like always, he'd committed the best features of the place to memory when they'd arrived. The building was old; the rooms had balconies and sliding glass doors. That was the ticket. "You got anything like a pry bar?"

"A what?" Nate asked it like Caesar'd gone mad.

"You know, one of those long pieces of metal you can beat people's heads in with."

"What the fuck do you need with a pry bar?"

Exasperated, Caesar sighed. "Not the time for question and answer period. Look, I need something I can get in the track of the sliding door."

Nate chewed on his bottom lip. "Hold on." Darting around the margins of the lot, Nate headed to his car. Once there, he popped the trunk. Following close behind, Caesar prayed that the guy on the stairs didn't see the trunk light. Quickly Nate rummaged through a big black bag in the trunk and came up with a tool. Maybe eight inches long, one end was flattened like a wedge, the other had a head that was half hammer, half spike. Cut into the shaft was a slot and in that was a blade. "This do? It's for getting someone out of a car…breaking windows, cutting seatbelts kinda crap."

Taking the tool, Caesar tested the weight. Decently heavy, it would work. "It'll do. Stay here." Caesar jammed the tool into his back pocket. "I'm going to get my dog. You want your crap?" He didn't wait for Nate's answer as he shimmied between the cars, avoiding the few lights, to where the building arms formed an opening. Their room sat three down from the end. He used the time to study the balconies as best he could.

Although it was dark, Caesar could make out that each veranda sported a cut out inset of pipes across the front. Someone's idea of architectural interest, they didn't merit more than a glance. The side walls grabbed his attention. Jagged, tan stucco, Caesar gauged them at around four foot high and a good foot wide. The hotel was reasonably theft conscious. Each first floor room had a patio, but they were low and topped with spiky wrought iron. He wouldn't be able to use those as a ladder. Well he could, if he really wanted to, but it wouldn't be fun.

Instead the designers had given him, and anyone else, the wall. They probably meant it to keep undesirables away from guests' cars. The masonry fence was just what he needed. Gray cinderblock formed a six-foot barrier between the hotel lot and the vacant land beyond. Ugly warred on both fronts. At least the desert was natural. The unpainted gray wall gave off a prison vibe. Caesar latched onto the rough-cast paver-caps and, with a grunt, jumped. Arms bulging and the toes of his work boots clawing bits of concrete, Caesar hauled himself onto the ledge. Balanced, unconcerned, he walked along the top of the wall. When he reached a point where he was looking through the slats of the closest balcony, he calculated the distance. About five feet of horizontal air, a bit of an angle and maybe two feet of lift spanned between the wall and balcony.

He smiled to himself, it was so doable.

Four steps back, he took a deep breath, then ran and jumped. Another grunt sounded, this one a little more earnest, as he hit the balcony wall. That was the only sound. His left arm hooked over the edge and his right scrabbled until he found the doorjamb. Caesar swung his legs over, quickly stepped to the opposite side and climbed onto the rail. He braced his left hand on the building then half-stepped, half-jumped onto the ledge of the next balcony. Moving just as fast he made the balcony to their room with the same maneuver.

He risked a quick glance for Nate. The cop watched the stairwell where the *other* cops had gone. That was just weird. Somehow Nate the cop had transformed himself from *them* to *us* in Caesar's mind. He even mentally used a different tone for the thoughts. No time for introspection. Caesar dropped and pulled the pry bar from his pocket.

The hotel needed some serious renovation, more than just cosmetic shit. He slipped the bar under the exterior edge of the sliding glass door. With a little prying upward, the panel shifted. Caesar tugged and it popped out of the track. Nothing that a cheap set of screws driven into the frame wouldn't have stopped, it was always the cheap fixes people missed. Then he just pulled the door off and set it aside. From across the lot it would look like someone had opened it. Less than a minute from parking lot to access, Caesar patted himself on the back...no one else would after all.

One black ear popped up, that was all the curiosity he merited from Ponchito as he stepped inside and flicked on the lights. "Come on, baby, let's get you out of here." He jogged across the room and grabbed both duffels. Poncho was a little more obstreperous. At Caesar's approach he launched off the opposite side of the bed. Then he dipped and snorted. "No time for this, Ponchito." Caesar hissed and dropped the bags by the patio door.

It took a few turns around the room before Caesar snagged the wiggling mutt. The game of chase ate up precious time. Finally caught, Ponchito grunted and tried to lick his face. Caesar hugged the little dog to his chest and grabbed the luggage with his free hand. Getting down would be fun. Normally he'd head out the front door, but that might mean running into the enemy in the hall. Not something he wanted. The bags could be tossed over. Hopefully, Nate didn't have anything breakable, but too bad if he did. Ponchito was the problem. Backtracking the way he came was not really feasible with a dog.

Once on the landing, Caesar scanned for Nate. Another cheap fix the hotel missed—brighter parking lot lights. He closed his eyes and counted to five to adjust his night vision. Then he blinked and looked again.

Below, Nate leaned against the Taurus, his arms crossed defensively across his chest. Across from Caesar's cop stood the two goons that beat him. Shit! Both wore equally confrontational attitudes. Caesar dropped below the rim of the rail, moving as much behind the solid portions as possible. Tickles under Ponchito's chin kept him fairly quiet. Good thing Caesar knew all the dog's weak spots.

A voice, an all too familiar and hated voice, sounded. "Look kid, do the right thing and walk away." At least he didn't call Nate a spick. That level of hate apparently belonged to Caesar alone.

"Excuse me?" Barely restrained anger wove through Nate's voice.

"We know you're just doing your job." Completely reasonable, the older cop continued, "You don't have a stake in this. Tell us what room and we'll take care of things. There's no IA Dick standing behind your shoulder, watching your every move. This conversation never happened. You went out to get some grub, and when you came back…." the thought faded off into the whine of cars on the road. "Everybody knows what these guys are like. No one expects you to stick your neck out. You're just doing your job."

More traffic noise. Poncho huffed. Caesar clamped his hand around the dog's muzzle. Finally, Nate responded. "I have no idea what you're talking about." Caesar wasn't sure he could pull off that calm line of bullshit under the same circumstances.

"Look, kid." That would be the black cop's voice. Far more hostile then his partner, the man spat out, "Don't bullshit us. You're babysitting that lying sack of shit and we know it." Maybe he was the *cabrone* who'd called Caesar a spick. Things had been awfully chaotic at that point.

"No, actually," Caesar could almost see the innocent expression on Nate's face, "I'm not." He'd lay odds Nate could lie like a dog for a polygraph and never make the needle blip.

"Then why are you here?" The older man jumped back in. Again, quiet, calm and persuasive, Caesar tried not to laugh. They were playing good cop, bad cop against Nate. "It ain't for the scenery."

"Not the outside scenery." Nate's tone dropped suggestively.

"What?"

"Look, I'm gay. I don't care who knows it. It's not something I hide. I got a few days off…screw job, but free time, and I'm trying to hook up. Maybe, just maybe, who I'm trying to hook up with doesn't want everyone and his kid brother showing up and knowing his business. So, hey, beach house. Sun. Sand. Surf. And a hell of a lot of privacy. So, I'm out there, minding my own business and ready to get laid and what happens? I got cops crawling up my ass. So I call, let's meet somewhere else. I show up here. I got cops crawling up my ass. What the fuck is your issue following me around? I just wanna get laid and you assholes keep scaring my date off."

"Don't feed me a line." The black detective snapped.

Nate snorted. "Did I check in with anyone? I'm sure you asked the clerk."

The older cop was surprisingly quiet. "Yeah, we asked." His partner's words, however, were delivered in a low, warning tone—a don't-fuck-with-me tone.

"And?" Nate's voice positively smirked.

Again the younger detective spoke. "He says you were alone."

"See." Nate paused. "He was going to give me a room with two full beds. And I wanted something a little more comfortable." Caesar could just imagine the completely suggestive but innocent look on Nate's face. "So he moved me to a room with a queen. Go check."

"We don't need to check." The black man groused. He'd swung from confrontational to grousing.

"Why," low and heavy, the other detective finally broke in, "the fuck come all the way out to Palmdale?" Caesar sucked in his breath. That was a flaw.

"Good God, you don't get it, do you?" Nate actually laughed. "There is a reason they call this part of LA County *Copburbia*. I needed to get out anyway, so I drove to him. I mean, there's a little more chance we might be seen together here, but we don't work the same department, so it probably wouldn't click."

Tense moments ticked by. Caesar could almost make out a hushed conversation. Maybe the two other cops were discussing Nate's story. Maybe they were planning a wedding or maybe it was the TV in the next room over for all Caesar could hear. Finally, the big detective broke the heavy silence. "We know how to find you."

"Great." A hollow thump sounded, like Nate had smacked the trunk of his car. "Fuck up my love life." There was a shorter pause than last time before Nate made a threat of his own. "So, now the other question is, do you just get the fuck out of here or do I call and have you popped for stalking? I'm sure you don't have departmental clearance for this cloak and dagger shit."

A car door opened and closed. Then another opened. "You ain't so smart kid." The implicit threat hung in the air.

"No." Nate grumbled. "I'm just horny and frustrated." An engine coughed to life as a door slammed. Then a steering column whine echoed across the lot followed by the groan of wheels on asphalt. Caesar hoped that meant they were leaving. He counted his breaths. From below he heard Nate calling him with a hoarse whisper. "Caesar!"

He bent to look through the railing. Nate stood alone below the balcony. A space next to the Taurus now stood empty. "They gone?"

"For now." Nate nodded and looked back across the lot.

Well, at least now he could use the stairs. "Be down in a sec." Caesar snorted. All that effort just to leave by the front door anyway. Poncho wiggled against him as he snagged the two bags and headed downstairs.

When he reached the lot, Nate turned from watching the entrance. He held out his hands towards Caesar. "Toss the shit in the car and give me the dog." Nate nodded towards the vacant lot and beyond. "See that gas station, you can barely see it over there?"

"Yeah." A blue and white lit sign was visible maybe a mile and a half away.

"Head there." Nate took Poncho, scratching the mutt's ears. Poncho licked his face. "I'll meet you over there."

Caesar popped the rear door and tossed the bags on the seat. "What do you mean? They split."

"Maybe." Always a handful, Poncho had smelled the leftovers sitting on the hood. He tried to slide out of Nate's grip. The cop held tight. "But if I was them. I'd be waiting just down the block to see who goes where."

Shit. "You think they'll follow you?"

"Yes and no." Nate must have realized what Ponchito was after. Kneeling, he grabbed the greasy carton and popped it open. Poncho didn't even wait to get down. Muzzle buried in the box, he wolfed down the mix. "They won't get too close, wouldn't want to risk crappy shadowing of another officer. You lie low, next to wherever they keep the dumpster. I'll pull up and run in for some coffee. The doors will be unlocked. Hop in, keep low and then we'll take off."

"Why don't I just lie down in the back now?"

"Where, in this car are you going to lay low?" Nate glared at him. Caesar realized the car was small, but not that small. If he scrunched down maybe only a little bit of shoulder would show above the window. "And they'll be really looking as I leave. I can almost guarantee they're right at a spot, across from some streetlight or bright store front where I'll have to pass. It'll back light everything and they can get a good view of the interior. Old cop trick. This way even if they follow me a bit, they'll pass me up when I pull in and then we can just zip onto the freeway. They can't tail me there…well they could but I'm guessing there's only one car and you can't effectively tail someone with one car on a pretty open freeway."

"I hate it when you use cop logic." Caesar grumbled.

"Go on, I'll meet you there in ten."

Once more Caesar was up and over the fence. He stuck to the shadows. Given that there wasn't much moon and no lights in the vacant desert, that wasn't a difficult maneuver. He really hoped there weren't any snakes or other nasty critters out there with him. Mostly, it was dodging the broken bottles and cast off bits of metal. Caesar angled for a spot a ways down from the station where the road was dark. Darting across the street, Caesar doubled back. He had to hop two chain link fences to get to the meeting place. Then he hunkered down behind the dumpster.

Minutes later, Nate pulled up. He backed the Taurus up to the air and water machine. Caesar watched him clamber out and shut the door. Nate didn't look around, just headed for the convenience mart inside. Faith in his skills, Caesar guessed Nate just assumed he'd make it. He crab-walked the few steps to the back of the car. Peering round the back, Caesar checked to see if all was clear. Just as he was about to move a glint in the wheel well caught his attention. A grayish blob of epoxy stuck almost dead center above the tire. Within it a sleek silver tube and flat base connected with little wires and gizmos. The whole thing wasn't much bigger than a golf ball. The only way to see it was if you were kneeling down looking up... like Caesar was now. Fuck!

Caesar stayed put and waited for Nate. When he heard the cop's footsteps approaching, he hissed. "Nate!" The footfalls paused and then wandered toward the back of the car.

Nate leaned against the back door. Although he could probably see Caesar from that vantage, he didn't actually look. Taking a sip of coffee from a Styrofoam cup, he whispered, "Why aren't you in the car?"

Keeping his voice low, Caesar explained. "Nate, there's a funky, monster wad of bubble gum stuck on the other side of the car. In the back wheel well." He felt like he was in some weird-ass spy movie. "With like a little antennae sticking out of it."

"Okay." Nate walked to the front of the Taurus. Caesar heard the driver's door open and Poncho woof. Then the door slammed and Nate appeared on the passenger side. A pressure gage stuck out of his pocket. Caesar smiled. Good choice, pretending to check the air. Nate knelt by the rear tire and Caesar craned around to watch. "What the fuck?" Nate growled. "Holy crap!"

"What, what is it?"

Nate risked a quick glance at Caesar. His eyes were wide in disbelief. "It's a fucking StarChase." Shaking his head, he clarified. "An experimental GPS locator. The department is starting trials right now. They're looking at permanent deployment throughout the fleet. Fuck!" He snapped, banging his hand on the rear of the car. Poncho barked in response. "No wonder they kept finding us. I can't believe I didn't think of that." Nate brought his voice back down. "Do you still have that pry bar?"

"Yeah." Caesar fished it out of his pocket and passed it over. Nate slid the end under the edge of the epoxy. "Careful," Caesar cautioned, "Don't break it."

Nate worried the glob, rocking the bar farther and farther under. "Why not?" Finally it came loose with a pop. Nate caught it before it dropped on the pavement.

"Give it here." The thief stuck out his hand. Nate stared at him for a moment then dropped it into Caesar's outstretched palm. "Be right back." Caesar slunk across the parking lot to where a UPS truck was parked near the fence he'd jumped earlier. A quick scan to make sure no one was watching, then he shoved the transmitter up into the springs of the driver's seat. He quickly retreated back to the car and slid into the back seat. Poncho bounced on his chest. He hugged the little dog tight as Nate slid into the driver's seat.

"They think they've got me nailed with the StarChase." Without looking into the back, Nate started the car. "Sit back, let the suspect go, and when he least expects it you show up and nail him. No wonder those assholes keep showing up." He laughed and pulled out. "It's still experimental and I'm guessing that they don't have authorization for this party. So, they'll be waiting until someone can sneak in, grab a quick look and report my location. We'll have some time before they figure it out."

"So where are we headed now." Caesar hoped they hit the freeway soon because his legs were already cramping up.

Nate glanced down at Caesar. "No clue, right now I'm just driving. Hopefully, I'll figure something out before I fall asleep at the wheel."

CHAPTER 24

Early morning, two days later found Caesar downtown heading for the Criminal Court building. The line to get in snaked out the front glass doors, across the pedestrian bridge and around to the sidewalk on Temple Street. Above his head loomed nineteen stories of gray glass and concrete. Nate walked ahead of him, all spit and polish in his deep-blue uniform. The District Attorney, Stevenson and the two lead detectives followed slightly behind and to his right. Dressed in a simple dress shirt and slacks, not even a tie, Caesar felt awkward. The only other time he'd gone into this building it'd been up the holding elevators in an orange jumpsuit. Not a memory he wanted to revisit. This time around he got special treatment of a better variety, rabbiting to the front of the security line. Still they patted him down when the steel toes in his work boots set off the sensors.

The elevator crawled up the floors. Caesar had just enough time to feel consigned to a personal hell; confined in a tiny room with three police officers and a DA. Do a good deed and this was his payback. God had to be laughing at that. The elevator disgorged them into a wood paneled hall floored in white marble and roofed with stained acoustic tiles. Hardly better, the place crawled with police and court personnel.

Then it was time for waiting. He grabbed a spot on one of the narrow wood benches lining the walls. When Nate plopped himself down next to Caesar, it surprised him a little. The detectives had found a place at the other end of the hall. They could watch, but not associate with Caesar from there. "Why don't you go hang with the rest of the cops?" By sitting where he did, Nate had stepped over the line in the us-against-them world.

"Why," Nate drawled the word, "would I do that?"

"Cause you're a cop, stupid." Caesar stared at his hands.

Elbows braced on his knees, Nate spun his cap through his fingers. "I'm also gay and sleeping with a guy who's on probation. So where do I fit?"

"I don't know, man." Caesar smiled and shook his head just a bit. "You are one seriously fucked up homeboy."

"Look who's talking." Stretching, Nate shifted his butt to the edge of the bench. As he leaned against the wall, Nate thought a moment. "So, after all this excitement is over, what are we going to do for entertainment? Life will go back to being real boring...not sure I want that."

"I don't know, *ese*, what do we do?" Caesar's eyes slid to consider Officer Nathan Reilly. There was no way he was offering what Caesar hopped he was offering.

"Well," Nate considered the ceiling, "I figure somebody's got to keep your butt out of trouble."

Still cautious, but more hopeful, Caesar asked, "Somebody?"

"Yeah, make sure you get a real job, show up to all your probation appointments." Nate's green eyes slid to lock sideways on Caesar. A mischievous grin wicked across his lips. "It's a dirty job, but somebody has to do it."

"You know anyone who wants to take on that kind of job...and a dog?"

"I might." Then Nate snorted, "Even if it comes with an overgrown rat-dog."

"Ponchito is not a rat-dog, he's a terrier."

"Rat-dog."

"Terrier."

Puppetting the sounds with his fingers, Nate teased, "Yip, yip, yip..."

Stevenson appeared at the door to the court. His face went blank with the same kind of startled look that people who don't really believe what they're seeing often sported. The DA shook it off. "Officer Reilly, if I could tear Mr. Serrano away from your scintillating discussion for a bit."

Caesar started to sweat as they both stood. This was it. Showtime. When he stepped forward, Nate grabbed his arm. "Okay, buddy," Nate whispered, "you tag 'em, I'll bag 'em. Got that?"

"Got it." Caesar flashed a half-hearted smile in response.

Nate's own smile was much more confidant. "Knock 'em dead." With that he moved off toward the other officers.

Caesar turned to Stevenson, who held the door open. "Come on." The DA motioned with his head towards the courtroom beyond. "It's time to tell them."

The District Attorney had gone over everything with Caesar. They'd keep his identity and testimony a secret, Stevenson promised. Although that hardly seemed reassuring; the assholes had found him before and tried to beat him into silence. Caesar would testify to that as well. Unlike a trial, he'd been told the Grand Jury would look at the evidence and decide if there was a strong suspicion that the crime had been committed. Most of their decision would be based on Caesar's testimony about what he'd found and events after, that of two alleged victims, and the pictures. Nate and the detectives would testify to the actual investigation, Caesar's beating and the other attempts to derail the inquiry.

The DA had decided on the route of Grand Jury because of who stood accused. There'd been enough obstruction of justice by officers thinking they were protecting their own. A Grand Jury would be the citizens' voice that this was unacceptable. Plus, if they went straight to indictment there was liable to be a lot of pretrial publicity. Any publicity in this instance might be prejudicial. And one of the victims was still a juvenile. It was better for her, keeping her out of the media as long as possible.

Twenty men and women sat in the room arranged about a u-shaped table. Caesar had been in many courtrooms in his life, but never one like this. Directly in front of the large table was a witness stand. To the right of that sat the court reporter, his hands poised over the stenographic machine. Instead of two tables for counsel, there was only one. District Attorney Stevenson took his place next to it and indicated that Caesar should proceed to the witness stand.

At Caesar's approach, one man rose from the group of jurors. A distinguished, older man of African-American decent, his close-cropped hair had grayed at the temples. He was the Foreperson of the Grand Jury and Caesar would never be permitted to know his name. All the jury member's identities were kept from the public. "Please raise your right hand." His voice was deep and rumbly, like he'd smoked for too long. "Do you solemnly swear that the testimony you are about to give in the matter now pending before the Grand Jury of the county of Los Angeles will be the truth, the whole truth and nothing but the truth, so help you God?"

Caesar swallowed. "I do."

"Thank you." As he sat, the man gestured for Caesar to do the same. "Please be seated and speak directly into the microphone during your testimony. Now, would you please state and spell your full name for the record?"

"Caesario Jose Payan-Serrano," he replied before spelling it out for the reporter. The clack of the keys faded into the background. Everything else came into focus.

"Thank you." A warm smile was offered before he spoke again. The butterflies in Caesar's stomach settled down a notch. "District Attorney, you may begin your examination."

Stevenson stood. His smile was professional, not reassuring. "Now Mr. Serrano, I'm going to go over some ground rules for you." Like everything else about him, his instructions were clipped and proficient. "It's nothing major, but only so we can be certain we have an accurate account of your testimony today. Please speak into the microphone, make certain that you answer verbally, a shrug or gesture cannot be transcribed into the record, speak clearly and think about my questions for a moment before you answer them. We want your best possible answers. If you don't know the answer to something, it's okay to ask me to repeat a question or say you don't know. Do you understand all this?"

"Yes."

"Okay. Good." Stevenson walked from behind counsel table. "Let's get something right out into the open for the Grand Jury. You're here on a deal with the DA's office, is that correct?"

Caesar nodded and then remembered he had to speak. Leaning into the microphone, "Yes it is."

"And what is that deal?"

"In exchange for my cooperation," Caesar paused thinking about how to state it, "testifying here and at trial, I won't be prosecuted for burglary...this time. And I've plead no-lo to four other charges, they've put me on probation and I have to make restitution of about twenty grand."

"By no-lo, you mean no-lo contendre, or rather that you pled neither guilty nor innocent, but that you declined to dispute those charges."

"That's right." Caesar wished he could be as self-assured as the man questioning him.

"Besides those, you have prior convictions for burglary, trespass, theft?"

"Yep, I mean yes." They'd gone over that this would come up, but it still was hard to admit it in front of all these strangers. "It's pretty much all in that nice little piece of paper you have there." Caesar pointed to the rap sheet held by the attorney. "I've never been a very good boy."

"Tell me why they gave *you* that deal."

This was it, what he was here for. A deep breath didn't calm Caesar's nerves at all. In fact, it made him realize just how anxious he really was. Shaking slightly, Caesar began. "Because on the morning of June 15, this year, I broke into a house I'd been casing for a while. And I'd pretty much gone through the whole house and gotten up to the master bedroom and in the closet I found one of those little hidey-holes that people think no one will ever discover."

"And was there something in that hidey-hole?"

"Yeah, pictures." Caesar closed his eyes, remembering the nastiness he'd found. He needed to picture it in his mind so he could make sure these people understood how awful it was. "Really fu... um, I mean, disturbing pictures."

"What was disturbing about the pictures?"

Caesar took a deep breath. He swallowed and then he told them. He described with as much detail as he could remember, what he'd seen, how he'd covered his tracks and run to Nate for help. From time to time, one of the jurors would break in and ask for clarification of a point. At first Caesar wasn't sure if he should respond to them, but Stevenson nodded and told him to go ahead. When he finished, and neither the DA nor the jurors had any further questions for him, the foreman stood.

The foreman had one last duty to perform before Caesar was released. "Before you leave, please listen carefully to what I'm going to say. You are admonished not to reveal to any other person, except as ordered by the court what questions were asked of you and what responses were given. In addition you are not to reveal any other matters concerning the nature or subject of the investigation which you learned during your appearance here, unless and until such a time as the transcript of these proceedings is made public. I will advise you also that a violation of this order can be the basis of a contempt charge against you. Do you understand?"

"Yes, I do."

"Thank you then. You are hereby excused."

Stevenson followed him to the door. As he opened it, the DA leaned in and whispered, "You did good."

Hesitating, searching for Nate in the hall, Caesar whispered back, "You think?" He felt Nate's hand on his arm and it startled him. He must have been standing just to the left of the door. Caesar leaned into the touch, drawing as much strength as he could from it.

With a warmer smile, the DA nodded. "Yeah, we're going to nail this son-of-a-bitch."

From inside, the foreman's voice echoed, "District Attorney Stevenson, do you have another witness for us?"

The attorney turned back towards the room, "Yes, Officer Nathan Reilly is right here."

"Good, let's get going."

Nate squeezed Caesar's arm before releasing it. Then he and the DA disappeared behind the wood paneled doors. Caesar found his place on the bench and settled in to wait for Nate.

CHAPTER 25

"Hi!" A tall Asian woman, all business, stood before an unremarkable metal door set into an unremarkable concrete box of a building. Except for the gate guard at the front, the place looked like a warehouse lot. Caesar shouldered the four shirts he brought with them. Nate stuck his hands in his pockets and drifted along behind, trying not to be obvious about drooling over Caesar's ass as he walked. The nice thing about unofficial-official bodyguard duties was a good deal of Caesar time.

She smiled and held out her hand to Caesar. "You must be Caesar?"

"Yeah." Matching her grip and her smile, Caesar asked, "You're June? Carol said I was supposed to meet June."

"That's me." She held open the door. A brightly lit chaos of lights, wires and monitors was visible just beyond her. With a clipboard clutched to her chest, June moved to let them pass. A short hall way opened onto a two-story room with walkways along the perimeter. Above the trio, various windowed offices and booths looked down upon a quiet frenzy. Men and women studied monitors or read through reports. The clack of keyboards drowned out almost all other sounds. "This is the actual newsroom. We're using their set up for today. It gets used for a lot of commercials and the like."

"Cool." Caesar glanced back at Nate. He was nervous, and had been on edge for hours. Nate tried to calm him down earlier with a good blow job. That strategy succeeded for all of ten minutes. Nate offered a grin and tried to be supportive. June looked at Caesar, then at Nate and back again to the thief. "Ah, I forgot to introduce you. This is my buddy, Nate. He made sure I actually found the place…didn't go all *loco* and freak."

"Nice to meet you, Nate." Her heels clicked on the bare concrete. "You're welcome to hang around." June stepped over a mass of cables strung across their path before leaning against a set of double doors. One swung wide from the pressure of her hip. "Now, this is the studio." Caesar's brown eyes went wide and he swallowed. Catching the vibes from his case of nerves, she smiled warmly. "Remember, this is just a screen test to see how well you work with the camera. We don't expect to see Matt Damon, just whether or not you have a presence on screen. Some people just wash out and come off flat." Another smile flashed. "I doubt that will happen here, Jeff and Millie have good instincts."

Both men leaned in to look at the dimly lit room. Flat black walls and a ceiling made of pipes and gantries didn't make for great scenery. On a raised dais to the left a long, red news desk sported the local station's logo in silver. Cameras of various sizes stood like sleeping sentinels around it. "The news studio takes up most of the room, but we're going to shoot you over against the far wall with the neutral black background." She used the clipboard as a pointer. "If we were doing a TV spot or commercial or the weather, that's where the computer would put the background behind you."

Letting the door swing shut, she ushered them along the wall toward a set of offices. "Don't worry about things. Today you just read off the prompter and try and act natural. Art Hoyle, who's already cast as the other half of the team, will be there. Jeff wants to see how you two look together, interact, that stuff."

Pacing them, a tall girl with bright red hair, a miniskirt and combat boots picked up the patter. "Hi, I'm Mandy. I do wardrobe for the show. Did you bring some shirts?" Caesar nodded handing over the four he'd picked out. Carol said they wanted a range of colors to choose from, but they should be something he might work in. Nate and Caesar spent most of the morning rummaging through his closet. They ended up with a selection of T-shirts and a flannel work shirt.

Mandy inspected the plaid and wrinkled her nose. "Don't like this one...." Without really looking, she shoved that shirt back towards Nate. He grabbed it before it could hit the floor. "Well, I like it but not for this, it'll go all wonky with the camera they're using." The other three T-shirts she held up for scrutiny. "Green? Red? Blue? No, no blue." That got tossed onto Nate's shoulder. He was beginning to feel like a clothing rack.

Oblivious to him, she alternated holding the last two up against Caesar's chest as they walked. "Green? Red? We're going with the red." Finally she noticed Nate. "And you are?"

"Just a friend along for the ride." He shrugged, dogging her steps.

"Okay, well then, hold that." She tossed the last shirt on top of the others and barreled through another doorway and then two more in quick succession. Since Mandy seemed to know where she was headed, they followed. Finally she stopped in a brightly lit narrow space. A long, white Formica counter and mirrors lined the entirety of one side. Large trunks holding bottles, tubes and jars of make-up were strewn across the surface. "Caesar put this one on. You," her finger jabbed toward Nate and then to the back of the room, "take the far chair over there. Just keep out of the way." Another young woman bustled into the room. Dishwater blond hair was held back in a bun by long paintbrushes jammed through at various intervals. "This is Jill, she'll be doing your make-up."

As soon as Caesar slipped his denim work shirt off and slid the red T-shirt over his head, Jill pushed him into a chair and set to work. Silent and efficient she compared tube after tube of color to his skin before choosing one. Then she began to smooth the foundation over his face. Caesar rolled his eyes and Nate bit back the snarky comments that threatened to rise.

As she worked, a bald man burst into the room. "Caesar!" His smile showed a set of tobacco-stained teeth. "Good to see you again, I'm glad you took us up on the offer." Bald, with bad teeth if Caesar's description was right, that would be Jeff, producer of *Housebreaker*. His smile went tight as he crossed his arms over his flabby chest. "You have been holding out on me."

"Holding out?" Caesar tried to turn to look at Jeff. Jill caught his chin with one sharp-nailed finger and held him still. "What do you mean?"

Jeff laughed. "You are involved in one of the biggest police scandals of the decade." His gravelly voice backed the habitual smoker profile. "Rodney and then Rampart and lo and behold Syd Price." More laughter, Jeff seemed inordinately pleased with himself. "And there's my boy, right in the middle of it. You can't buy that kind of publicity." Jeff glanced up and caught sight of Nate. "Who are you?" The tone of his voice lingered somewhere between annoyed and attracted.

Somewhere between annoyed and more annoyed, Nate mumbled. "Just a friend."

It seemed like Jeff was about to say something more, when a tall man, his red hair fading toward white stepped in and pounded Jeff's shoulder. A voice, twice as large as the man who spoke, boomed through the room. "There you are my man." His bright smile was framed by a huge, silver handlebar mustache. "And this," gray eyes flitted down to consider Caesar, firmly pinned in the make-up chair, "must be my partner in crime." The penetrating gaze flicked to each person's face before coming to rest on Nate. Narrowing his eyes, the man stared for a moment. Nate stared right back. The smile returned after the briefest absence. "You're LEO."

"Yep." Nate nodded.

Jeff broke in. "Art, what the hell is LEO?" He seemed peeved that someone would dare steal his thunder.

Sidling past Caesar and the make-up artist, Art answered, "Law Enforcement Officer." Then his attention swung again to Nate. "Where?"

"LAPD." That was the basics. For clarity Nate added, "Northwest Division."

Art nodded. Jerking his head toward Caesar he shot out another one word question. "Babysitting?"

No way in hell was he going to explain that situation to a cop he didn't know. Sooner or later, Art would get the run down, but not just yet. He shrugged. "Something like that."

The answer seemed to suffice. Art dropped into one of the other chairs and studied Caesar. Bending in close, he growled. "I'm not sure yet whether I like ya."

All Caesar could move were his eyes. He stifled a snort and managed. "I'm sure you scare the shit outta me."

"Good." Art belted out a laugh. "We might be able to work together then." Another young man forced his way into the room. Any more people and it would resemble stuffing a phone booth. "I ain't scary, not me. Right, Lane?" The last comment was directed to the newcomer.

Jeff spoke instead. "Lane here is my assistant. You'll get to know him well, Caesar. He takes care of just about everything."

"I just got off the phone with the bonding company. It's not going to work." Lane leaned against the doorframe and scowled. "There's no way the bond will come through. The insurance company is having an aneurysm about Caesar's record."

Art snorted. "Hard for a company to have an aneurysm."

In the midst of the insanity Nate's phone rang. He fished it off his hip and plugged one ear with his finger. Pressing the speaker to his other ear he answered. "Reilly here."

"He didn't come in." H.M.'s voice was barely audible over the discussion in the room.

Nate backed into the farthest corner of the tight space. "What?" He yelled into the phone.

"Price didn't come in like agreed." Shit. Lawyers on all sides had spent days arranging the voluntary surrender. No one, not the department, not the District Attorney, not Price's own counsel wanted to see a big scene. Price apparently had other ideas. Without pausing the Sergeant barked another question. "Where are you?

"Down on Santa Monica," Nate looked up to catch both Caesar and Art staring at him. He shook his head and continued, "Hollywood area."

"Okay, then." Adrenaline already pumped through Nate's system. He focused on the voice on the other end of the line. Everything else was a blur. "We're assembling at San Fernando. Obviously, IA is in on this and they're coming from downtown with Metro SWAT. The plan is to stage at the Los Feliz Community Service Center. Know where that is?

"Yeah, that bank building over on Hillhurst, above Sunset right? Why?" Somehow, Nate already figured what the answer would be.

"Got your warbag?"

Already pushing his way out of the room, Nate answered. "Always, it's in my car."

"Good, get your ass over there."

He paused when he reached Caesar and put a hand on the thief's shoulder. Caesar covered it with his own. "Sarge, I'm still *technically* on suspension." They were still going through the motions of a formal ethics inquiry.

"Yeah, right, whatever. We'll see you in twenty." The line went dead.

The room had dropped silent. Nate swallowed and offered a thin smile to Caesar. "Something's gone wrong. I've got to bail. I'm sure someone here can make sure you get a ride home."

"No problemo," Nate's gaze jumped to Art's face. The retired officer smiled. "You don't worry about this pedestrian shit. Go kick ass."

Nate let out the breath he didn't know he'd been holding. "Thanks." He squeezed Caesar's shoulder before backing out of the room. "See you later, okay?"

"Take care of yourself, Nate." Caesar's voice held the same tenor as his mom's had every time she said good-bye to his dad.

He offered up his dad's standard response. "Always do." Then he ducked through the building and out to his car. Shit, shit, shit...bad news Price not turning himself in.

Nate drummed his fingers on the wheel as he dodged through midday, mid-city traffic. By map he wasn't more than ten minutes away. It took Nate thirty before he pulled into the lot behind the red brick and smoked glass building.

H.M. stood with several other officers off to one side of the parking area. Several wore the grayish blue tactical uniform of the LAPD SWAT. They clustered around the hood of one of the many patrol cars. As he slid out of the Taurus, Nate hesitated. He felt odd dressed in just his civilian attire. And although he'd trained for SWAT and put his name on the list, there were always more volunteers than openings. He'd never worked with one of their teams.

The Sergeant turned at the sound of Nate slamming the car door. "Got your gear, Reilly?" He called across the lot. Nate nodded and popped the trunk. Then he hefted his warbag, slammed the trunk closed and jogged over to where everyone else was gathered.

On his heels, two unmarked vehicles turned into the bank parking area. As Nate clipped his extra sidearm to his belt and then struggled into the heavy Kevlar vest, H.M. passed him a mike set up. The Sergeant nodded to the new arrivals walking their way. Nate recognized Renee Chavez, the lead IA detective and Martin Black who'd been with them at the courthouse when Caesar testified. All four of the Internal Affairs men wore the police issued T-shirts and jeans. It was the bust uniform of most detectives.

Robinson, commanding as ever, stepped up to meet them. "Gentlemen, Northwest Division is at your disposal."

"Thank you, Sergeant." Chavez nodded and then launched into business. "Alright, here's the plan. We're going to try to make this nice, easy and painless." A few customers of the bank wandered past eyeing the cadre of police. After a series of hard glares from the assembled cops, they moved along quickly enough. "I've got about as much hope of that actually happening as I have that my wife is going to stop spending all the money I don't have. My guess is, if we're lucky, we're a half-step ahead of the media. We're probably not lucky and there's a herd of reporters converging on the Turney address while we're here with our fingers up our butts."

"Craig is the designated media liaison." Chavez jerked his thumb at a detective Nate didn't recognize, then he swept his hand to indicate a few of the boys in blue. "You uniforms are under him and mostly responsible for making sure the yahoos from the press don't fuck up shit. Now, we've talked to Marian, Syd's wife, she said he was at home as of an hour ago when he called her...." He nodded towards Detective Black, indicating it was he who spoke with Syd's wife. "She said it came up on the caller ID. She and the kids are at her folks. Which means we probably won't have a hostage situation, but Syd doesn't have any reason to make it easy on us." A hard sigh echoed the unease all of them felt.

"Remember, no matter what, the guy's LAPD. Keep it clean, quiet and as respectful as we can. Nick Jefferson, the District Attorney on call, is meeting us at the scene with the warrant. That's it, head out."

As the cops moved towards their vehicles, Chavez stepped up to Robinson. "Sarge, I'm going to want you with us. Somebody at his level to help with the arrest, it'll give him a little dignity and maybe make it go down a bit easier."

"Sounds like a plan." A curt nod acknowledged the order disguised as a request. Then the Sergeant turned to Nate and gave one of his own. "Reilly, leave your car here. You're riding with me. Stick to me like glue, got it? We're bending things a little, but you should be in on this."

"You got it, Sarge." Nate acknowledged the order.

For a moment Chavez sucked on his tongue. Then he looked at the Sergeant. "I thought we had Reilly doing desk-jockey time."

"Not necessarily, he's just off patrol for the time being on special assignment. You okay with that?"

"You're his commanding officer. I'm good with just about anything you are." Chavez crossed his arms over his chest and dropped into the standard, wide-legged police stance. Then a hard smile crawled across his face. "Good, kid, you started it, you should finish it."

Nate swallowed. "I'm not sure I want to see it finished this way."

"None of us do." Chavez sounded emotionally washed out, drained. "Let's roll."

Sitting in the passenger side of the Sergeant's car Nate considered those few blocks the longest short ride of his career. Uniformed officers had already shut down all traffic along the street and set up a perimeter around the house when they pulled up. Neighbors, drawn by the reporters converging on the scene, were pushed back to a safe distance.

Chavez quickly assessed and outlined the totality of the situation, briefing them as they jogged from their vehicles to his side. If Syd wanted to make things easy, he would have come in. They needed to move fast and precise. God knew they didn't want Syd to know how they were going to hit the house because he was watching them on Channel 7. The DA flashed the warrant so that Chavez could see they were clean. Then he and Craig headed off to the knot of cameras and news vans relegated to a side street with a partial view of the scene.

The diversionary team ran toward the back of the house. The rest of the arresting officers scuttled, weapons drawn and bodies stiff, to the front door. From what they knew of the layout, too many windows in back made that entrance far riskier. The open garage wasn't even an option for entry. Although Chavez flicked his wrist and a set of uniforms peeled off to guard it, should Price try and use it for escape.

All of them breathed in a rapid-fire staccato. High-risk warrant entries were not level playing fields. The moment Rene Chavez yelled out, "Syd Price, Police! We have a warrant!" they were targets. Somewhere in that house, Syd Price waited for them, maybe waiting to take some of them down with him. Nate almost laughed—a cop suiciding by cops.

What else did Syd have to lose? A police officer and a child molester...his life expectancy after conviction would be measured in minutes.

They waited, blood frozen halfway to their hearts, for a sign that things would be uncomplicated. No one expected that at this stage. Sitting ducks gathered around the door, Syd could pick them off right there. Any decent handgun around, and all police had decent handguns, could penetrate the exterior walls. They huddled down where the brick facing might give them a better chance.

From the back of the property came the shattering of glass, their cue that the show was on. Without further instruction, a uniformed officer broke the door with a large pry bar and they spilled through the fatal funnel into the house, back-lit, exposed and vulnerable. A cadre of SWAT charged up the narrow, central stairs...arguably the riskier area to search. Nate blinked rapidly to adjust his eyes to the dim interior.

They had a vague idea of the floor plan of the premises, but lacked time to get a bearing on their surroundings. Darting through the rooms like a fucked-up screenplay for some daytime cop drama, Nate, Chavez and his Sergeant covered the dining room and kitchen. Another three-man team would be dancing the same steps through the living room.

They met at the back, in the family room as the shout of, "Clear," echoed from above. One door left. Everything focused on that door.

Syd's turf, he knew what he intended to do. Nate and the officers could only guess whether he was armed and intended to fight, flee, or surrender. From behind that thin, thin barricade came the unmistakable snap-click of a round being chambered. Time pulled like taffy.

Nate didn't want to die and the flimsy interior wall sure as hell wouldn't stop a bullet. He swallowed and tried not to piss himself as the sound ricocheted to conclusion.

Chavez jerked his chin at H.M. Robinson. The Sergeant took a breath and nodded. "Come on Syd, don't do this." He pleaded in the most reassuring and reasonable manner Nate had ever heard.

"Go to hell." The voice on the other side of the wall was so soft, for a moment Nate thought he'd imagined the words.

Robinson took a breath. "Think of your kids, your wife." His tone was soothing and calm. Nate watched the sweat trickle down the Sergeant's skin and realized the man speaking was anything but. "They love you no matter what. You've been to too many funerals with family…it shatters them, you know that. There are other options. Open the door, Syd."

The loudest concussion ever to assault Nate's ears answered.

Chavez screamed, "No!" His shoulder landed hard on the door. The frame splintered, but the door didn't budge. Nate joined the effort, pushing on the wood. Something large and heavy was propped on the other side. Three of them shoved in concert. A loud crash and they were through, climbing over an old metal file cabinet, pushing it out of their way.

Dressed in full uniform, Syd Price sat on the couch in his home office. His service revolver rested loose in his right hand. The left draped casually across his lap, resting atop the case containing his service ribbons and Police Star for Bravery. A study in casual repose, his eyes were shut, his mouth relaxed. If it weren't for the ungodly amounts of blood staining his shirt, slacks, shoes, sofa and congealing on the wall behind him, you might think he was merely sleeping.

A blue set of rings around a hole the size of Nate's thumb marked Price's temple. Black flecks of un-burnt powder dotted the cherry-pink muzzle imprint stamped around the edge of the wound. Nate knew, but had trouble processing, that the stain probably was a result of incomplete combustion—carbon monoxide mixing with fresh blood. Otherwise the fluid was viscous and dark like merlot thickened with strawberry jam. The cloying copper smell of blood and other bodily fluids gagged him. One of the detectives backed into the hall and retched.

Nate managed to hold it until he was in the yard.

CHAPTER 26

"A high ranking member of the Los Angeles Police Department shot himself yesterday afternoon. Detectives from the department attempted to arrest Sergeant Syd Price at his home in the Los Feliz area when he failed to turn himself in as previously arranged." Nate looked up from his clumsy attempts at chopping zucchini. Oh well, it would still taste okay. Chicken was already baking under a layer of canned tomatoes in the oven. Nate leaned on the island and absently popped a slice of squash in his mouth. He'd put the TV on earlier for noise. Now it had his attention.

In the living room a peppy, sincere reporter voiced over a shot of a man in the uniform of the LAPD. An older officer, with a heavy mustache, gray hair and florid cheeks, stared from the screen. "Sergeant Price, a twenty year veteran of the force, was indicted last Thursday by the Grand Jury on several counts of possession of child pornography and molestation." The camera cut to a young, female reporter in an expensive suit and streaked hair. Behind her loomed the gray slab front of Parker Center, LAPD HQ. "It is not known at this time how many victims there may be…but sources say, based on the number of photographs found, there could eventually be dozens."

It looked like everything would shake out fine career-wise. The rookie had recanted the whole crotch-grabbing story when the details filtered down. Tuesday Nate reported for desk duty. I's still had to be dotted and T's still had to be crossed, but at least Nate was in uniform. Sergeant Robinson gave it another week before Nate could go back on patrol. Two days of being a desk-jockey and dealing with the administrative side of a bust gone very bad.

Half the department was in crisis debriefing. He, and those who'd actually witnessed the aftermath, were set up with departmental shrinks. Nate still saw the image of Syd Price on the couch every time he shut his eyes. Relying on Soma was the only way he managed to sleep. God knew he didn't want to start drinking to cope.

"On June 15, detectives began investigating Lieutenant Price after an attempted burglary uncovered evidence of child pornography." Now another photo appeared. This time it was Caesar's mug shot. Years out of date and as bad as most, Caesar still managed to look rather dangerous and sexy. "The alleged burglar, Caesar Payan-Serrano, turned over materials he found and agreed to cooperate with police in this matter."

"Detectives obtained a search warrant for Price's home." The house on Turney came into view and he caught the grainy image of his own form crashing through the door. Thankfully no one had filmed him puking in the backyard afterward.

Nate spared a moment to wonder how many neighbors were sitting at home angsting over whether anything had happened to their kids. "During the search, officers found numerous sexually explicit photographs and videotape recordings of small children. Receipts led them to a nearby storage unit." On cue the orange and gray façade of a pay-by-the-month place appeared. "Apparently rented by Price, where additional photographs and videotape recordings of children were found. After examining the videotapes and photographs, the police determined that they contained child pornography of both boys and girls, six to ten years of age, many engaging in sexually explicit acts. Over one hundred videotape recordings and photographs were seized."

A knock on the patio door startled Nate. He turned to see his twin pointing at the latch. Swinging his eyes back to the news he wandered over, unlocked the sliding door and pushed it open for her. Carol handed him a Trader Joes' bag as she wandered past. Bottles clinked inside.

They cut to a shot of the lead detective. The IA Dick stood on the steps of Parker Center, surrounded by a sea of microphones. "It is a tragedy of immense proportions any time a child is victimized." The detective's tired voice carried both anger and hurt. "That the perpetrator was a member of our own law enforcement community, someone who should have been there to protect them, saddens every officer committed to upholding justice. We encourage anyone who has suffered to come forward."

The reporter came back on screen. "Although Caesar Serrano was given immunity from prosecution in exchange for his testimony before the Grand Jury, he has been sentenced to probation for a string of Southland burglaries. Mr. Serrano declined to comment for this story."

Carol leaned over the breakfast bar and snagged a slice of zucchini. "Why the hell are you watching that crap?"

Nate stowed the bag on a spare square of counter. Then he grabbed the knife to finish chopping. "Not much else on right now." Sighting down the blade, Nate implicitly threatened his twin if she stole more. "So are you staying for dinner?" Nate hoped the response was no.

A snort answered him. Another piece of squash disappeared into her mouth. "With your cooking...hell, no." An inability to cook ran through the male genes in their family. The only two things Nate could manage that didn't come prepackaged was the chicken dish in the oven and spaghetti. "I just wanted to drop that stuff off before I headed out."

"Thanks for running to the store for me. I always forget shit." Nate yanked open the oven door, grabbed a towel and pulled out the rack. He slapped Carol's hand before she could thieve more. Then he dumped the cut vegetables on top of the tomato and chicken mix. Slamming the stove closed, Nate tossed the rag into the sink. Another twenty minutes or so and he'd call it food.

"Yes, you do." Carol teased. "I should have just brought it with me this morning. I knew you'd run out of time after our game." Every Sunday they played basketball. Carol usually skunked him. B-ball had been *her* sport in high school. He'd almost begged off, but reconsidered; keeping with regular routine, just like the head doctor instructed. "I have a nice Chilean at home a client gave me. I'll never drink it." As he was about to say something snarky back, the doorbell rang. Carol sprang off the stool, waving at Nate to stay put.

"Wait, wait, wait." She chanted, heading for the door. "I'll get it." His sister literally bounced across the living room. When she hit the door, Carol checked through the peep-hole.

Spinning, she flung open the door and threw her body into a tradeshow model presentation stance. "Officer Nathan Reilly," Caesar, dressed in his standard jeans, T-shirt and work boots, stood in the doorway, looking at Carol like she had grown two heads. Carol winked at him then added another flourished wave. "I would like to introduce you to the newest client of Barten-Lane Management and co-host of the new show *Housebreaker*."

Without taking his eyes off Carol, Caesar threw a question at Nate. "Are you as nuts as your sister?"

Nate ignored Caesar's query, but had one of his own. "How come you told Sissy before you told me?" He leaned on the counter and glared with mock hurt.

Caesar stepped into the room. "Well, first, she's my agent." A kiss landed on Carol's cheek at that. Caesar shut the door behind him. Then he turned and his smile was all for Nate. "So I kinda have to. And second, I was coming over and I wanted to tell you in person." Thumping the back of her head, Caesar headed towards the kitchen. "I didn't know she was over here. Or that she'd ruin it."

"I so did not ruin it." She moved past the couch to hit the off button on the TV.

Nate came around the counter to meet Caesar part way. "So I take it the screen test went well after I left?" Without waiting for a response, Nate slipped one hand behind Caesar's neck and pulled him into a congratulatory kiss. His other hand slid down to cup the man's ass. Warm arms wrapped around his middle. Goddamn, Caesar was a good kisser. As he lost himself in the taste of Caesar's mouth, it hit Nate that this was the first guy he'd ever kissed in front of his sister. None of his other relationships had lasted to the family introductions stage.

Since he was otherwise occupied, Carol answered for Caesar. "Well, with Millie and Jeff, unless he was a complete dud…they already knew what they wanted."

Pulling back, Nate ran his knuckles down a strong, brown arm. "So what about the whole insurance thing? Is it going to be a problem?" His other hand still held tight to a firm butt.

Caesar didn't let go either. "Nothing's a problem, apparently, if you're willing to throw enough money at it." He laughed and shook his head. "I don't know what the fuck the bond was, but everyone indicated it was a lot."

"Well boys, I'm out of here." Oh yeah, Carol was still in the room. Nate glanced over to catch his sister smelling her sweat-stained T-shirt. If she was acting like that, she already considered Caesar part of the family. Non-family never got to see the tomboy side of her. "Uhg, I stink like a guy. See you both later. Have fun."

"As soon as you leave we will." Nate shot the comment at her back. She flipped him off as she let herself out the door.

Caesar's tongue teased the stubble along his chin. The pressure of Caesar's body backed Nate into the kitchen and against the counter. "Oh, somebody's in the mood to celebrate." Fingers fumbled with Nate's fly. The heat in the kitchen ratcheted up another twenty degrees. The heat between Nate's legs ratcheted up about a thousand.

"Yes, I am." Caesar whispered against his skin and the words made Nate shiver. "I was..." Nate tried to pull back. For some reason his hips had other ideas, thrusting up against the touch. "Going to grab a shower before you got here."

"So glad you didn't. 'Cause now you smell like a guy, not soap." Caesar's teeth worried the V of his T-shirt.

Caesar's hand snaked under his shorts, stroking and pulling. Oh shit, right there, right then...Nate had been planning on a romantic dinner and then sex. He tossed those plans and lifted his hips into the caress. As he yanked Caesar's shirt out of the waistband of his jeans, Nate hissed. "You know my neighbors might see." That sentence was almost more than Nate could manage.

"Good..." Caesar's other hand unbuckled his own wide belt. "For your neighbors." Then they were both pushing clothes off hips. Hard, burning kisses wound fire into Nate's prick. The feeling of Caesar sliding against him drove him nuts.

"We should go in the bedroom." This protest was as half-hearted as the first.

"Why?" Caesar sounded desperate. It was an *I don't want to stop* kind of desperation. Shit, Nate'd had sex more times in the last five weeks than he'd had in his last two relationships combined. They were both still so incredibly hot for each other.

Why indeed? Nate didn't want to break things off right then either. However, he didn't keep the kitchen stocked with those types of supplies. "All that shit's in the bedroom."

"I…" Caesar nuzzled in the hollow of his throat. "Came prepared. Wasn't sure where we'd end up. You know how crazy things seem to get for us."

"Then fuck me hard, 'cause I am so good with prepared." Nate panted.

Caesar worked his way back up to Nate's mouth. The kisses were softer, but no less intense. They lingered on Nate's lips even when Caesar pulled away. Slow and easy, that strong hand moved over Nate's length. Nate shuddered when he saw the desire burning in the dark stare. Caesar's chest heaved once, twice, and then he managed to growl. "Turn around." It was good to know Nate wasn't the only one over the edge.

Caesar's fingers whispered across his skin as he turned, tightening Nate's stomach. Light touches crawled across his ass. Nate sensed Caesar kneeling behind him. Anticipation ate him inside out. "Fuck!" Elbows braced on the counter, Nate pushed back as Caesar licked his hole. "Goddamn yeah, rim me." Nate shuddered. That hot tongue tracing the tender flesh sent him soaring. Caesar grabbed one cheek, squeezed then pulled so he could get his mouth exactly where it needed to be. "Shit, Caesar, shit." Nate leaned forward and spread his legs. His own hand wandered down to his aching cock. Twisting it in time to Caesar's explorations, Nate was in heaven.

Fire crept under Nate's skin as Caesar's other hand drifted up Nate's leg. Two more intense kisses fucked his ass. Then Caesar stood and pushed his already slick cock in deep. Nate groaned and arched his back. They stilled for a moment, savoring the first heady rush. Caesar pulled all the way out, and then slid back in. Strong hands gripped Nate's waist, ran down the small of his back and over his cheeks.

Appreciative murmurs wound into Nate's babbling. Caesar pulled him back onto his hard prick, rocking them both. Nate braced himself with his hands and looked back over his shoulder. Caesar's face was lost in pleasure. He pulled out his cock. Running it along the crack of Nate's ass for a moment, Caesar toyed with Nate's want. "Fuck yeah!"

Once more he pushed deep inside. Then he began to stroke Nate inside and out. Nate matched the pace. God, it was so good. The shudders started in his legs and crept through his frame until he was drowning in his orgasm. Caesar kept stroking through it. A moment before Caesar's grip jerked, Nate heard him moan, "Oh *tío bueno*." Panting, Caesar collapsed against his back. Nate collapsed over the counter. It was just about perfect.

Nate shifted, pushing back and twisting until Caesar was pulled hard against his chest. "I like it when you speak Spanish to me."

"Really," Caesar's touch danced along Nate's arm before he purred, *"Solamente mio. Mi's media naranja."*

Only his, in a very possessive way and it was so very true. There was that other phrase again too. "Caesar, what does it mean when you say I'm half an orange. It can't be literal."

Caesar tensed, like he'd been caught backing out of someone's window. He swallowed. "I forgot you speak Spanish."

"Un poco, puedo son pobre." Nate smiled, catching Caesar's hand and bringing it to his lips.

"It means," Caesar paused and shook his head, almost like he was embarrassed to continue. Finally he answered in a near whisper, "It means you are my other half, you complete me."

"Really?" Caesar's other half? Nate's chest went tight, and it was hard to tell whether from fear or want or absolute insane thoughts of love swimming about his brain...or fear and other things combined. "I'm, ah, yeah." Damn, he couldn't even form a complete sentence. "Shit, I ah, think I've pretty much fallen for you, too. Scary to think you might be in love with someone you didn't meet that long ago."

Caesar leaned in. His chocolate eyes were so deep and soft, Nate could happily drown in them. "Do you think you are?"

Nate pushed a loose strand of hair back behind Caesar's ear and thought. Then he pressed his forehead to Caesar's. "Yeah."

"Good, I didn't want to be the only one who completely lost it in this pair." Slowly, Caesar moved in and kissed Nate. It was warm and easy and one hundred kinds of wonderful. After a time of sensual drifting, where they kissed and touched,

Caesar pulled away. He sniffed and then sneezed. "Shit, what's burning?"

It took a moment for the words to register. "Oh, fuck!" Nate pushed back. Nearly tripping over Caesar, he tried to make it to the stove and yank up his shorts at the same time. "Dinner's what's burning."

"Don't worry about it." Caesar danced out of the way. "We can order in." Laughing, he struggled with his own pants. "Carol warned me about your cooking anyway."

"Shit!" Nate fought with potholders, the oven door and a ruined casserole. With a clatter he dropped the pan on the range top. "Thank you, Carol, for jinxing me." The chicken wasn't flambéed, but it was way past edible. "I'll owe you another dinner."

Caesar leaned against the refrigerator and crossed his arms over his chest. After chewing on his lower lip for a bit, he sighed. "You know, this job's going to take me out of town a lot. There'll be weeks at a time where I'll be gone."

"I will." Nate smiled.

"You will what?" Pushing his hair behind his ear, Caesar just stared at him. "I didn't ask you anything."

Nate left the ruined dinner smoking and stepped up to Caesar. "Yes, you did." He slid his hands into Caesar's pockets. Another condom and sample packet of lube were in the left. The thief had definitely prepared for a celebration.

"What did I ask you?" Caesar kicked at Nate's leg, teasing him.

"To watch your little rat-dog for you."

Caesar's eyebrows went up. "I asked that, huh?"

"Yep." Nate nodded and pressed in close. "Of course that means that I'll have to find a place where I can have a dog. Maybe a workshop. I'm sure with two incomes I could find someplace nice."

"Two incomes, are you asking me to move in with you?" Caesar was laughing again, this time it betrayed disbelief. "We've known each other for about a month. And you've got that weird-ass satanic picture in the bedroom, I don't know if I can sleep with that thing around."

"I'll move the picture. It'll look good in the living room." Caesar groaned and rolled his eyes. Jabbing him in the ribs, Nate got serious. "And I know you better than I know some people I've known for years." He pushed Caesar's hair off his face and stared into those deep brown eyes. This was so right and it was so good. "Besides, you'll be out of town a lot. You don't want to leave your place vacant. Someone might break in, steal all your stuff."

Caesar pulled Nate up against his chest. More laughter vibrated through both of them. "Asshole."

ABOUT THE AUTHOR

James Buchanan is an award winning author of, primarily, gay erotic fiction. James grew up in a small Southwestern town, hours away from any other small Southwestern town. A stint at the State University, where he ostensibly majored in English, garnered him a degree useful for being someone's secretary. The absolute lack of employment opportunities led James to Southern California. After a stint in County Mental Health (administration not client) he ran screaming into the field of Law. James has been practicing for nine years and someday he might even get it right.

James has published several short stories and novellas as well as six novels with various publishers.

You can visit James on the web at:
   http://www.james-buchanan.com/

Printed in the United States
118939LV00001B/16/P